TO JOHN
A TRUE FRIEND.

SARDINE PACKING

Morton Morelli

Published by Morton Morelli
www.mortonmorelli.com

Copyright © 2015 Morton Morelli

All rights reserved. This book or any portion thereof may not be reproduced or used in any manner whatsoever without the express written permission of the publisher except for the use of brief quotations in a book review.

All characters appearing in this work are fictitious. Any resemblance to real persons, living or dead, is purely coincidental.

First Published 2015

ISBN: 978-0-9934541-0-3

Acknowledgements

I would like to thank my friends and family who supported me
during the writing of this book, you all know who you are.

I also acknowledge Stephen King's book 'On Writing',
it was my bible on how to do it and I recommend it to anyone.

Thank you to Matt Maguire of Candescent Press,
for the cover design and his guidance on publishing.

And finally a special thank you to my editor Kristina Walters
who was there from the start and whose skill I would recommend
to anyone.

A heartfelt thank you to you all.

And thank you Dear Reader for buying my book,
I hope you enjoy my tale.

Woody Allen:

I don't want to achieve immortality through my work. I want to achieve it through not dying.

Book 1

Chapter 1

The road to Rittershoffen was little more than a dirt track that wound through the surrounding temperate forest of evergreen and deciduous trees. Hans Grubber was sitting in the front passenger seat of an open top car, with an old map of the region laid open on his lap, leading a convoy to the village.

'We should soon reach the lake', Hans said to the driver, who apart from acknowledging instructions had hardly said a word.

If Hans was right, they should almost be there, but as Rittershoffen was nestled on a hillside, it was hidden from view. The road veered sharply to the right and then looped back upon itself as they came to a crossroads. Hans then looked up from his map to get his bearings, 'Turn left here' he said. As they bounced along, Hans started to think he had taken a wrong turn when suddenly they came out of the shadow of the trees into the open and there, with the warm summer sun reflecting off the crystal clear water, was the beautiful Eau Claire Lake.

Hans said, 'will you look at this place! Are we still in Germany?' He didn't expect a reply, it was a rhetorical question anyway. Rittershoffen in Alsace sat right on the border between France and Germany, Hans was aware that its ownership has been disputed, and today he could see why.

They followed the lake road counterclockwise and soon came upon the village. Hans thought the timber framed chalets had a Swiss influence with their beautiful shutters, heart shaped eaves and other fine details chiseled into the deep, red, Heart Pine. The larger properties had fancy balconies with carved handrails above sculptured struts, and black slate roofs with wide eaves. All adding the finishing touches to the picturesque village.

Before the trip, Hans had read all he could on Rittershoffen and thus far it had lived up to his expectations. They passed a wonderful old horse drawn carriage, abandoned at the roadside, and drove on until they reached the village square.

'The wonderful scent in the air is from the lavender,' Hans said, pointing to the delicate blue flowers. His colleague seemed nonplussed, but for Hans it took him back to happier times, as it reminded him of home. Just last year, Rittershoffen had been a thriving community, but now all useful resources, and that included men and horses, had been commandeered. It was the summer of 1940 and the World was at war.

∞

In a war torn Europe, Rittershoffen had previously been an overlooked little paradise, now it had become completely immersed into the ongoing conflict. The German 4th Light Infantry Battalion had arrived en mass to the small Jewish community. The villagers were terrified, as these armed forces had a harsh reputation that well preceded them. It was common knowledge that the soldiers pledged unconditional loyalty to the Fuhrer, and would fight to the death. Making them an enemy anyone would face with trepidation. The village was to be a valuable German outpost, and the properties were required as a base for the Third Reich. Within hours of arriving, the soldiers had taken complete control.

'That went perfectly'. Hans looking resplendent in his Schutzstaffel uniform, raised his glass to his commanding officer, and replied, 'With all of the men on the front-line, there were only the old folks, women, and children. With respect Sturmscharfuhrer it was never in doubt that this mission would go perfectly'.

'Don't be so disparaging, enjoy our victory. Our orders were carried out perfectly; *take command of Rittershoffen without damage to the buildings*. That was our primary objective, and that is exactly what we did,' said Fischer.

Sturmscharfuhrer Fischer liked Grubber, as did all the men. Hans had a confidence that belied his age, at just twenty eight years old, he ranked second in command to Fischer on this sortie. Hans, a proud German, wore his SS badge with pride, and had a reputation of being even handed. He also had the distinctive racial purity that was seen as essential to the Nazi party, and he was expected to quickly climb through the ranks.

'When will we get further orders on our on-going responsibilities in this village?' Hans asked.

'All I know, is that this is a strategic move that will play a much larger role. Beyond that Hans, you know as much as I do. I would tell you if I knew.' They hadn't known each other more than two or three months, and even though they got on well Hans would never forget that he was talking to his commanding officer, and he choose carefully what he said, and did in front of Fischer.

They were standing in the Village Inn, an Inn which had been dry for several months until today, the SS had with them ample supplies; particularly for the Officers. Quite contrary to the rationing of food for many people in this War, some divisions such as the Stormtroopers had very good access to all manner of supplies. Including the fine Brandy that Sturmscharfuhrer, and Hans were now enjoying.

'What I can tell you is that we are to receive some very high level VIP guests during the first three weeks.' Fischer downed his glass in one, and began to refill it immediately.

Hans didn't have the man's tolerance for alcohol, and he had no intention of trying to keep up. He therefore chinked again with his existing full glass. From today, the Inn would become the recreational area for the officers, and soldiers alike. Grubber and Fischer sat, and admired their surroundings, the hostelry had already been draped in German flags adorned with the swastika, the German symbol of hope, and belief in a better future.

It was just around the first anniversary of the war, and they were a long way from the frontline. There was no doubt that Hans held a privileged position that came with, not only ample supplies, but very little actual fighting anticipated. Even though he had been largely shielded by his rank, and success, he had still suffered along with millions of others from both sides of the conflict. He now hoped the plans for Rittershoffen would give him the chance of recovery, and relative peace that he needed.

Chapter 2

Before arriving at the village Hans had suffered acute grief. He hadn't shared this with anyone, and he had managed to put on a front that didn't show the internal stress he was still going through. It had been only eight months since he has lost his wife and child, just after the start of the war. He still had feelings of overwhelming guilt, that were heightened when he saw the overwhelming beauty of Rittershoffen. On this first day, while walking in the morning sun, he thought, *How dare I still enjoy life*, Hans felt that he was somehow letting his family down. Regardless of grief, and feelings of guilt, Hans still had a job to do, and he was intent on keeping his internal strife to himself.

In the SS weakness of any kind would not be tolerated. Hans was also quite spiritual rather than religious, and he considered himself fortunate to have something to believe in. He planned on throwing himself into his work here, at Rittershoffen. Deep down he knew that life had to go on, it was not his time yet, and he fully believed that he was on this planet for a greater purpose. The very next day he found his purpose.

It was the first morning of the occupation, and the residents had all been secured in their own homes. In a coordinated manoeuvre by the infantry, the villagers had been placed under house arrest. Down one of the lanes there were four cottages in a row, these were the residents in which Hans would personally interview the individuals of the three cottages that were currently occupied, and explain to them the rules of the house arrest. In the first cottage there was a mother and daughter, the dad was off to war, the young girl, just 17, had a very unusual name, Paris. In the second there was a young couple, Maria, and Andreas Da Silva, who had avoided war. Andreas had lost a leg in a farm accident, and because of this he had failed the army medical exam, and was declared unfit. Hans noted them down as a bright and pleasant couple that were devoted to each other. It was in the third cottage that Hans meet Sophie.

As Hans walked to their door, he could see a young girl, who he would learn was called Alicia, perched at the window.

'Mama, a soldier is here.'

Hans could clearly hear the girl call out, and her mother's response. 'Go to your room, quickly.'

The first thing Sophie noticed upon Hans' arriving at her door was how immaculately dressed the SS were. The very trendy German designer Hugo Boss was responsible for the tailored black uniform, and the black was very deliberate as it tended to intimidate people. Sophie was no exception to this. It was forced labour that turned out the high fashion uniforms, and it was in this black uniform that Hans had his first conversation with Sophie.

'Madam, don't leave your house under any circumstances. As you may have gathered, the Third Reich has taken control of your village, and you and your daughter are now prisoners of war.'

Hans quickly explained that he had a few questions that he needed to ask her, and that she should have no fear, her life was not in danger. She invited him in, and he completed some paperwork in relation to her circumstances, covering things such as what provisions were available to her, and her daughter. Within twenty minutes he was about to leave.

'Please take my advice, and cut your hair short, and change your appearance.'

Sophie replied, 'I don't understand?'

'Trust me, I have my reasons,' he said.

She caught on quickly, and asked no more questions concerning her appearance, but she did question his motive.

'Why do you want to help us?'

His reply was from the heart. 'I saw your daughter through the window, and just for a second . . . look I need to go. Please stay inside.'

Right from the first time he laid eyes upon her, he found Sophie constantly on his mind. As he lay on his bed in the old Scholl Hall, he thought about her so much that he couldn't sleep. As a privilege of his rank, Hans was free to choose any home for the duration of the stay, and he had been asked to mix within the Jewish captives of the community. This was all part of the propaganda machine intended to demonstrate that the Germans had tolerance, and even compassion towards Jews. Hans didn't think they would fool anyone as recent events had shown him that the animosity between Germans, and Jews was far too deep rooted; but nevertheless it suited him.

∞

He called again at Sophie's cottage on the morning of the second day, and every morning following with the food rations that all of the prisoners were to receive. Because the cameras would soon be rolling, the prisoner rations were very good, as they needed to look healthier than they did now for the filming. Within a matter of days the villagers started to look much improved, and Hans thought how it was quite extraordinary just how fast they came back to life.

This transformation suited the psychological strategy implemented by the Germans, since they intend to show the outside world how they were re-housing all Jewish families in areas like Rittershoffen. Hans had no reason to believe that their motives were anything but genuine. On the fifth day of the occupation, Hans entered Sophie's cottage from the front door, as he had each day previously, and now stood in the kitchen. It had not taken long for him to make Sophie feel comfortable in his company, and she soon trusted him to the extent that she introduced her daughter to him.

'This is Alicia.' The little girl stood before him wearing a smile, clutching a teddy bear. Hans bent down to Alicia's height before speaking.

'Hello, you have the same big brown eyes as your mommy.' The smile widened, and lit up her face. He asked, 'who is this?' pointing to her teddy.

'This is Mr Pickles,' she replied. It was a teddy her best friend, Paris, had given her.

Hans said, 'now you be a brave girl for your mommy, and I will do my best to help you. Here take this.' He handed Sophie a little extra meat at his disposal.

'Thank you. I don't know what to say.'

The meat alone was more food than she had seen in months. They had been suffering absolute poverty, and were very near to starvation before the troops arrived. It seemed like a blessing in disguise that these soldiers were in Rittershoffen, handing out such generous rations. Rittershoffen had fertile soil, and the villagers had been growing a very modest crop that was nearly depleted.

The skilled farmers were all off play their part in the war. The food that had been harvested, and the animals that have been slaughtered for meat had gone to the front line. It was never anticipated that the war would drag on as long as it had, and the handful of villagers left in Rittershoffen has been living off very little. The food rations were a blessing. Just as he was leaving Sophie called to him.

'Wait, please tell me your name?'

'I am Hans, Hans Grubber.'

As he left, Sophie managed a grateful smile.

∞

When Hans called again the next day he saw that Sophie had finally done as he asked. She came to the door with short cropped hair, but she still looked just as beautiful as she had with long hair. She was wearing a simple cotton dress down to her knees, and Hans couldn't help but look at her long slender legs. Sophie diverted her eyes, slightly embarrassed.

'I'm sorry,' he said. 'Do you have anything else to wear to cover your legs?'

'I have some work trousers.'

'You must start to wear them.'

He warned Sophie of the rapes he knew of, and with his encouragement she started to try and make herself look less attractive. Though Hans thought that it wouldn't matter what she did with her appearance, for her beauty shined from within.

Hans had decided to use the empty cottage next to Sophie's as his residence, and he wanted to secure the location before his comrades caught sight of Sophie, and for that matter, sad to say, her daughter. He had already called on Sophie to tell her he would be her neighbour, and that he would try to make their lives as comfortable as he could under the circumstances.

Hans told Sophie that he was concerned that once the filming was complete the rations would be reduced, and she would be given heavy manual labour work where she would be in contact with the regular soldiers. He offered for her to come and cook and clean for him, to keep her from being allocated for manual labour.

Sophie wasn't stupid by any means, and had come to realise that Hans was an insurance policy, and was quick to accept his offer. It was did not take much time before it became apparent that Hans was spending all of his free time with Sophie, and her neighbours. Paris was always more than happy to occupy Alicia, and Maria often helped Sophie. Hans also found Andreas very good company, he was such a comical person, especially for a man who had a missing leg, and was a prisoner of war.

Even though he found all his neighbours to be wonderful company, it was Sophie whom he was constantly drawn to and who he spent the majority if his free time with. A couple of weeks into the occupation Hans found himself completely free one Saturday afternoon, and asked Sophie to join him for a picnic by the lake.

Sophie quickly accepted his offer, and dropped Alicia off with Paris before walking down to the lakeside. During their outing Sophie began to open up to Hans, and discussed her life in Rittershoffen before the war.

'We have always had a peaceful, and quiet community here,' she told him, 'I have always felt that we live in a small piece of paradise.'

Hans was quick to agree with her, for the peace and beauty of Rittershoffen had already greatly affected him, and felt that he was finally beginning to heal after the loss of his family. Their conversation soon turned to the war, and Sophie commented that she couldn't understand why the Germans hated the Jewish people so much, they were suffering the same economic hardships as everyone else in Germany, and she didn't see how one group of people could be the cause of the entire country's difficulties. Hans surprisingly found himself agreeing with her more, and more.

As they returned to the village, Hans found himself deep in thought about their afternoon together, and about all he had learned of Sophie. He thought that she was, quite simply, one of the nicest people it had ever been his pleasure to meet. She was strong, intelligent, and very determined. She was a force of nature, and in the short time he had known her she had already drastically changed his view of the Jewish people, and he hated the thought of anything happening to her and Alicia.

Hans had never thought of himself as a bad person, but up to this point in his life, he had believed that the Jews were largely responsible for the economic turmoil the Germans had suffered since the end of the first World War. The government had done much to influence German people towards seeing Jews in a negative light. The movies he had seen in Germany were full of propaganda, but up until now he hadn't necessarily seen it that way, and he wasn't alone. With a country brought to its knees through economic sanctions, and a charismatic leader promising a better future, who could blame them for falling under Hitler's influence.

Hans was well educated, and felt that he should have known better, but everyone had suffered such draconian sanctions on almost all foreign trading, and he like every other German citizen were hoping that change would come. It was not surprising that people were prepared to back Hitler and the Nazi party. Sophie quickly had such a profound influence on Hans that he had come to the conclusion that he would help them at any cost, including his own safety. If his intentions were known, it would be the death penalty for him for sure. He was no use to them dead, so for now he decided that he would keep his head down, and get on with his job. With this thought, he left Sophie as her door, and quickly returned to his cottage, contemplating how he was going to go about helping her, and Alicia, and above all, keep them safe.

Chapter 3

Paris was playing upstairs with Alicia at Sophie's house while Maria, and Sophie made lunch. They could hear the girls upstairs laughing. Before the German occupation there seemed little to laugh about, and they couldn't believe that things had changed for the better. They still couldn't believe that they had bread, and cheese, no butter, but still a reasonable amount of food. It was just so unexpected.

Sophie turned to Maria, and asked, 'what do you think of Hans?'

Maria said, 'he seems a really nice man. I have to say, he has made me realise that not all Germans are bad. Why, what do you think?'

'Promise not to say anything to Andreas.' Sophie wouldn't say anything until Maria swore that it would be their secret. 'I think he is very attractive, and I believe he likes me as well. I know he is friendly with all of us, but I catch him looking at me, and he spends a lot of time with Alicia and I. I also swear he is starting to flirt a little when no one else is here.'

'You may be onto something there,' Maria said with a smile. It hadn't slipped her notice that Hans was spending more and more time around Sophie. Sophie was taken with Hans that was clear, and Maria was fairly sure that Hans was taken with Sophie. 'When he first came to the door I was absolutely terrified. My heart was pounding, and I got the shakes, I thought we would be taken out of our homes straight away. So come on Sophie, tell me what did you think?'

Sophie replied, 'I was put off a bit by his presence, especially in those awful uniforms, but I was also calm. He looked at me, and he had such kind eyes, I thought *this is a good man,* and I was right, I am sure of it.'

Maria already new that her friend liked Hans, that was clear and she was pleased that Sophie shared her feelings with her. Maria was going to ask, *What if her husband was still alive,* but she decided it was unfair, as there had been no contact for well over six months now, and he was almost certainly another statistic of this horrendous war. Sophie had received a telegram a few months ago listing him as missing in action, but Sophie has already suspected that something had happened. He had always written to her, every chance he had, and after a few months had passed with no letters, she knew he was never coming home.

Sophie, and Maria were more than just neighbours, they were also great friends. It all came about when Andreas had a terrible accident on his farm, and lost the bottom half of his leg. Sophie stepped in, and took over. Without her, Maria didn't know how she would have managed. Andreas would almost certainly have died, but Sophie, without a medical background, put a tourniquet just above his knee, and it was this that stopped him from dying. Maria never stopped thanking Sophie, and the lack of a leg seemed to be a blessing in disguise when Andreas couldn't go off to War, although Andreas didn't see it that way as he wanted to go, and fight saying he was "stronger than most men with two legs."

'Maria . . . do you think I could be with Hans when the war ends?' Sophie was clearly serious.

Maria hesitated, not sure what to say. She hadn't contemplated the end of the war, but she corrected herself, she was desperate for the war to end, and she found herself feeling she didn't dare to hope for the end for fear that in some way saying the words would guarantee it would go on forever. Maria didn't consider herself superstitious, but she certainly leaned that way. Maria started to silently cry, the tears were rolling down her cheeks.

'What's the matter Maria?' Sophie asked as they threw their arms around each other. Maria burst into floods of tears, and Sophie couldn't help crying too.

'We won't survive this war. I know they are feeding us, but for how long. We are really in serious trouble Sophie. My jaw is so tense from worry through the night. I am okay sometimes, but most times I know we are fucked. I just can't see any of this coming to a good end,' she sobbed.

Sophie had never ever heard Maria swear before, but she understood. It was desperate but should they give in or should they hold out some hope. Surely everyone would eventually realise that the war was not doing anything other than killing people. But Sophie had to admit, until Hans turned up she had almost given in. Life had been so hard to bear, what was the point, you may as well give in. But Hans had given Sophie hope, and she now thought, *please God save us.*

Chapter 4

There was always a lot to do in the village, and Hans quickly fell into a routine. He was in charge of all provisions, and he had to give his approval for any spending, and the rationing of all supplies. He had twelve soldiers under his direct command, and as long as his men knew their tasks for the day, it freed him up for most of the afternoon.

The village was heavily guarded, Hans wasn't sure why. The villagers had been given leave to move around the village at designated times, albeit this was for the benefit of the cameras, and the rest of the time they were to stay in their homes. Thus far there was nothing that justified the intense security. Unfortunately Hans could do nothing about this, since it was his commander's duty to oversee the safety, and security of Rittershoffen.

Due to her position as his housekeeper, Sophie was allowed out of the cottage for an hour in the morning between 11am, and noon, and again for one hour in the afternoon between 4pm, and 5pm. Everyone else was only allowed out for one hour in the evening, which was indicated by a siren each day. Despite her greater freedom, Hans rarely saw Sophie go out alone. He believed this was a result of being scared of what the other soldiers may do. She had heard lots of rumours of very poor treatment, in addition to the warnings Hans had given her about the soldiers. However, much to his relief, none of this clouded her opinion of him.

They were spending hours just getting to know each other, and the days were flying by. Hans had begun to feel that Sophie was his soul mate, he considered himself a normal rational man, and as such felt slightly uncomfortable with the idea, but nevertheless, no other expression quite captured his feelings for Sophie so succinctly. He still thought often of his wife, and child, but it seemed to Hans that he, and Sophie belonged together, and he very much hoped that she was feeling the same way too. For Hans it was a completely unexpected turn of events and, if at all possible he was going to stay on at this camp so that he could stay with her. With his thoughts centred on

Sophie, Hans made his way to her cottage and let himself into the kitchen where he was greeted by warm smiles all around from Sophie, Alicia, Andreas, Maria, and Paris.

Paris' mother has taken to her sick bed, so she never joined them, but Andreas, Maria, and Paris came most nights during their free evening hour to Sophie's cottage, and Hans tried to join them most evenings. There was never a "them and us" between Hans, and his prisoners, and they were all becoming firm friends. Paris was a very charming girl and she was equally happy talking to the adults or to Alicia, and she always knew just the right thing to say to put people at ease, displaying a maturity beyond her age.

On a similar evening when they were all discussing how they were dealing with many of the hardships caused by the war, she quipped to Hans, 'the shares are in a safe in a hotel.' Apparently, Paris was always making comments like this. None of this really phased him, it was Sophie who completely captivated him. They grew close very quickly, which they put down to the extreme circumstances they have endured in this atrocious War. Later, after everyone had left, Hans was lingering in the kitchen, as he turned to leave Sophie spoke to him.

'Hans we are so lucky that you came into our lives.' Sophie said this while standing at the sink staring out of the window, in a dress that was almost see through after having been washed again, and again.

'It was pure chance, but it feels to me that it was meant to be,' he replied. 'And it is me that is the lucky one Sophie.'

It had been a very hot summer's day, and the sky was still bright, and as blue as a flawless Sapphire. Sophie's cottage looked like a picture postcard from the outside, but sparse inside. In the kitchen she had white café style net curtains, very threadbare, but hung in place with a level of dignity that Hans admired.

He stood behind her, and put his arms around her waist, hoping she wouldn't reject his advances, she responded positively, and lay back against his shoulder, and held his arm.

From this window they could see the village green, with the beautiful old limestone church.

'It's beautiful here,' Hans said.

'The locals call the church *le petite Notre Dame,* and can you see over there, in the distance' she pointed, 'that was a beautiful old smokehouse, there is not much left of it now.' The smokehouse chimney was a wide rectangular wooden structure at the top of the building. It was vented at the sides rather than the top, and this allowed the meats to be hung, and air dried.

Sophie said, 'when I had my windows open, it would always smell wonderful from the hams, and sausages hung inside.' They both continued looking into the distance, Hans reluctantly pulled away from Sophie, and made his goodbyes for the evening.

A few days later, when Sophie came over to clean his cottage, they found themselves sat in his kitchen enjoying some of the sweet, summer beets that Hans had procured from the officers rations. They both were finding it hard to come to terms with how much their lives had changed, virtually overnight. Sophie told Hans of how Alicia had been longed for by both of her parents, and that her arrival had been made all the more precious as Sophie miscarried twice.

'My physician said a third attempt at pregnancy would most likely kill me.' But despite the doctor's educated, and well-meaning advice they did try again. 'Even the birth was a challenge, she was premature, I was only 33 weeks.' Telling the story now she was happy, showing her wide smile. 'She was only 4lb 3 oz. It was a miracle that she survived at all, and now look at how happy and beautiful she is.' Everyone said Alicia was going to be stunning, like her mother. 'She was a fighter, and she gripped tightly to my finger.'

It became a symbol of her fighting to hold onto life, one that they continued. As Alicia grew, mother and daughter would always hold hands by linking their fingers in almost the way a golf player would grip his club with Alicia's small finger between her mother's ring, and middle fingers. When they linked hands like this, it seemed to bring them closer together. It was slightly odd, very deliberate, and it felt more personal than just holding hands.

Hearing Sophie talk about Alicia reminded Hans of his own daughter, and for once he had a smile on his face as thought of her.

The pain of losing his daughter, and wife was fading each day. He felt that Sophie was helping to heal him.

∞

Hans had the day next off, and he spent it with Sophie while Alicia was visiting next door with Paris, they had the whole day to themselves and they talked nonstop. Sophie really opened up, and it seems they both constantly had something to say. She told him of her husband.

'Kris was a good looking young man, full of life, and a hard working family man. I loved him more like a brother, and I still feel guilty, because he deserved more, he was a good man and a great father.' She told Hans how she met Kris at just fourteen on a trip to Spain, 'he was half Spanish, and living there with his mother, he had no other family. He was my first boyfriend, and when his mother died suddenly, he decided to come to Rittershoffen with me.'

She had inherited her grandmother's cottage, so they moved in together. Before she had really known what she wanted to do with her life, she was living with Kris, and pregnant. But she was happy, particularly when Alicia finally came along; out of respect for his mother's memory, Kris wanted to name their daughter after her. That was how they ended up living a very simple, peaceful, and happy life in Rittershoffen, before the war took it all away.

Sophie was always very demure when she spoke to Hans, and tended to look down, but he was well aware that he was a German Officer, and she was one of his prisoners of war. He started to believe, or hope, that they are falling in love. After losing his family, Hans wasn't expecting this, and the fact that Sophie was Jewish made no difference to him whatsoever; after all she was so very special to him, and he loved everything about this stunning woman. She looked up and fixed her eyes on his, and asked him to tell her all about his childhood.

'I was very fortunate Sophie, I had a real privileged upbringing. My father was a very successful industrialist.' As Sophie knew Hans was a grounded individual without airs, and graces, for her it said a lot about his family.

'Did your father have a big influence on you?'

'Oh yes . . . he was a great man. One of my special memories was just him, and me, alone in the forest. We had a summer house, and while there, he would take me hunting. I sat next to him in the hide, holding my breath, while the beaters were driving the wild boar in our direction.' It was Hans' turn to look away to get the words out, he hadn't spoken of his father like this to anyone, and to his own surprise, his eyes welled up. He composed himself to push on.

'I will never forget how calm he was when we had the boar in our sights; my heart would race. He would let me take the first shot, but if I missed or wounded the animal he would instantly kill it.' Sophie put her hand on his and squeezed. 'He taught me to respect life, and we only ever took what we needed. He hated cruelty, but he said it would be hypocritical to distance ourselves from the death of the animals that we eat.' She could see how much Hans admired him.

'On the way home, he would always know what we could forage, and he would point out wild mushrooms, and herbs that were good to eat. We stopped, and picked berries, and we would eat them straight off the tree. "Don't tell your mother", he would say, if she was there, we both knew that she would insist that we wash them first, but they were so good that fresh.'

They sat down to eat their lunch, Sophie made a sandwich, with the bread and meat. As they sat together eating, it was as if the outside world, for one day at least, was forgotten. Hans said, 'when we first reached the outskirts of your village it was those same smells at the lake that took me right back. My dad had cancer, and when I lost my little girl he seemed to give in. He was fighting it, but . . . it was his only granddaughter.' He didn't finish, some overdue tears finally came. Sophie took this big man in her arms and whispered, 'Hans, you are our guardian angel.'

Chapter 5

Hans expected to be in Rittershoffen for some time, and he intended to make the most of his new surroundings. He wanted to go down to the lake to swim, and possibly fish, and he was going to ask Fischer's permission to take Sophie, and Alicia, and if possible, Andreas, Maria, and Paris, but everything was about to change. Today Hans was to discover the true reason for their occupation, and events were about to dramatically change forever. Sturmscharfuhrer Fischer finally had information on the VIP's, and Hans was about to meet the head of the SS, Heinrich Himmler. Moreover, Himmler would soon be joined by the Fuhrer himself, who was due to arrive at Rittershoffen any day now.

They still knew nothing of the plan of action, other than knowing who the VIP's were, but they were about to find out, as Heinrich Himmler had called a meeting of all senior personnel. They were to be briefed about the Fuhrer's up and coming visit, and to learn more about the overall strategy, and the role Rittershoffen was to play in the war effort. Hans made his way to the village hall with hope that the relative peace they had enjoyed since their arrival would continue. Sadly that wasn't to be.

Around the perimeter of the village, watchtowers had been set up, four in all. Guards were stationed there 24 hours a day. As none of the villagers were armed, Hans thought that the security measures were excessive. As he went past the East watch tower, and acknowledged his comrades, it occurred to him that the security must be for good reason and maybe he was about to find out.

When he arrived, all eight officers were present. Having never met Himmler before, Hans was prepared to make his own judgement of the man the soldiers refer to as "little Hitler". They shook hands, and the first thing Hans noted was Himmler's personal hygiene left a lot to be desired, and he thought from the smell of Himmler's breath, it was doubtful that the man knew what a toothbrush was for. Himmler was seen by most of the soldiers as someone whose rise to power was based more on who he knew rather than what he is capable of.

They were all about to find out that he had a purely evil intent for this particular tour of duty, and that Rittershoffen would only be the beginning. Himmler stood, and addressed the group.

'Gentlemen welcome. You are all here as part of a unique experiment. I believe that if this goes to plan, it will help return our fatherland into its rightful place as a dominant commercial, and political force on the world stage.' He wasn't very charismatic, but position was everything, so everyone was listening respectfully. 'A Germany for us all to be proud of.'

This opening gambit was met with a round of applause. Hans found it hard not to stare at the grease stain on Himmler's shirt. He went on: 'We are here to start the demise of our nemesis, the Jewish people.'

The more he said, the more Hans thought it was becoming obvious that Rittershoffen was to be nothing more than a death camp. They were to transport prisoners to the village, and execute them without mercy. Himmler's lack of any empathy whatsoever startled Hans. Himmler continued:

'We call this experiment *Sardine Packing.*'

Hans had to stop himself from outwardly showing his disgust, he felt like retching as the words sunk in. Himmler was asked why it is called Sardine Packing by one of the officers.

He replied, 'we take the strongest prisoners, and get them to dig out trenches. We then line the prisoners up at the edge, we shoot them, and they drop into the ditch. They fall in a tightly packed group, just like sardines in a tin.' His delivery is almost matter of fact. It is like he is looking for praise for his ingenuity, and sadly it didn't lack support from the men in the room.

Hans' head was spinning as he thought of Sophie, and Alicia, and the fate that awaited them. He couldn't comprehend how his countrymen could be so evil. These were not the loving, caring Germans of his youth that he knew, and loved. The Jews were seen as the enemy, and the hatred of them by the average German person was absolute, but to kill them like this seemed completely barbaric. Maybe he would have felt different if he hadn't gotten to know Sophie so well, but he didn't think so. This was the lowest point in his entire life. They were talking about taking the lives of humans as if they were exterminating rats in a cellar, on this day Hans was ashamed of the uniform he had worn proudly for years, and what it was coming to represent.

Himmler had written to the Fuhrer with a paper he called "The Final Solution" outlining the idea of his death camps. Before Hitler took ownership of this solution, Himmler wanted his audience to know that he was the pioneer of this strategy.

'What are the cameras for?' someone asked.

Himmler replied, 'the film will show a beautiful place that Jews will want to travel to without resistance. How many do you think we would get here, if we told them it was a death camp?' The men laughed.

'This is the first facility of its kind, but if this is successful, the scheme will be rolled out across Europe.' So complete was the deception, that Hans wouldn't be surprised if some would even pay for the train tickets. The message was, "Jews will have a better standard of living in designated camps". If only they knew. The German psychological warfare was very advanced, and focused on people's belief systems, and was created to reinforce attitudes, and behaviours of the German people against the Jews.

Himmler went on with vehemence. 'The sooner these pigs are all dead the better.'

Hearing this was shocking to Hans, Himmler didn't just want to win the war, he was proposing genocide. Himmler even smirked as he delivered his plans; it further sickened Hans when the information was received with a round of applause. His peers seemed to take this in their stride as if it was an obvious solution to all of the German trials and tribulations. Completely eradicate the Jews, and life would return to the glory days when Germany was a respected nation. Hans could only see this as making the German people reviled throughout history.

Hans heard a rumour that Himmler was bullied as a child, and this added to his personal hatred of the Jews, and he was seeking revenge. He didn't know if this was true, but he thought that Himmler came across as both clever, and manipulative. He wouldn't trust the man, and Himmler would never command his respect. He was however the superior officer, and Hans felt helpless, and didn't know what he could do to stop this madness.

Over the next hour or so the plans were debated. Not the validity of the Sardine Packing, just the execution of the instructions they have been given.

Himmler said, 'the first of the camps imported prisoners are due tomorrow. I want the men to make ready the graves for their countrymen.' The trenches needed to be ready in three days, as there were just over a hundred of the first prisoners to be brought to the village for processing.

Processing, Hans was disgusted at this term, process; these human beings were to be treated like lumps of meat. The plan was to drive them to trenches, make them hand over all valuables, and then execute them. This is what was meant when they speak of processing them. Hans didn't know if this term was meant to deliberately dehumanise the Jews, but either way, no one seemed to care.

Maybe some felt as Hans did, but they didn't have the nerve to expose themselves. Hans surreptitiously glanced around the room, no one looked particularly perturbed. Either way, this job would be done efficiently, and without question. It was fair to say that they were all very aware that not following orders would have potentially severe consequences; nevertheless Hans was still surprised at the apparent indifference shown by the Nazi officers present.

Himmler continued, 'We are expecting something like 800 poisoners over the next three weeks, they are coming from temporary camps. I want to create temporary shelters on the outskirts of Rittershoffen, so none of the village residents will be aware of what is happening. Once the filming had been completed they will also be subjected to Sardine Packing, and the village will become your residence.' Himmler boasted, 'the village will then be a permanent death camp. In Rittershoffen alone I want to process at least 1000 prisoners a day.'

Hans was flabbergasted, this would be a staggering number of people to be wiped off the face of the earth at the hands of this mad man. He just couldn't believe how painful this would be for Sophie, to know your daughter will be shot was quite sickening, quite appalling. He couldn't keep it from her, but at the same time he didn't know how to tell her. He had no choice, he would have to prepare her. The more he reflected on this, the more determined he became to help them. That night he cried for the second time in his adult life, and he vowed to help as many of these poor people escape as he possibly could. He started to make plans that very night.

Chapter 6

Hans has lived next door to Sophie for three weeks now, and he has come to realise, that under the surface people were all the same. Their relationship was different to any other, and he knew that deep down they had connected. He knew he had completely fallen in love with Sophie and Alicia, and he was sure they felt the same.

Sophie was exceptionally attractive, but it was a far more complex feeling that she had stirred in him. He longed to hold her, and he wanted to consummate their relationship but he feared that she may reject his advances, after all, she was his prisoner of war. Now, with the plan for the Sardine Packing revealed, he was even more cautious of approaching her, and above all he wanted to protect her and Alicia.

But he could do nothing until he told Sophie, and her friends about the Sardine Packing. He would feel deceitful if he kept it to himself. He calls round to her cottage very early the next morning, to speak to Sophie, and tell her right away before Alicia woke. The cottage was open as always, so Hans walked in, and called quietly to Sophie.

'Sophie? Sophie I need to speak with you,' he didn't want to shout, so that he wouldn't wake Alicia.

He went up the stairs, and called softly to her again. She still hadn't responded to his calls, he thought he could hear her moving around in her bedroom, and the door to her room was slightly ajar, he opened the door a little further, just an inch or two to peer in, just in case he was mistaken, and she was still asleep.

When he looked in he saw Sophie standing over a bowl of water washing her naked body. Hans was unintentionally voyeuristic, like a rabbit frozen in the glare of a lamp. All thoughts of telling her lost to the moment. Her jet black hair with a natural light curl, had grown out some, and lay on her shoulders. Her body really was perfect. She has long slender legs with no visible hair, leading up to beautiful buttocks. She was sideways to him and he could see the curve of her breast on her left side with a pert nipple protruding in his direction. The size of her breasts seemed smaller when she was dressed. She was perfectly proportioned, and he his honourable intentions were deserting him, he wanted her there, and then. He lost track of time as he lingered there appreciating her body, but before he could retreat, and pretend he wasn't being lecherous, Sophie turned and looked at him.

Sophie had known he was there all along, and there was a part of her that had wanted him to appreciate her body. She had been alone for a long time, her feelings for Hans had been growing and she knew that she loved him more deeply than she had ever loved her husband. A part of her felt guilt over this, but at the same time she felt liberated. She beckoned Hans forward as she knew that he wanted her as much as she wanted him.

As they embraced she wrapped her body around his, they felt like they belonged together, like two parts of the same whole. They were ready for each other, and that was obvious to them both, but suddenly they heard footsteps just outside the bedroom, it was Alicia. Sophie reluctantly pulled away from Hans, and wrapped herself in a towel, and went to greet her daughter.

Hans knew the moment was lost. He quickly greeted Alicia before leaving, as he went out the door, turned and looked to Sophie. The look they exchanged suggested he wouldn't have to wait too long, before resuming where they had abruptly left off, but he knew that he had to talk to her first.

Chapter 7

Hans had only spent time in the main village, and he couldn't avoid it any longer, he needed to make a trip to the recently constructed camp, situated at the top of the hill, some half a mile from the main village. Nicknamed S camp, short for Schussweite, simply translated as, the firing range. Hans had the budget responsibility for the whole operation, so he had to go and inspect the S Camp books, where Sardine Packing was already underway.

None of the villagers had been sent to this camp yet or were even aware of its existence, as the soldiers wanted to keep the morale in the village artificially high for the cameras. The film that would eventually be released should show the Jews the benefits of being transported from the ghettos to a designated site. By issuing decent food rations in the village, the people had an air of relief about them as the soldiers coming had lifted them from starvation, and it all played well for the cameras. Little did they know that it was all part of the plan.

As Hans got closer to the camp, the first thing he noticed was the horrendous stench. It smelt like rotting animal flesh. He arrived at the main gate, and was greeted by the camp Kommandant, and despite knowing each other for several months, they formally saluted.

Jürgen said, 'Hans, welcome to my world,' as he slapped Hans on the back, with a nervous laugh. 'Don't worry, no matter how malodorous, you will get used to it.'

'What on earth is making it smell this bad?' Hans asked.

Jürgen said, 'it's the Sardine packing.'

They walked through to his office, and he offered Hans a drink. He also held out a box of snuff which did reduce the smell but only just. Hans had a job to do, and quickly got down to the finances. It was just his job, and he hadn't really stopped to think too much about funding in general. Suddenly it was so obvious that they were simply stripping the Jews of all of their possessions. Hans didn't know why he hadn't really contemplated this, possibly because today he was so much closer to the source of the funding. He had a budget before he arrived in

Rittershoffen, and thought nothing of it. But here he was discussing the new income, and it was literally anything, and everything that they could, and had confiscated from the prisoners.

All portable possessions, the notes, and coins of many varied countries, and of many denominations. Rings, watches, bracelets, if it could be carried, it would have to be carried. If not, it would be left behind. After all the Jews had no choice, where else could they put the valuables they had. And whatever they had was taken from them, glasses, boots and clothes . . . literally everything.

Hans didn't want to be here doing this, but what choice did he have. He told himself that he would never cause anyone harm, and yet he was still a cog in the system. If they all refused to play a part surely this would come to an end. As Jürgen placed a glass of vodka in front of Hans, and their eyes met, Hans realized that as his superior officer Jürgen was waiting for his instruction, and the pause, albeit brief, had led Jürgen to think he had done something wrong. Hans snapped back into his role, he had to focus on his girls back at the cottage, and just get through the day. They chinked glasses, said salut, and got down to work.

They went through the books, and Hans found it quite surprising, they already had pages, and pages of entries listing all of the items confiscated. It was headed, "Sardine Packing Income Proceeds". Someone at the top had realised that the total valuables that they were likely to confiscate could be substantial, and further fund the war effort. Hans could see that they were stripping everything from the Jews, and it wasn't just here at the camp. There would be far greater value outside of the items that can be carried. What about property, art collections, cars, it didn't matter, they would just take it; Hans was speechless, he thought, *how abhorrent*.

Jürgen, and his team were diligently listing every last item no matter how small. The notes, and coins were under lock and key, as was the jewellery, and other valuables. In the safe there were no papers. Hans thought about what Paris had said, realizing she may have been speaking in earnest, he picked up some papers from a waste paper bin, and they were Share Certificates.

Hans turned and asked, 'why have we thrown these away, they may be of some value?'

Jürgen said, 'They are not bearer shares, so each of those will be registered to the owners, and I am certain that we won't get any value off them. But I will keep them to be on the safe side, if you like?'

It occurred to Hans that he was probably overly influenced by what Paris had said, and conceded that they could be thrown out. Jürgen showed Hans a warehouse, and it was full of coats, boots, and on it went.

'How many prisoners have you had so far Jürgen?'

'We have already had somewhere in the region of 800 prisoners. They generally give up all of their possessions straight away. After all, we are heavily armed'

Hans asked Jürgen, 'do they resist?'

He replied, 'yes, but only very occasionally. We shoot the odd difficult customer, one shot straight through the head at close range tends to set the tone. Most understand that resistance really is useless.' The body language was that of a very stressed man, and he was wiping at an invisible mark on his chin as he said this.

It was a hot, and humid summer day, but the windows and doors were all closed. The smell wasn't too bad in doors, and after a couple of hours of auditing the figures; you could almost be in any office environment. There were no prisoner deliveries scheduled today, and so Hans was spared that particular experience, at least for now.

Jürgen was a complete professional, and Hans satisfied himself that the books were in order. In business Jürgen would be a real asset. His team respected him, and Hans could tell that he got his results through leading by example, and he would keep whatever hours necessary to deliver on his workload.

Hans was satisfied, he nodded his goodbye to the various staff, and they saluted to their superior officer. Jürgen saluted too, but Hans reached out to shake this man by the hand. He couldn't say anything, but he felt that Jürgen was as disgusted as he was with the whole purpose of this camp. Hans could tell Jürgen was determined to do what he had to do to the best of his ability. Hans believed that he would want the death of his prisoners to be over as quickly as possible. There was no gallows humour to be had here. As Hans stepped outside, the smell seemed much stronger than when he arrived.

Jürgen said, 'it's the sun, Hans.' He had read his thoughts, or more likely saw Hans screw up his face as he tried to not breathe through his nose.

'The worst part here are the flies. The bodies are laying there for no more than three or four hours before they are rife with maggots. If the prisoner's skull was shattered, and the brain exposed, the maggots always seem to find that first. Do you want to go to the edge of the trench?'

Hans now knew why his colleague had bags under his eyes; Jürgen would have those images embedded into his mind for the rest of his life. Hans thought that he should, but he didn't want to.

'No, I have seen more than enough, thank you,' Hans left to go straight back to the cottage. They were running out of time, and come what may, he had decided that he would help Sophie and Alicia escape. He had a plan, it wasn't great but it was about the best he could come up with.

Chapter 8

There was no easy way to say it, but that night Hans told Sophie all that he knew. 'This is so very painful to say,' Hans said to Sophie, he was shaking, and pale. 'Sophie, I'm so so sorry.' His face told her in advance that this wasn't good. She urged him on, she needed to know. 'Some of the transported prisoners have been assigned the task of digging trenches that will be a mass grave. Tomorrow all of the prisoners in the village will be marched out to S Camp where they will be executed.' Thankfully Alicia had already gone upstairs to prepare for bed, so Hans whispered to Sophie to make sure they did not alert Alicia.

'The Fuhrer is expected tomorrow, he will make his inspection, afterwards . . .' Sophie buried her head in her hands, and sobbed silently. 'Listen to me. I want to help you escape . . . when you are told to line up, I want you to go to the front of the line of people. As you are marched up the hill, I am going to make sure I am next to you. When I give you the signal you are to run, and hide in the trees. Wait there until I come back for you.'

Sophie asked, 'why can't we just hide here, we could climb into the loft?'

'It is not possible. The camp has a record keeper who has a list of all of the prisoners, and he will make sure everyone is accounted for.'

'Thank you for trying to help Hans. You are a good man.' Sophie insisted on saying goodbye. Hans would have none of it. He had found the lady he wanted to spend the rest of his life with, and they will get through this.

Sophie kissed him. He pulled away and looked at her. Then he kissed her back. He just couldn't stop the tears. This last night at the cottage was not the time to consummate their relationship, that will have to wait, it was simply too painful, but also Sophie wanted to spend the night in bed with Alicia.

The way that Sophie dealt with this news was extraordinary. She decided to tell Alicia they were going on a trip to their next life. She told her that all would be ok, and that Alicia would finally see her daddy once again. Instead of being scared, Alicia went to sleep happy in the knowledge that she was going to a new home, and a new life. Hans thought it was an incredible way to deal with the awful pain of knowing your daughter would be executed.

Once Alicia was asleep, Sophie asked Hans to lie with them. She had her back towards him, and she faced Alicia. Hans wraps his arm around her, and they hold hands.

'Hans, we must say goodbye.'

'No, I refuse to give in, I will help you escape, and we will be together after this war is over, it can't go on forever.' Hans whispered so he would not wake Alicia. Sophie held it together so amazingly that you would think it was Hans going off to the trenches.

'Hans you must know that I have fallen in love with you, but tomorrow I will die, I know it is my fate.' He was lost for words. 'When we go to heaven, I will be reunited with my husband. You understand don't you?'

'Sophie please don't think about dying, I will do anything to make sure that you escape.'

'Hans I believe that you will do your best, but I still have to be realistic. The chances of survival are slim, and I need you to understand about Kris.'

'Of course I understand. If I met my wife in heaven, I would have the same dilemma, but what if you survive, would you want to be with me?'

'Yes'

'I love you Sophie.'

'I don't want to think about being in heaven with you, and Kris there. I will trust in God to take care of us all. If tomorrow we live, then I won't think about heaven, but if we die tomorrow, I want you to know that even if I am reunited with Kris, I will never ever forget you.' She was repeating some things he already knew, she went on. 'I didn't love him, I was very young, and pregnant and we ended up together. But he was a good man, and a good father. I have to do what is right.'

They lay awake for most of the night, and they hardly spoke as they had said all there was to say. Sophie was happier planning for the worst, and hoping for the best. Hans' final thoughts before they drifted off to sleep were full of determination, the escape would be a success.

Chapter 9

The Fuhrer arrived in his open top Midnight Blue Mercedes Benz 770K with his large entourage, seen as befitting of a leader of his stature. The prisoners, and guards alike were to line the road leading to the makeshift Headquarters at the village Hall. His presence seemed to command respect. He even waved towards the Jewish villagers lined up for his arrival, and with the pomp, and circumstances surrounding his visit some even wove back. After all, the well fed villagers still have had no idea at this stage that their fate had already been decided.

As one of the most senior trusted soldiers at the camp, Hans was positioned at the door of the village hall. The Fuhrer shook his hand as he entered, and it was from this vantage point that Hans heard the conversation between the Fuhrer, and Himmler.

'Heinrich my loyal comrade, please come, take a seat.'

'Thank you mein Fuhrer.'

Himmler sat, but Hitler remained standing, and said, 'I was intrigued by your letter outlining the "Final Solution to the Jewish question", and of course, I had to see it for myself first hand. Tell me of our little experiment here. Do you think it will be cost effective?'

Himmler loved the praise, Hans could tell with the way he replied. 'Absolutely. We arrived here less than a month ago, and took control of the village with just 48 men. Granted there was little food here, however we have confiscated a substantial amount of money, and jewellery, and of course the real-estate. It really will be self-funding, and that's the exciting part.'

Himmler had the attention of the Fuhrer, and continued. 'This is totally scalable. I think we can process up to a 1000 Jews with only 10 men. The secret is to take the strongest prisoners, and set them to work. Here they have already dug all of the trenches that we need.'

Hitler remained standing, and replied. 'Excellent. Excellent. I am proud of you. You have indeed listened to me, and I can see that this solution has come about through my strong leadership.' At this point

Adolph was animated, and shouting while banging the desk at which Himmler sat, and continued.

'I follow my course with the precision, and security of a sleepwalker.'

Himmler for his loyalty, and commitment to the Fuhrer had risen to the head of the SS, replied.

'This village is an experiment in extermination, and a model that, with your blessing of course, I would like to roll out, and oversee. We can have purpose built extermination camps. At these killing factories we could process far more Jews than we ever could Sardine Packing.'

Himmler was like a puppy, looking up to his owner for any praise coming his way. 'It is good Heinrich, very efficient. Do you realize that you are in the presence of the greatest German of all time?' Hitler offered, modest as ever. 'I note that you have requested to select several women for the pleasure of your troops. But tell me why your soldiers want these ugly bitches? They are sub-human, they smell like pigs, and God knows what diseases they carry.' Despite the rumour that Hitler was gay, to Hans he came across as more asexual.

'With respect Adolph, these men are all red blooded young males, and they are much easier to control when they have their needs satisfied. If not these women, they will simply rape fellow servicemen, and women. The Jews are simply sex slaves that serve a purpose. In fact our scientists have run some experiments, and they have proven that if we encourage extreme sexual domination, the soldiers are desensitised of any moral compass they may mistakenly have felt.'

Hitler, referring to the scientists replied. 'These impudent rascals who always know everything better than anybody else. Okay Heinrich, you have my authorisation. I want the whole episode filmed for my perusal. Now tomorrow I want all of the prisoners lined up for my inspection. I want to see the fear in their eyes first hand. Remember that conscience is a Jewish invention. It is a blemish like circumcision. Unless you are prepared to be pitiless you will get nowhere.'

Some of Hitler's ramblings didn't seem to be linked, even though each word had meaning to him. It was almost like he verbalized every thought without it all making sense. Despite this Himmler hung onto his master's every word, certain to further his career. As their discussion came to a close, it was clear that both men were very pleased with the plans. They both shared a look, like the cat that got the cream.

As they walked out together Hans couldn't help noticing that Hitler had a high heel on his boots making him around 6ft tall. He saluted Hans, and Hans snapped the response as they walk past him heading to the accommodation set aside for the Fuhrer. Hans reflected on his first encounter with his leader.

The way he had felt prior to being here in the village, this would have been the highest honour to personally serve the man who had inspired a generation. But Hitler's immediate, and complete adoption of the Sardine Packing was enough proof for Hans to be convinced that he was nothing but a charismatic mad man. It was with a very heavy heart that he returned to the cottage.

Chapter 10

Hans left at 6am, after telling Sophie that they would have to leave their home at the 7am siren. Sophie, and Alicia step outside to join the crowd, some were neighbours but most had been transported to the village that day in cattle trucks. They all stood around bewildered. After roll call, Sophie, and Alicia fell in line with everyone else. They were waiting to be marched up the hill that lead out of the village.

Sophie could see Hans, and she made her way to the front as he had instructed. Hans had to go to the centre of the village to accompany the visiting dignitaries. Before he left, Hans made eye contact with Sophie, he hoped she understood; they meant to say *I will come back*. Throughout the new arrivals, grown men were moaning out loud. Women, and children were crying. The new arrivals hadn't had the benefit of the rations of the last three weeks, all of them looked gaunt, and dishevelled. To a man, they looked beaten both mentally, and physically. Hans found it strange that no one was actually hysterical or resisting.

The atmosphere was so tense you could have cut it with a knife. The noise started to increase as the people began to sense that they were no more than animals being lead to the slaughter. Hans noticed that the line of SS soldiers seemed to be enough to keep people in line. He thought, *If I had been starved, and beaten, and my physical endurance was so depleted, would I fight back?*

Judging by these poor people it would seem not. The enemy they were facing were heavily armed, which was enough to remove the last vestiges of any courage they might have otherwise had. They were all lined up for the inspection that was to be made by Hitler, and his entourage. Hitler's entourage comprised of the various dignitaries that he always had in tow.

Hitler marched along the line of prisoners. Himmler was walking proudly with his great leader mirroring the body language of the Fuhrer; hands behind their backs, sporting a cane, and shoulders back. Hitler looked much taller than his actual height, which made him look even more imposing. There was a certain charisma even though it was that of a despot. As Hitler passed Sophie she did not want to stare, but she can't help it. The man was infamous after all; their gaze meet, just briefly. She knew she would remember those black soulless eyes forever. Hitler suddenly spotted something amongst the prisoners, was instantly outraged, the crowd fell silent in absolute terror.

'You!!' He gesticulated at a prisoner with his cane, and gave instructions to one of his group, who in turn spoke to Sturmscharfuhrer Fischer who shouted to two of his men, 'hold out his hand.' On the man's hand was an old ring. The two soldiers quickly had the man pinned to the ground. Hitler was venomous as he shouted at the prisoner:

'What is the meaning of this!'

The poor man, he must have been at least 80 managed to say, 'please sir it is of no value, it was my mothers, please.'

Sturmscharfuhrer Fischer spoke to Himmler, and then spoke quietly with one of his men, who quickly left, and then returned a moment later with an axe. The poor prisoner on the ground, arm outstretched with his hand held out ready. The axe came down with crunching force, and chopped through the hand in a diagonal line from the outside wrist bone across to the thumb of the left hand. The soldier then bent, and picked up the severed limb, the ring now very accessible. This soldier removed the ring, wiped it of blood, and then handed it to Hitler's outstretched hand. The Fuhrer held it up between his thumb, and index finger. He closed his left eye, and seemed to stare through the hole in the ring. Like a diamond merchant looking for inclusions. He started to speak again, softly at first but soon turned to a shout.

'Prisoners, I command you to hand over anything of value to my men. This is our rightful property, and the consequences of non-compliance bear a heavy price.'

At these words, Sturmscharfuhrer Fischer made a single command, and the axe was buried deep into the skull of the offending prisoner. The point was well made. Hitler had seen enough, and was ready to leave Rittershoffen. As he departed he gave his half-hearted, infamous salute to the soldiers, and they saluted in return with the fully raised arm accompanied with an emphatic, 'Heil Hitler!!'

Chapter 11

With Hitler out of the way it was now time for Himmler to select three women for his personal use. To help him make his decision he wanted to see them naked. Himmler had studied much about slavery. To his mind there was much to be understood about the psychology of slaves that translated well to prisoners of war.

'Bring her to me.'

He pointed to an attractive girl, it was Paris. She stood out amongst the other women, because just those few weeks of rations had brought the vitality back into her body. Whereas the prisoners who had been transported to the village were looking desperately ill. Paris was dragged from the line by a big ugly brute of a man.

'Remove her dress.' The solder simply ripped it off revealing her shoulders, small breasts, and stomach.

'My baby, my baby.'

These were the last words Paris's mother wailed as she courageously ran at the soldier, and began beating his chest with her firsts. The soldier laughed out loud, Hans was disgusted right to his stomach, making him feel physically sick. The brute took out his luger, and shoot Paris' mother straight through the right eye. The bullet exited through the back of her skull, and the blood arced three feet in the air. It sprayed some of the prisoners of war, much to the merriment of many of the soldiers.

As she watched the quick execution of her mother, Paris' bladder gave way, and she would have fallen to the ground if not for the soldier who was holding her up by her arm. She stared ahead mutely; she would never speak again. Himmler's face didn't betray even the slightest change of expression or emotion. The ever present look of indifference was still planted firmly on his face. He walked over to Paris who has just become an orphan. She shook uncontrollably with her arms instinctively crossed over her naked chest. Her eyes staring blankly ahead.

'Take off your underwear.'

Himmler grunted, but heard no response from the girl. She has gone too far inside to hear, and her eyes remained unfocused.

Himmler repeated, 'take off your underwear. I only want a virgin, do you hear me. Are you a virgin?'

The soiled underwear eventually went the same way as the dress. Himmler decided to find out the answer for himself. He pushed his middle two fingers of his left hand between her legs, and up inside her body. He wasn't sure if he felt her hymen break or not but he pulled his hand away, and there was a trickle of blood. This seemed to satisfy him. He picked up the girl's discarded dress to wipe his fingers.

'You! Take her to my quarters. No one is to touch her. I want her as soon as this job is over, do you understand?'

All the soldiers in unison replied 'yes Reichsfuhrer.'

Paris had fallen so far into herself that was no longer aware of what was happening to her, and unable to move. The soldier, using his initiative slung her over his shoulder. Unfortunately for him, her bowels now give way as he did this. There was sudden snickering around him, as most of his comrade's thought this was hilarious. The Reichsfuhrer raised his voice.

'Enough. Take her away, and have her cleaned up.' The men fell silent, Himmler never needed to ask twice.

Himmler forced three other young, attractive women in turn to undress, and there was no further attempt by anyone in the crowd to stop this. He pointed to two of the women, 'you two back in line.' To the third he commanded, 'you, go with that soldier.' He then pointed to another villager, one who was not as emaciated as the prisoners that had been recently transported.

'You will be treated well if you don't resist,' Himmler lied. She was grabbed firmly by the left arm, and led away. With nothing on her feet, and the rough terrain underfoot she found it difficult to keep up.

Many of the soldiers enjoyed taking batons to their chosen women, but never to their faces. They claimed it spoiled the women's looks when the face was covered in bruises or bleeding. As women were pulled from the group of prisoners many were struck to subdue them. However, with rape being so common in war time, many of the women selected hoped to avoid death by being very compliant, this woman was amongst them. The prisoners that had to witness the selection process were sickened by the sheer cruelty of this degrading scene. But still, no one, other than Paris's mother, has come to the defence of any of the women. This was about to change.

Hans was grateful that Sophie had changed her appearance, and was standing well away from the centre where Himmler stood making his selection. If she hadn't he was sure she would be selected. Himmler, still looking for his third girl, went into the crowd of prisoners to get a closer look. One or two were managing to hide their faces against shoulders of loved ones.

Himmler thought that some of the prisoners from the village, that have been fed reasonably well, looked quite attractive, for Jews. He grabbed the long black hair of a woman, and turned her to face him. She was older than the other two, and in Himmler's opinion probably not untouched. He preferred virgins, as he was sure not to catch any of the venereal diseases that were rife, but she was attractive, so he decided to make an exception, 'undress.'

This was his only command. What choice did she have? As Maria removed her clothes her eyes were locked on Andreas in the crowd. It was too much for him, and despite the hindrance of his false leg; he rushed towards Himmler as fast as he could. He hadn't gotten very far when two bullets from different soldiers hit him at more or less the same time. Both shots deliberately didn't kill him. The soldiers were under strict instruction not to kill people in the village as it wasn't efficient for them to then have to clear up the mess. Himmler held up his hand, palm open to his men, to remind the soldiers not to shoot to kill. There was going to be something worse than death for Andreas to endure.

Thankfully Hans wasn't selected to assist. Two of his colleagues have to grab Andreas under the arms, and they hold him captive facing Himmler awaiting his command.

'Is this your wife?' Himmler asked. He repeated the question, and still has no reply until Maria answers "Yes" for him.

Andreas said, 'you bastard, kill us now you fucking bastard. We will see you in hell.' It was unbearable for Andreas to see the love of his life treated in this degrading, and vile way. There was nothing Hans could do, he would be better off keeping his head down, and helping from within whenever he was able. If he stepped in now he would only achieve his own death, and possibly that of Andreas. The soldier to his left raised Andreas head by the hair so he could see Maria not ten feet away. Andreas said, 'you touch her, and I will kill you.'

Himmler now had two other soldiers each side of Maria, they each had a wrist, and ankle, and hoisted her feet off the floor, legs spread. If anyone had any fight left in them it was about to be extinguished. Himmler walked over to Maria, and right in front of Andreas he inserted his luger right up inside her vagina.

'Do you like that eh?'

The words spoken to Maria, meant to torment Andreas. Himmler turned to him, and said,

'Is your little Jewish cock getting stiff?'

'Please no, please I will do anything,' Andreas said.

Many of the villagers turned their eyes away from the depravity before them, others looked on with horror, and found it hard to turn away. There was almost an incredulity about it that made them keep looking. Hans hated Himmler, but he knew he had to keep his thoughts to himself. He didn't know who he can trust; almost all of the soldiers seemed to think this behaviour was perfectly acceptable.

Himmler said, 'she likes that see? My gun is the first really stiff thing she has had for a long time.'

The soldiers don't laugh at this, it wasn't meant to be funny. Domination suited a lot of them, you could see it in their faces, they loved it, it really turned them on. Himmler loved it too. He was the dominant, not just over the woman, but over the troops too. War time suited men like these.

It seemed to Hans that it allowed domination to come to the surface. Shown through killing and brutality. It would seem that many men had desires based around these themes, especially in war time when there might not be a tomorrow. The Germans watching were also thinking about the women for later. The Jews were no more than pigs to the soldiers, but still worth fucking.

'You bastard leave her alone.' Andreas managed to cry.

'Why, are you jealous?' Himmler replied, as he plunges the gun in, and out a few times making exaggerated panting noises. Maria, was crying silently, too terrified to utter any sound. With the gun right up inside Maria, as far as it could go, and with Andreas being forced to watch, Himmler, the Reichsfuhrer, pulled the trigger. Thankfully death came almost instantly for Maria, and the torment was over at last.

Andreas's dying cry was a high pitch whine; a bullet straight through the back of the head brought an end to the mental torture he had endured. It had the desired effect on the crowd; they were now more than ready to die, most felt that death couldn't be any worse than this. Hans didn't know what he would have done if it was Sophie that Himmler had selected; at least he didn't have to find out. It was so horrendous seeing his friends treated like this, and it did cross his mind that they are picked because Himmler has heard they had made friends with Hans.

The third, and final woman selected would have been better off dead. She had to endure the same humiliation as her predecessors, clothes off, fingers inserted, but this time when the Reichsfuhrer pulled his fingers out of her, he sniffed them like he was smelling the cork of a fine wine. When he did this, she had enough spirit left, to spit right in his face. She hadn't really thought it through, but probably somewhere in the back of her mind she hoped this would get her shot. . .if only that were true.

Himmler simply wiped his face, and had her sent immediately to his quarters. Later that night, to facilitate oral sex with her, and without the risk of Himmler being bitten, the Reichsfuhrer would first break her jaw in five places.

Hans wanted to follow the story of all of these women, and find out the full horror of this War, but he couldn't do it, it was too painful. By morning, the talk in the camp would be of such horrors as slicing through the one woman's perineum just for fun, three broken arms, a broken hip and much worse, Hans would find it all incredibly disturbing, and he hated his inability to do anything to help the women. In a way Paris escaped the ordeal, as she had gone so deep inside her own mind that her body wasn't responsive. By all appearances she was lifeless, and was left alone. Hans could only hope that these would rest in peace soon.

Chapter 12

Sophie and Alicia didn't see the full horror of the scene unfolding down the hill. That said, the crowd were still picking up on the fear, and are now absolutely terrified. There were only 48 SS soldiers at the village, and history would record that they had a total of 2787 prisoners to process. Moreover there were only 20 soldiers in the Einsatzgruppen, roughly translated as the killing squad. It was hard to imagine the kind of men that could do this.

They have nearly 140 Jews each, so they had to kill at least one every five minutes, twelve an hour: it was a very long day. The Einsatzgruppen complain that the soldiers in the village had the best of the women by the time their shift is over. They also say that it was a lot harder than it sounded, processing that many Jews in one day. If each death was a single shot, and the bodies dropped straight into the ditch it wouldn't be so bad. But, as well as shooting each prisoner, they then had to go through the mouths looking for gold teeth, which occasionally lead to them being bitten by those not yet dead.

They then had to smash away at the jaw bones to remove the teeth, and that alone could take five minutes. For the prisoners dressed well there was always a possibility that they have slipped valuables inside the rectum, and so the soldiers have to open up the gut. They say that it stank horribly when they did this. There was no doubt about it, Hans is grateful he had not been assigned to the Einsatzgruppen.

As the morning wore on, the command came from Himmler. 'Get these pigs moving faster, raus! Raus!'

Hans immediately went to the front of the line, and stood very close to Sophie, and her daughter. The crowd obediently shuffle forward. In complete contrast to the horror of the occasion, the sun was shining, and the pine trees, tall and proud, were releasing their scent as they always do. The walk to the edge of the village only took 5 minutes, and the reason for the trenches soon became apparent to the prisoners.

Although most, by now realised that the journey would lead to certain death, no one really expected to be staring down at their own final resting place. There were already two or three layers of decomposing bodies in the trenches, and with the day being so hot the smell was uniquely putrid. Those who strayed too close, quickly found themselves bent at the waist vomiting.

The Jewish prisoners didn't look human anymore. The way the starvation had forced the body to cannibalise itself, meant that faces were gaunt, almost ghost like. Teeth protuberant, eyes sunken and bodies so thin, they were almost skeletal. Hands, and feet looked abnormally large as the rest of the body became smaller, and with their heads shaved they look so different.

Hans heard Alicia say, "mommy the people look funny with no clothes on". Alicia was surrounded by people being forced to strip, and had made this observation without fear in her voice. Hans wondered why there wasn't any resistance, as the prisoners far outnumbered the troops. Most of the 20 brown shirt soldiers of the Einsatzgruppen assigned the sardine packing duty enjoyed dishing out pain. Whenever they had a smaller amount of prisoners to process, they took difficult shots, such as aiming for ankles, moles, breasts, and other more difficult to hit targets.

Some say that they needed to do this to keep their aim sharp, others confessed, it was purely for pleasure, for some the more pain they dished out the better. Today they were processing a much larger amount, and the senior officers like Hans had to be in support for any prisoners who tried to escape. He was sure that his escape plan would work as there was nobody standing by him. He put himself between the other prisoners, and his girls. His instruction was for them to run into cover as soon as they reached the perimeter of the woods. They were 20 feet away, and poised and ready to run.

Hans' heart sank as Himmler's car raced to the front of the crowd. He was stunned, and didn't know what to do. Himmler had instructed his chauffeur to drive to the head of the line, and he saw that Sophie, and Alicia were not in the main throng. So he fires his Luger above their heads shouting for them to get back in line. Several soldiers of the Einsatzgruppen had turned to look at what the commotion was all about.

If Sophie and Alicia were to run now they would be gunned down. Hans didn't know if Himmler suspected him of being complicit in their potential escape. He did seem to watch Hans more closely. It was the lowest any man could ever sink, and a part of Hans just wanted to die with them. He could do nothing other than stand and stare at Sophie, and Alicia through their final moments on this earth.

The execution of his beloved girls was in the hands of a young soldier standing directly behind Alicia, and Sophie. He was well aware that any shots that were not fatal would extend his working day, and he wanted to kill with a single bullet whenever possible. At the trench he could see Sophie holding her daughter close. Alicia with her eyes tightly closed focuses on all of the promises her Mother had recently made, and amazingly kept a smile planted firmly on her face. Mr Pickles gripped tightly under her right arm. For his part, Hans felt helpless, even worse that he had no choice but to watch.

Thankfully Alicia's death was instant. She landed on her back in the ditch. Hans had eye contact with Sophie, she said so much with that one last look, then she mouthed the words, "never forget me Hans". She took a shot to the lower back. The force of the impact took her off her feet, and she too landed on her back in the ditch. Hans looks down, and she was barely alive. He felt sure that Sophie could see Alicia's smile from where she lay. She was the bravest woman that he had ever met, and she has done all she could for Alicia. Hans was desperate that he couldn't do more, and has failed to save them.

With her dying breath Sophie wondered why she felt no pain, she saw a light that at first seems far far away but it is coming closer. She believes she heard Alicia say, 'Mommy you were right Daddy is here.'

As Sophie faded from her physical form. The feeling of love was all around her, she was aware of her daughter in a new way. They were part of the same whole. Her final thoughts were to forgive the soldier that had shot them both, to forgive Himmler, and she even forgave the Fuhrer. Whether it was just the thoughts of a dying woman or not, she only felt everlasting love as her soul returns home.

Book 2
Present Day

Chapter 13

It was the first night of a brand new Evening Class at Washington University, entitled "How to diagnose and treat Post Traumatic Stress Disorder". It was scheduled to run every Monday evening for the next 12 weeks, and the eminent psychologist, Dr David Prost, was the guest lecturer. Prost had his own busy holistic therapy clinic, and thanks to savings and a substantial inheritance, he certainly didn't take the role of lecturer for the money. He took it because he had always found it hard to say no to projects that kept his life full of new experiences. He saw this course as giving students an introduction to the disorder, and he expected to attract professionals and amateurs alike.

When the students paid their tuition fees they had an information booklet that contained all they needed to know, including the classroom location, what to bring with them and so on. It said the start time was 7pm, but by 6.30 most students had already arrived, and were helping themselves to coffee. There didn't appear to be anyone in charge, so the group mingled awkwardly. Stilted conversations broke out here and there, with the more outgoing students, while others made more of the notice board than the contents deserved, and avoided eye contact.

A tall well-dressed man casually strolled into the lecture hall, and he had such an air of confidence about him that everyone guessed him to be the lecturer. The first thing he said was, 'well . . . good evening everyone, I hope I'm not late,' he moved his head back as he said this, to move his eyes further away from his watch, to bring the hands into focus. As his watch tended to lose time, for confirmation, he looked up at the large clock on the wall, but as that said ten past two, it wasn't much help.

'I am Dr David Prost . . . but by all means, David please . . . though I will answer to most names.' His thick mop of blond hair, cut in a youthful style, made him hard to age. 'As you can tell, I am not the leather patches on the elbows, sort of lecturer.' He left a suitable pause before adding, 'Yet,' and quite naturally laughed at his own joke. He added, 'In fact this is the very first course I have ever taught, so bear with me as I fumble through.'

He grabbed himself a coffee, and went about connecting his laptop to the in-situ overhead projector. He had always been a little hopeless with technology, however he was ready for the 7 pm start, by which time his students had all found a seat. Prost did a headcount, and noted 14 students in attendance compared to a list of 15 anticipated. 'Can you put your hand up if you are not here.' Prost joked, this time when he laughed, the students joined in. While working, he had a wonderful way of making people relax. Just then number 15 burst in apologising and blaming traffic, after she got her coffee she sat at the front, Prost realised straight away that he knew her.

He displayed a single slide saying 'PTSD', and perched on a desk at the front, and said, 'shall we begin. Can we start by introducing ourselves?' He looked at the last lady to arrive, and he gestured for her to begin. She stood, and addressed the room.

'Hello everyone my name is Emily . . . Emily Myers, right . . . well . . what can I tell you about me? I am 34, I am single and well emmm . . . as you can probably tell I am English. I have a wonderful family, and I am so close to my mother and my sister, they still live in England, but we speak every night on Skype or we text, email or Facebook and so on.'

Dr Prost was smiling inside at how much Emily wanted to say, but he felt no compulsion to stop her, he was relaxed as she continued.

'I often talk a lot, especially when I am nervous . . . as you can tell, in fact I am told I go on too much sometimes, other times I am so focused on what I am doing that I zone everything and everyone out, if you know what I mean.'

Prost used the opportunity to gather his thoughts, and check his outline of an agenda as Emily pushed on, 'I can worry about anything and everything and usually do. My sister, Eleanor, the pretty one, said I could worry about having nothing to worry about. So I am here to learn techniques to control stress.'

This was not unusual, as people attracted to the profession often come through suffering some sort of trauma in their own lives. Emily looked at Prost to indicate she had finished.

'Thank you Emily.'

Prost then gestured to Emily's right, this lady remained in her seat and said her name. She had read the Information Booklet and it said, when invited, you should state your name. Prost raised an eyebrow to the right of her, and so it went around the room as it dawned on Emily what she should have said. She gave Prost a look that said, "I can't believe you let me stand there and say all that". He smiled a cheeky smile, but he didn't have even a twinge of guilt, he did however hope she would see the funny side.

The two hours flew by, and with plenty of group participation through a variety of activities, most left feeling they knew several of the other students, and they looked forward to next week. As everyone was filing out, Prost was putting away his laptop, and Emily walked over to him.

'Did you recognise me straight away! Probably not, as I am old and fat now?' she asked.

She looked young and she was certainly not fat, but David recalled that she always had a tendency to be self-deprecating.

'Of course I did, it's only been, what . . . seventeen years or so.' He said, with his light jocular style. 'I saw your name on the student list, and I wondered if it would be you. I thought there was a chance because I had heard that you are living in Washington.' David was born in England and the Prost's had been neighbours and close friends of the Myers for over twenty years before they emigrated. 'How is Eleanor,' he asked. He tried to sound casual as he asked about his old girlfriend, but failed.

Emily replied, 'well you know what she's like, so very positive, if I ever feel down, I can call her and she will pick me up straight away. I am hopeless and usually pessimistic. I call Eleanor the "Eternal Optimist". I love America, but I do miss her so much, and mom of course. Saying that, Eleanor has a new job, and she will probably travel the world. So I am hoping she gets to come here as her new company has their Head Office here.'

David had been very close to Emily's sister when they were teenagers, they were all very close. Emily asked David if she could see him professionally as she was dealing with a level of stress that she wanted help with. David had taken over his Father's practice, Dr David Prost senior, and it was a pure coincidence that Emily and David found themselves both living, and working in Washington DC.

David asked, 'do you know why you feel stressed?' He was so laid back in his approach that she found him easy to talk to.

Emily replied, 'with all the terrorist activity around the world, and the various wars that are being fought in Syria and other volatile places, I have started to feel really sorry for the innocent people caught up in it. I also keep watching programmes on World War 2, even though I find it all quite repulsive, I can't stop. I have started working on my family tree, as I want to see how our own family were caught up in the second World War. I think that might give me the answers I need.'

He gave her his business card, 'please book in, and come and see me. If our personal relationship is an issue for you, I have a business partner that I can recommend.' She assured him that the relationship would actually help her. He said 'I am going to have to be rude, I have a table booked at 9pm, but will you please call me?' She promised that she would. 'It was great to see you again, please remember me to Eleanor.'

Chapter 14

Eleanor Myers was on an all expenses trip to meet with her new employer, Mr Richard Weiss, the Chairman of Weiss Investment Banking Corp, W.I.B.C, based in Washington DC. She was heading to the French Alps, to the exclusive ski resort of Val D'isere. By pure coincidence, Eleanor had spent many winters as a young girl with her family in Val, but this was the first time she had flown into the resort, and her first time in a helicopter.

Eleanor was surprised just how much the rotation of the blades shook the aircraft. She turned to the pilot, and asked, 'what are those animal tracks?' They were flying low, at around two hundred feet and she could see a lot of paw prints. The area wasn't exactly covered in them, but nevertheless enough for her to wonder, *what on earth do they find up here to feed on*?

The pilot, Michael Morgan said, 'they are Alpine Marmots Miss Myers.' He hadn't said a lot so far but he seemed to be concentrating on flying. 'Do you mind if I ask what you will be doing for Mr Weiss?' Michael asked.

'I have signed a 12 month contract as his personal translator,' Eleanor said. She knew it was rare for a personal translator to secure such stability.

'If I know Mr Weiss, I would imagine he is paying you very well.'

'You're not kidding . . . about twice what I could get anywhere else,' Eleanor replied. She had never worried about money, for that matter she hadn't really worried about anything.

Michael said, 'well I know that he will see it as value for money, he spends a lot, but he isn't wasteful. You will find that he will recoup that cost and some, but he will look after you, of that you can be sure, you just wait and see.'

'Do you know what he wants me to do Michael?' Eleanor enquired.

'Not really . . . well actually I have heard that he is looking at purchasing a French company. My guess is he sees you as important for that deal, but I would rather not try and second guess Mr Weiss,' Michael said.

Eleanor thought the views were always breath-taking, but this bird's eye view added a new dimension, she had always thought that the Alps were a truly awesome spectacle. From up here she could see that most of the area was completely inhospitable, sheer, snow covered slopes that could never be tamed. Eleanor recalled when the family used to travel to Val D'isere by road, that there were buildings throughout the area, albeit not overly dense, however from this height she had a different perspective, and realised that only a very small percentage of this vast space had any human habitation.

Michael interrupted her reverie, 'we are about to begin our descent.' He kept his eyes straight ahead as he spoke, very focused on landing and added, 'I expect it to be quite turbulent, but that is perfectly normal for these conditions.' Flying in this location had its own set of challenges. Michael was flying without a co-pilot, with his passenger in the free port side seat. He said, 'we are flying well within the acceptable range for this aircraft, so don't be concerned if we get a lot of yawing during the landing.' As he spoke he demonstrated the anticipated movement with his free hand. He had complete command of his aircraft, and Eleanor was completely relaxed, although she was oblivious to the challenges of flying in this environment.

Michael said, 'the vision is often compromised as the downdraft tends to kick up the loose snow, but we can land safely by the instruments if necessary.'

'Thank you, don't worry about me,' Eleanor said, 'I'm loving it . . . it is stunning from up here.'

The whole trip, Michal had insisted on formality, constantly saying Miss Myers, and Mr Weiss, and it had created a professional barrier between them, however it wasn't uncomfortable. Michael had an air of professionalism, and Eleanor knew she was in safe hands. Despite Eleanor's tendency to make conversation where there wasn't any, today she was preoccupied with the views.

As she uncrossed and recrossed her legs, Eleanor was unaware of the reflection in the chrome dashboard. The pilot felt guilty not confessing to the rather splendid view up her skirt. He realised that this was the first person he had ever dropped off in Val Desiree, in mid-winter, wearing stockings, and high heels.

Eleanor knew how cold she would be, but thought first impressions were far more important. She also knew that she wouldn't be outside for too long, and thought it a price she was prepared to pay. She wasn't a big fan of fur either, but the extravagant coat seemed far more acceptable in France, and there was no doubt, it completed her look and kept her warm.

∞

The benefit of the bubble canopy of the helicopter was the full hundred and eighty degrees aspect, an advantage for Visual Flight Rules. Landing created an effect like a shaken snow globe, but they touched down without incident. They transferred to the waiting vehicle, and Eleanor had to smile at the "Weiss 1" number plate. She was surprised that the pilot not only disembarked with her, but he now sat in the cars driving seat. The car had been pre-warmed, and the windscreen cleared, in readiness for their arrival. As it was fitted with winter tyres and snow chains, it was a perfect vehicle for the conditions. Eleanor saw the dashboard thermometer, it was minus three degrees. Outside everyone was dressed accordingly, and no one seemed to really notice the cold, even though the vapour created on exhalation served as a constant reminder.

Eleanor had feelings steeped in nostalgia, with a good mix of anticipation, and confidence for good measure, as the resort was very familiar to her. They passed a bus completely rammed with skiers, and their kit. Whatever the bus manufacturer's recommended maximum passenger capacity, it must have been at least three times over that stated limit. It trundled along the main road leading through the village, and they pulled out just behind it. The main road was very busy, as it always was during the ski season, but it was on the move, as usual, despite the heavy snowfall. The car handled the well-worn ruts in the snow as if it was on rails.

Eleanor took in the fresh air. The "Alpine Spring" scented candles try to capture the essence of a smell, but the real scent was a much broader attack on the senses. She took a deep breath, and it made her feel good, it was a feeling deep rooted in her psyche, from years of pleasure here.

Eleanor asked, 'are you finished for the day?' It wasn't idle chit chat, she was genuinely surprised that the pilot of the helicopter was now the chauffeur. Michael hadn't brought any of her luggage, so clearly there were other staff involved in her transfer.

Michael said, 'I'm what we call an 8k employee.' As the sun had gone down he placed his sunglasses on the top of his head. 'I am literally full time, available to Mr Weiss twenty-four hours a day, three hundred and sixty five days a year. Hence, around eight thousand hours.'

She was slightly irritated that he continued to insist on the formal Miss Myers. She thought, being professional is one thing, but it was almost rude to not acknowledge her on first name terms, especially as they were now work colleagues. What he had said just sank in, her mental arithmetic was fast, and for a basic stab at most people's working year, she calculated forty hours by fifty weeks, two thousand hours.

'That's incredible. So you are available to fly or drive anywhere at any time?'

'Essentially yes, but in reality my role is far more comprehensive. My official title is "Personal Transport Director", and I have a large team.' Michael had one eye on the road, and one hand on the wheel as he adjusted the air-conditioning to clear the windscreen of the condensation that had suddenly appeared.

This is the most he had spoken since the journey started, and he was upbeat while speaking, it was a subject he clearly felt comfortable with. 'We have two jets with two pilots for each. In air travel, we also have two helicopters and pilots for each of those. We have a ground support team consisting of four people; they take care of the luggage, prep the aircraft's fuel and so forth. We then have the yacht, and its full time crew of eight, and four part time.' He went on and on, clearly proud of the job he did.

With no sarcasm intended she said, 'and you drive as well?'

'I started working for Mr Weiss fifteen years ago, I was his personal pilot. As his business grew, so did his need for transport, and my role grew organically. Mr Weiss still prefers me to be at the helm of all of his personal travel, and now my total budget is seven million dollars a year.'

'So the team you run, do they all work for W.I.B.C?' Eleanor asked while applying fresh deep red lipstick.

'No we all work for a subsidiary of the bank. The team that I manage effectively all work exclusively for Mr Weiss. He has such a busy International schedule, and getting him to where he needs to be on time is our modus operandi.'

They could see the wonderful Hotel Les Barmes de L'Ours, this was the hotel that the Myers used to stay in, it was a firm family favourite and it always made Eleanor feel at home here. It served a classic cheese fondue in the same original fondue sets. It had the distinctive French Chalet sloping roof with icicles two feet long, and very thick, their eventual journey down the mountain would be some months away.

The restaurant had a wall of fame, and Eleanor wondered if the Myers family photo was still there. It was a picture that told a tale as it featured the sisters as young girls, and they looked very similar. However, even back then, Eleanor had always wanted to look her best, and shopped with her mother for the latest high fashion ski items, while Emily always had very basic salopettes, usually boys. Try as she might their mother couldn't get Emily to wear nice girl's clothes. "I look like a fat lump in those" she would say, despite being very slim. Emily's hair was also cut short in more of a masculine fashion, and this core difference carried through to their adult lives.

Eleanor continued to freshen her make-up, as they sat in silence for the remainder of the transfer, she was thinking about what Michael had told her. What a team of people, and they were just on transport alone. She knew Weiss was a wealthy man, but he was clearly far richer than her Google search suggested. As they pulled up outside the Chalet Blanc, Eleanor's face was a picture. The Chalet was breathtaking. Although built with an eye on tradition, in typical French ski resort style, incorporating lots of natural wood, this building had an unmistakably modern twist about it. The door to the underground opened automatically.

'Michael. What is it like working for Mr Weiss?'

'I absolutely love my job, and Mr Weiss is great to work for, very generous. You will soon see that we get to travel the world, eat in the finest restaurants, stay in the best hotels, and I wouldn't change places with anyone. I think you will be pleasantly surprised just how good it is working for him.'

Chapter 15

The garage area had a double door system to keep out the snow and cold. The first door opened into a pristine, but nevertheless, typical garage area. Waiting staff removed the chains, and then Michael drove onto a rolling road, where the tyres and wheels were cleaned and dried. At the same time two people wiped down the vehicle to get rid of the bulk of the snow. The second internal door opened onto an immaculate parking area. This floor was a stunning, highly polished light grey marble with silver flecks. The two cleaners followed the car through, and started to polish the car even before the occupants had alighted. Michael walked around the car, and opened the door for Eleanor.

Michael said, 'I would like to introduce you to Victoria who will take care of you from here. I am sure you will get on well with her, everybody does . . . and I look forward to working with you.'

With that Michael excused himself, leaving Eleanor in the capable hands of Victoria who was waiting to greet Eleanor in what looked like a reception area of a luxury car showroom. Victoria was dressed in a black Versace knee length skirt, buttoned up the back seam. Which was finished off with a lime green pashmina, and a broad smile to complete the look.

'Hello Eleanor,' Victoria said, 'and welcome to Chalet Blanc, I will be your chaperon for this trip. Did you have a good flight?'

Straight away Eleanor felt comfortable with Victoria. She had a bubbly personality that was warm and genuine. Eleanor was relieved that the formality adopted so rigorously, by the Pilot, was not company policy. She put out her hand to shake, at the same time Victoria stepped forward, and gave her a friendly hug saying, 'I can see you and I are going to get on like a house on fire.'

Looking out the window, Eleanor replied, 'what an unbelievable view. Why is it called Chalet Blanc?'

'Weiss translated in German is white, I think that was all it was.' Victoria answered.

The chalet was built on the main black run into the village, La Face. From here they had a full view of the resort; the view took in all of the nursery slopes that nestle in the valley between the two main peaks, where the restaurants prepared for the "Après Ski" crowd. 'Yes it's absolutely stunning. It is also ski in ski out, and we will have plenty of time on the slopes,' Victoria continued. 'Please let me show you to your room.'

Victoria led the way, past the floor to ceiling wall of glass with the view. Victoria walked almost silently, if she was walking on carpet, each right heel imprint would be filled by the left. She managed to saunter as if she was on a cat walk. They went down a marble staircase to the entrance of the Madeleine suite. Beyond the doorway there was a hallway with a seating area, and cloakroom. Eleanor slipped into some soft slippers, left to encourage those who enter to remove their outdoor shoes.

The opulence of the suite was in evidence in every single aspect of the various rooms, finished in style while remaining inviting. There were large displays of beautiful fresh flowers throughout the Chalet. It was quite unusual to see such a variety in the mountains, especially at this time of year. They were colour coordinated with the decor, deep yellows, almost gold. The flower vase included the delicate Angel's tears, a pale cream narcissus with delicate rounded cups, and Dianthus, with their deeply serrated petals giving off a clover scented aroma that filled the air. Clearly, great care and consideration had gone into their selection.

'Dinner is at eight, if you want to meet me at the top of the stairs at seven thirty, I can give you the grand tour.' Victoria said.

Once alone, Eleanor ran a bath. The first surprise was the fact that her luggage had not only arrived, but the contents had already been unpacked and put away. The second was the leather bound guide, detailing every last aspect of the trip. This itinerary included a full tailoring session where Eleanor would be measured for the range of uniforms; including the black outfit that she admired on Victoria. She sat in a dressing gown and rolled down her black stockings. She could see through the windows but no one could see in from the outside as it was mirrored glass. But she still felt self-conscious as she slipped out of her knickers with people going by. She knew they couldn't see her, but it still felt strange undressing in front of them. There was an exhibitionist quality to the way she felt; looking out at people who couldn't see her while she watched them as she undressed.

Once naked she headed to the en-suite to soak in the bath. She placed her neck on the headrest, and looked at herself in the mirrored ceiling and reflected on her journey to this point. It seemed surreal, but with an overriding sense of pride. She had worked extremely hard as a student and she had straight A's as the evidence of that commitment. But she had to say there was an element of luck that she should be here in this role today. She thought of her father's words, *If you follow the right path, everything will flow*, how right he was.

∞

Eleanor met Victoria as arranged, and in turn was introduced to the staff at the chalet. They were all very pleasant, and she knew she would fit in. The chalet continued to impress. The two rooms that stood out were the music room and the office. The music room, even without instruments, was a fantastic space. It had twice the ceiling height of the other rooms with a black gloss grand piano as the centrepiece. There were drum kits, keyboards and dozens of guitars. A separate mixing room full of electronic equipment.

Victoria explained, 'Richard is an accomplished musician.'

By contrast the office had a completely different vibe. Where wood was the main feature of the music room, the office was all high-tech. There were several sixty inch Ultra High Definition, Plasma Screens covering the walls. Each displayed various charts and stock market information. News channels were on mute, with the sound available through headsets. There were six people in this room; each raised their head from the screen to say hi. Eleanor was due to have dinner with Mr Weiss, but he sent his apologies. He would join her at some point tomorrow.

Victoria said, 'Richard often changed plans at the last minute.' This gave Eleanor the chance to get to know the team. The girls got on famously, and Eleanor just seemed to be accepted as one of the group. Weiss has four chefs for him and his close team, and the food served was exquisite. The dining room became full of laughter as the girls played a drinking game where they took it in turns to say "I'll take a drink with anyone who?" adding a confession. Each person was to tell of a real life situation and anyone who had also experienced the admitted transgression had to raise a toast. Each person then had to tell the tale in question. The more the alcohol flowed, the more outrageous the claims became. None of which caused any offence, but the odd one or two brought tears of laughter to the group.

After dinner, Eleanor invited Victoria back to her suite to finish off the champagne, and Victoria accepted. They hit it off so well, they were so comfortable that they both felt like they had been friends for years. Once they had said goodnight, Eleanor lay on her bed and just as her eyes went heavy and she was drifting off to sleep, she thought that she couldn't have wished for a better introduction to W.I.B.C.

Chapter 16

Eleanor woke at 7am, the agenda said breakfast was at 7.30, so she was up, and ready to start the day, thankfully, with no sign of a hangover. After breakfast, Eleanor met Victoria in the boot room. The agenda said that Richard would be joining them for the morning's skiing, but Victoria said.

'Richard needs to work, he said he would join us for lunch.'

The girls worked in "Direct Internal Support", D.I.S as they called it, and they all referred to the boss as Richard. Eleanor wasn't sure if the difference was the fact that this team were all girls, or more likely that they didn't generally work outside of the inner sanctum, and so "Image", wasn't an issue. As she squeezed into her ski boots she briefly thought that not meeting Richard yet was building up the tension a little, but she soon focused on the skiing.

The conditions were perfect, as it had been heavily snowing for the last four days. Today was one of those paradoxical days where you are surrounded by snow, and yet the sun is shining and it feels relatively warm. The agenda said that at the start of the day they should meet in the village where they would be joined by a ski instructor, come guide, as she knew the safe, off piste areas where they could carve through fresh snow. They set off to start the day on an easy green run, so the instructor could get a feel for the ability of the group. The standard was high, and so straight away the intensity increased. Black runs, and some off piste areas were skied well, but after an hour or so, Eleanor's thighs were burning. Her technique was still good, but her legs were working harder than they normally would.

They were going down a challenging red run as a group of French children skied past in a snake behind their teacher. They were no more about six or seven years old, and they followed in the teacher's tracks, who was traversing while looking over her shoulder, and shouting, "á l'envers, ensemble". As the day progressed, and everyone had gotten their ski legs, they took on a difficult mogul section. It was a steep black run, and the sign at the top said, "Experienced skiers only".

Marie, the ski instructor said, 'this is more of a challenge but you are all perfectly capable of getting down this run.' She didn't give the group an option, and they followed as instructed, as they worked slowly down this challenging descent, an elderly gentleman of at least seventy, skied straight past them at speed. He had a lit pipe clenched firmly in his teeth, on his extra-long skis with his hands behind his back, in this completely relaxed posture he was able to ski almost straight down the mountain, the top half of his body relaxed with just the knees bending. He went flying down the slope without a care in the world.

Eleanor and the girls skied well, and apart from the occasional snow boarder going too fast, and out of control, this was one of the best mornings of skiing she had ever had. The girls covered a lot of ground, and arrived at La Brevieres in plenty of time for lunch. The restaurant lay about a hundred meters from the centre of the small mountainside village, and no sooner had they removed their skis, staff were there to carry them off for safe storage. It was such a relief to not have to carry her own kit, Eleanor thought, *I could get used to this.*

The restaurant was the most exclusive eatery in the resort. They were greeted at the door by a very effeminate m*aître de*. He had a high pitched voice that had a rising inflection at the end of each sentence. With his hands clasped tightly together at chest height, palm to palm, and bending down in almost a bow. He kept saying Bonjour Mademoiselles, Bonjour, as he escorted them through the dining area to stairs at the rear. Eleanor had eaten here with her family but she had no idea that there was an additional exclusive dining room in the basement literally called "Le Sous-sol".

As they entered the private dining room, the first thing they noticed was the incredible aromas from the cheeses, and dried meats that were stored here. The room was rectangular with the wines arranged in racks around the walls, displayed behind frosted glass. They were behind sliding doors on chrome rails, each featuring a region in France. No other wines, just French and Eleanor thought, *why not.*

∞

Richard Weiss was standing at the head of the table removing his jacket. As he looked occupied with the four people with him, Eleanor was surprised when he immediately acknowledged her with a nod of the head, and a smile. Richard excused himself, and came over to greet her properly. He didn't reach out a hand to shake, but instead he held her upper arms, leaned forward, and kissed her on each check. It was a friendly gesture and for Eleanor it broke the ice.

'A pleasure to meet you Eleanor, I'm so glad you could make it . . . are the girls making you feel welcome?'

'Hello Mr Weiss.' she replied formally, she assumed that she would also be expected to in a public place.

'Richard please . . . all of D.I.S call me Richard, unless we have clients or guests. This trip will give you a chance to get to know the team. Victoria will run your induction, and this week is all about you settling in. Now can I get you a drink?' He reached down to adjust the tension in his large boots, but he was a tall man. Big and muscular, exuding a confidence expected of such a successful person. His Armani aftershave reminded Eleanor of a previous boyfriend.

'Just a "Cafe Au *Lait*" will be fine, thank you.' It occurred to her that it may give the wrong impression if she started drinking in the afternoon.

'Were on holiday,' he replied. 'Relax and have a drink, I have ordered pink champagne for the girls, and I also have a beautiful Sancerre on the way.' Richard raised his right eyebrow to someone over her shoulder.

'Thank you, that's very kind.' Eleanor said as she removed her coat and draped it on the back of her chair, 'I love a good white wine, but I will join the other girls if you don't mind.'

No sooner had she put her coat down, it was instantly removed to be dried, and returned to her when the meal was over. Richard pulled the chair out for her, she was seated next to Victoria. The waiter, who had been listening to the conversation, came over with her drink. The champagne was served in the most exquisite glasses that had a long elegant, stem, which went thinner from the base to the upturned bell like shape and a very thin edge. The glasses were also noticeably pre chilled.

Richard said, 'I like my champagne served a little colder than is recognised as ideal. A sommelier will serve it at nine degrees, and will tell you that you lose some of the depth, or spectrum of flavour if it's too cold, but I tend to feel that it's a fine balance between the overall impression on the mouth compared to the complexity you get from the length of the wine so I drink it at around seven to eight degrees.'

She felt comfortable talking about wine, she was no expert, but she felt that she could hold her own; she had a good palate, and a reasonable understanding of the basics, but she hadn't contemplated the temperature champagne is served at, but she had to agree that it tasted quite delightful. 'The flavour is all at the front of the palate, but it has a long finish.' Eleanor said.

She thought, to describe the overall taste as summer berries wouldn't be quite right, maybe summer berries caramelised in Demerara sugar with a dash of raspberry liquor would be a bit long winded, but certainly closer to her take on it. The general, oohs and ahhs said enough.

The sommelier heard Eleanor talking with Richard about wine, and with great enthusiasm asked if she would like to see the wine collection. She knew the sommelier's role was to enthuse about the wines to make a sale, but this was different. The selection had been made by Mr Weiss, so Eleanor directed her response to the sommelier.

'"Ce qui m'a fait plaisir"

As the sommeliers new guest was fluent in French, the conversation continued in his language. According to Pierre, the sommelier, the 2005 Petrus was even better than the world renowned 1998, and it would just keep getting better.

He said, 'it is the single best bottle of wine in all of France'.

Pierre accepted that there was the potential for a single wine grower to have a one off special bottle, but as far as commercially available reds were concerned, this was his bottle of choice, and he assured her that €34,999 was a good price, adding, it will only grow in value. Eleanor couldn't help but like Pierre because he clearly loved his job. She thanked him, and returned to the table. When she resumed her seat, Richard stood, and addressed the group.

'Now ladies, I'm not staying long, we are heli skiing this afternoon and we want to make the most of the conditions as we may not be able to fly beyond about two, as the weather is forecast to change.' Richard had a deep voice and he spoke quite loud, with a tone that commanded attention. The waiting staff were poised and ready to serve the first courses, but they were waiting for him to finish speaking. 'I will join you this evening for dinner. Please be my guest and have whatever you wish this afternoon. We have transport to take you straight back from here. But the lifts are open until four thirty if you would prefer to ski back.'

Smiling, he took his seat again, and signalled to the staff to serve. Eleanor and Victoria were deep in conversation as the waiting staff descended with beautifully presented food, all assembled with height on the plates. Eleanor was served by a bubbly girl who only looked fifteen.

'She is a really conscientious young worker that is a credit to the youth of today.' Eleanor said to Victoria.

Richard finished his drink, and the little charcuterie he had been eating and he was off with his entourage. As they got ready to leave, they were banging their boots on the tiled floor as they were stretching the buckles across to the hooks, pulled tight and latched into position. Before they left, three of the four in turn, came over to Eleanor, shook hands and introduced themselves. One just stared at her, and didn't say anything, she thought, *very odd*. She asked Victoria about him and apparently he was Richard's personal surgeon Dr Blake Gibson.

'Just ignore him, everybody else does,' Victoria advised.

He had stood out to Eleanor throughout lunch as he was constantly in and out, each time he came back in and walked past Eleanor, he reeked of cigarettes. He had a smokers cough too, constantly retching, as his lungs tried to expel the 70 or more cancer causing chemicals. Eleanor didn't want to judge him negatively just because he smoked, but nevertheless he was someone she felt that she wouldn't get on with.

∞

After lunch, the girls decided to ski back. On route they saw Richard and his group tackling a very steep couloir.

Eleanor said, 'Richard is either brave or stupid.'

Victoria replied, 'or just very good . . . bloody show off.'

The girls skied back at a leisurely pace, and returned to the village after an hour or so. They finished the day with the Après Ski crowd in a busy bar with skiers packed in like Sardines. To say there was standing room only would be an exaggeration as there was no room at all, but still people managed to push their way in.

Victoria shouted to Eleanor, 'there are quieter places, but this one has a real buzz.'

Eleanor couldn't believe her luck, what a fantastic first week at work this had turned out to be. Her new boss was a gentleman. The great location, and the added benefits of the excellent restaurants, and accommodation, was the icing on the cake. It was six deep at the bar, but the girls managed to eventually get served. Like moths to a flame, the busier the bar the more people were attracted to it. The girls had *Vin Chaud*, an après ski must. By the time Eleanor, and her new friends climbed into the private transfer waiting to take them back to the chalet, they were all part of the same team.

Chapter 17

Emily had started nursery school on her third birthday, just two weeks before she became a sister to Eleanor, she was really pleased, as she never wanted to be an only child. She was a gifted A student, and at the age of eighteen she took a place at Harvard University in Massachusetts. Moving from the UK to the USA was just one of her options as she was also offered a place at Oxford. Her father before her, had earned his Doctorate at Oxford, and the opportunity to follow in his footsteps was tempting. But Harvard was ranked the number one in the world on Life Sciences; her specialist subject is "H20". The origin of water on Earth was the specific area of her doctorate that still fascinated her, and she was still involved in specific, inconclusive studies in this area. But her particular interest, and specialisation was the access to free fresh water for everyone, both today, and for the ever growing population.

Emily's PhD's foreword encapsulated the project's *Raison d'être*, and in it she covered the most accepted research on population growth, which suggests the population will level off at eleven billion. Therefore, the question posed was, "Can the planet sustain that many people". To provide fresh water for crops, governments allow countries to use underground water, known as aquifers. She highlighted one of the largest aquifers in Africa that was estimated to hold something like a thousand, trillion litres, but she noted, if it is siphoned off at the current rate, it will be used up by two thousand and twenty four.

It was a great university where she completed her PhD, and there were lots of opportunities that opened up for her future. Emily never returned to the UK after completing her Postgraduate Studies, as there were a lot of job opportunities in the USA, and the first role she took was at her university. The position appealed to her because it meant that she had the chance to do both lecturing, and some research of her own. This in turn, led to her relocating, and eventually settling in Washington DC.

∞

Emily and Eleanor's Father, Philip Myers, was a self-made man who had instilled in the girls a good sense of right, and wrong. His success came about because he had a perfect mix of both technical prowess with a natural entrepreneurial spirit. His profitable business enabled the sisters to be privately educated. It would be fair to say that Emily had her father's intelligence, while Eleanor had his single mindedness. Not to suggest that Eleanor was a fool by any means, on the contrary, she had always had a flair for languages, but she was in her sister's shadow from an academic achievement perspective.

Philips smile can still be seen in his daughter's today. Eleanor and Emily were very similar, but even as teenagers, Eleanor always looked glamorous, wearing frilly bras well before she needed to, while Emily looked a little frumpy, hair tied back in a simple ponytail, always wearing a frown. The sisters lost their Father when they were young, he died prematurely in a light aircraft he was piloting. At the time of the tragedy, air-crash investigators confirmed that it was engine failure, rather than pilot error, that caused the incident, but that was of little comfort to the grieving family. At the time, Emily suffered emotionally, and never really fully came to terms with his death.

∞

The sisters still communicate on a daily basis. They both embrace the "Facebook" generation, and constantly updated their status. They regularly emailed each other, and had weekly face-time calls. Emily was really pleased about Eleanor's new job, but being pessimistic made her think, "If something sounds too good to be true, it probably is". Eleanor's take on life was the polar opposite to her sister. She was an optimist, and could see the good in everyone, and everything. Right from the first interview for this job, she had an instinct that it would be good. She went to the same prep school as Richard Weiss, albeit he was there four years ahead of her. It was his company, in fact that had first approached her about the role.

Eleanor got back to her room in time to call Emily with an update. Under Emily Myers in Eleanor's iPhone was a picture of the sisters holding hands. They always held hands by linking their fingers with Emily's small finger between her sister's ring, and middle fingers.

'Hi Em, you okay?'

'Yes I'm fine, I am just fixing dinner. How's your first week going?'

Emily was preparing a pasta dish, she had a girlfriend coming, and as usual was running late. They were on the land-line, and Emily had the handset jammed between her left shoulder and ear, leaving her hands free to continue with the spaghetti. Emily's multi-tasking would have to include going to the door as the doorbell had just rung.

'Oh I love it, it's fantastic. The girls I'm working with have been really friendly. There's this girl Victoria that I really get on well with, and she is taking care of me.' Eleanor was lying on her back on the bed with the phone on speakerphone lying on her chest. 'She is making sure I meet all of the team and find out what they do, she knows everyone, and everything about the business. She's a real genuine person, I feel like we have been friends for years.'

'Is she the one who posted on your Facebook wall?'

Eleanor was back in the living room, sitting in front of the mirror again, this time removing her make-up. After the day's skiing, her long black hair was looking very lank, so she had it up in a hair claw clip. She had got used to people passing the window, and so sitting in her skiing long johns and topless seemed perfectly normal.

She said, 'yes. She is the "Senior PA".'

'What do you mean, senior PA! Is there a junior?' Emily handed her guest a glass of wine, and indicated that she would just be a minute. 'And don't tell me she's intelligent too, no one that attractive deserves to have brains as well.' The pan was now smoking, and it set off the fire alarm. 'Owww!!! damn, damn, damn. It's alright, I just burnt my hand?' Emily said as she dropped the red hot spatula covered in sauce onto the floor, just missing her jeans.

Eleanor said, 'there are five.' She hadn't picked up on the fact that Emily was no longer really listening, and went on regardless. 'You should see Val, it's so lovely here.'

When Philip was alive, the family had the same three weeks every year at Val D'isere. Their mother, Elizabeth, also a keen skier, still travelled to Val over Christmas with her best friends. Eleanor joined her mother every other year; she only usually managed three or four days, according to her schedule, but Emily had never returned, mainly because of living in Washington and the distance was an issue, but Eleanor and her mother believed that Skiing reminded Emily too much of their late Father.

The sisters were very popular at school, and had lots of friends, but they always liked each other's company best. While growing up, they did most things together. Philip used to say they were, "Joined at the hip". But there was never any jealousy when one of the siblings had other friends to play with. As adults they were still just as close, even though they didn't get that much time together these days, but they both knew, they would pick up from where they left off as soon as they were together again. For now online facetime would have to do.

While talking to Emily, Eleanor moved from the living room to her bedroom and sat naked on the edge of the bed examining marks on her stomach, and ankles from where the tight thermal underwear had been. The phone, now standing on its bottom edge, was still on speaker.

Emily was waving a tea towel under the fire alarm and said, 'I better go babe, my dinner is burning, and my friend is here.' They promised to speak again soon.

Once they said goodbye Eleanor got dressed, and went to dinner with the girls. It was a more subdued affair than the previous night.

Victoria said, 'after a day's skiing I feel really hungry, do you?' Everyone had a real appetite, ate well and drank plenty of champagne, it went down very well. Eleanor sat with Victoria, and they became more than just colleagues whilst chatting.

'I feel like I've known you forever,' Eleanor said.

'You know I was going to say that to you,' Victoria replied.

Richard Weiss only managed a brief appearance that night, and Eleanor didn't really see him again on this trip. By the end of the week she knew what was required of her, and she was ready to start. The opportunity to begin came sooner rather than later, as the whole team were heading off to Monaco, and Richard wanted Eleanor to go too. She willingly accepted.

Chapter 18

Following the week in Val D'isere, Eleanor travelled home for just one day to pack for Monaco, and her first official day at work. The chauffeur picked her up, and headed to Oxford Airport, an airport for private flights only. On route they picked up Victoria, and they flew together down to the south of France. From Nice Airport on to Casino Square in Monaco, they travelled in Richard's luxurious modified Bentley Mulsanne. They pulled up outside the Hotel Du Paris, at the bottom of the grand entrance steps, Eleanor recognised the staff in attendance from the ski trip.

'Aren't they support staff from the Chalet Blanc?'

'Yes. Richard has taken over the hotel for three days.' Victoria replied as she gathered her belongings. The heat was quite extraordinary for spring in the south of France today, almost as warm as southern Spain. Victoria added, 'the hotel staff assist, but the interaction between Richard, and his personal requirements are always catered for by his own people. We do everything including our own security. The Hotel cameras are off, so he has complete privacy for his guests.'

The car was attended by two doormen in uniform with peaked caps. Eleanor sat in the offside rear passenger seat, and she twisted her hips to take her legs out together, and to step out with her modesty intact. As the girls were climbing out of one of the best cars in the world, to enter one of the best hotels in the world, it made them walk tall, with an air of importance, it was unavoidable. They were also immaculately dressed, young, attractive women, and the eyes of the people in casino square followed Victoria and Eleanor, to see if they could identify who they were, these VIP's, that most assumed were of a celebrity status. While they climbed the steps Victoria continued.

'One of the exceptions of Wiess overseeing his own affairs is the phenomenal restaurant here. Alain Ducasse, the Three Michelin Starred chef will still be overseeing the food.'

Eleanor said, 'I thought you had to book this place months in advance?'

Eleanor assumed they were heading towards the reception to check in, but as Victoria was on her left hand side, and was walking instead directly to the lifts, Eleanor followed. Clearly, the room arrangements had been made in advance. Victoria continued her explanation.

'Mr Weiss is here for a meeting that only came together about a week ago. I had to pay a large premium to secure the booking . . . we only need two floors, but we had to take the whole hotel.'

Eleanor picked up on the formal use Mr Weiss, as they were now, essentially, in a public place. She could only see members of staff, but nevertheless she was careful to be as disciplined as Victoria. There was a line of hotel staff to greet them, five people in all creating a chevron towards the lifts. They stood with their hands behind their back, apart from the only gentleman at the end of the line that held his left lapel with his right hand, and had his arm out, unnecessarily indicating the direction to the lifts that were only five feet away, and clearly visible. They all smiled, and nodded a welcome as the girls walked by.

As the entered the lifts Eleanor continued her query. 'So if Mr Weiss only wanted to book the trip a week ago, how come the hotel could accommodate? Where are the usual guests?' Eleanor came to the simple conclusion that there must be an on-going amount of advanced bookings. Furthermore, she had heard that this particular hotel is fully booked six months in advance.

Victoria replied, 'the guests who reserved rooms will be told that the hotel has unfortunately been double booked. They will be offered an alternative hotel, with complimentary food and drink.' The clicking of their heels echoed in the cavernous foyer. Their timing was almost in sync, and sounded like a walking horse. They could smell the aromas coming from the kitchen, it was like a refined version of frying doughnuts. They entered the lift for the top floor, to the Penthouse, Diamond Suites. A lift that was almost silent, Eleanor could hardly tell they were moving.

Victoria continued, 'on top of that they will get an alternative date at the Hotel Du Paris, again at no cost.' The doors opened onto a high ceilinged hallway with a huge crystal chandelier. 'Basically, we get invoiced for all of those expenses.'

Eleanor exclaimed, 'incredible! It's hard to believe that happens . . . It must cost a small fortune?'

'It probably doesn't occur that often, but it certainly happens. This three day stay will cost eighteen million Euros.' Victoria said as they reached their rooms.

Eleanor kept being surprised, and this latest revelation was one of them. It was also apparent that Victoria took this in her stride; it must be the way Richard always operated. How could any deal he was here to do, be worth an expense investment of eighteen million?

Chapter 19

Eleanor shut the door to her suite, and walked over to the balcony, to look out over casino square, she promised herself that no matter how much she made, she would never waste it. As she tried the bed to see how soft it was, she changed her mind, she had to remind herself that it was Richard who had made his fortune, and you don't gather money if all you ever do is waste it. The deal he was here to do must be worth it. She decided to see what she could learn about how Richard thinks. This trip would no doubt be another eye opener.

Eleanor was only a baby when the family business allowed a good standard of living, so she had always been comfortable financially. But the level of wealth on display today was in a completely different league. Richard had money to burn, and she could see that with extreme amounts of money came power. There was certainly power demonstrated here, Hotel Du Paris clientele were of a high net worth, but how many of them were forced to change their planned trip because of the guy with the deeper pockets. The one thing she could accurately predict, was that the coming months would be memorable.

Eleanor's suite was typically French, exquisite antique furniture, predominately black with gold inlay. There was original art on the walls, one showing a grand prix car going down the hill towards Mirabeau with Casino Square in the background. She realised that as the car was travelling down the hill, the angle of Hotel Du Paris in the background highlighted the very room she was in. So it was a commissioned painting with this very room in mind. She wondered if Victoria had the sister painting with a slightly altered angle, highlighting her room. The artist had signed A Hill; she would Google to see if he or she was famous.

The room was teeming with luxury; from the plush thick pile carpets to the marble floors in the bathroom. The sitting room was over thirty feet wide. The French doors right in the centre of the outside wall, with heavy golden coloured curtains draped from the centre, with a thick plush pelmet. It was a classical feature of an "old school" hotel suite. An antique clock chimed 12 times to signify the middle of the day.

Eleanor went into each room to get a feel for the place. There were two bedrooms off the sitting room and a separate office space, one wall adorned with framed photographs of former French Presidents that had stayed in this suite. She particularly liked the large round water bed in the master bedroom. The sunken bath in the en-suite had been filled with an Aloe Vera based oil. A bottle of the pink Dom Perignon nineteen ninety five was on ice, waiting on a small side table. Eleanor thought this seemed to be a hell of a lot of room for just a Personal Translator.

Eleanor took her hotel welcome letter, poured a glass of champagne, and sat outside on the balcony. The letter informed her that she had three staff in attendance this afternoon. Her mobile phone rang, it was Victoria, she called to ask if Eleanor was happy with her room and Eleanor responded, somewhat bewildered, 'I have a private yoga session that concludes with a full body massage.'

'I know . . . I booked it; you also have a hairdresser, and makeup appointment all in your suite.' Victoria said. 'We can do yoga together in future, but I wanted you to meet Rainbird for the first time by yourself.'

Victoria said that she hoped she has a nice day and that dinner with Richard goes well. They had to end the call when a metallic blue Bugatti Veyron went by because of its very noisy engine; it attracted lots of admiring glances, as well as Eleanor's.

She went back inside, and with the window open she could still hear the noise from the square. Several people were grouped together watching some sporting event on a large screen. It wasn't clear what sport was being played, but every now and then she would hear a large cheer. Eleanor closed the French Doors, and couldn't hear a thing; the walls of this old building were thick, they blocked out the outside world, and it created a pleasant stillness to the room.

Someone knocked on the door, Eleanor answered, and in burst Rainbird. Eleanor's first impression of Rainbird was a bubbly, iridescent character that instantly draws your attention as she walks into any room. 'Hi Darrrling, you must be Eleanor, come . . . let me look in your eyes.' With that Rainbird got within 10 centimetres of Eleanor's face, not staring each other out, more like an ophthalmologist looking right through the eye.

Rainbird said, 'right let's get started.' She went back to the front door, and carried in her portable massage bed, and a large rucksack with two yoga mats under the flap. 'Make yourself at home,' Eleanor said. The sarcasm was meant fairly light hearted as clearly Rainbird was going to be fun, but her comment made no difference anyway, it was not heard or simply ignored as Rainbird carried on making the room ready for Eleanor's treatment, and yoga session.

Rainbird was light on her feet, and more or less bounced everywhere she went. Eleanor was bemused; she poured them both a glass of pink champagne without even asking. Her timing was good as Rainbird appeared ready. Eleanor handed her a glass, Rainbird beamed a smile at her, and raised her glass; 'Cheers.' They clinked. 'The first of many I'm sure darrrling,' Rainbird purred.

She was a revelation, she was Richard's' full time personal yoga teacher come masseuse, but what Eleanor found most surprising was that she was also Richards's spiritual guide. She was a psychic, and Richard had Rainbird comment on the deals he was considering. He gave her a business card, and asked her to tell him about the person. She didn't know if he acted on her profiling, but he always seemed happy with the results. She was also employed to deliver a daily routine of meditation, yoga, and massage.

Rainbird said, 'I could do much more if he would let me, but so far he has resisted.' Eleanor would never have guessed a business man like Richard would believe in psychics, never mind actually using one. What a fascinating man; she was looking forward to getting to know him.

The yoga was fun, Eleanor was much better than she imagined she would be, and was quite flexible, which was amazing as she did little if any stretching. But the treat of the day for Eleanor was Rainbird's extraordinary massage. She had real strong fingers that worked deep into the muscle tissue. As she worked she made comments about

Eleanor's body. The most intriguing one was when she said, 'You had an injury here when you were three', pressing her thumb into the bottom of Eleanor's right calf. She had no recollection, of an incident to cause that, but Rainbird was not asking, just telling, and not looking for confirmation.

Rainbird had so many stories, she could talk on and on without any input from Eleanor, she would ask, "How are you finding it, working for Richard?" and then answering herself, with "I know you are enjoying it". She also offered these words of wisdom, "No one is in your life by mistake, even the bad ones," and "We are the only ones who can turn away from the abundance that life has to offer". What she meant was never made clear, she just seemed to say random thoughts out loud. And she did this all afternoon. When Rainbird had completed all of the treatments, she repacked ready to go.

Again, completely without promoting she said to Eleanor, 'when your boyfriend is ill you are to call an ambulance immediately.'

Eleanor giggled, 'sorry that was a champagne giggle,' she said, not wanting to be disrespectful. 'I laughed because I haven't got a boyfriend.'

Not put off in the least, as Rainbird headed for the door she said, 'I didn't say when darrrling. Oh I nearly forgot.' She handed Eleanor a letter, and without a by your leave, Rainbird bounced out of the room, and was gone.

Eleanor tore open the envelope. It was a handwritten personal note off Richard. He had used a fountain pen in purple ink, a habit he had unashamedly copied from Enzo Ferrari. It said:

Please join me for dinner at eight. It will be a chance for you and I to get to know each other and I can talk through my reasons for creating your role. I would like to take this opportunity of thanking you for starting earlier than your contractual obligation. As I need you in the negotiations for a business I am looking to purchase. I will explain over dinner.

The note was simply signed *Richard*.

Chapter 20

Eleanor arrived at the entrance of the restaurant at precisely 8pm; this was more luck than judgment. She had tried on no less than five different outfits trying to choose the right one for the occasion. In reality, they were all of exceptional quality, and looked very good on her. In the end she plumped for the black business suit that was the uniform that Victoria had worn the first time they met.

'Bonsoir Madame Myers . . . please let me show you to your table on the terrace on this beautiful evening. Is the room to your liking?'

'It's wonderful, thank you, as is this beautiful dining room.'

The Maître d introduced himself as Ricardo, a proud Italian who had crossed the border specifically to work at the Hotel Du Paris, rumour has it, some say started by Ricardo, that he was headhunted, he led the way to the table.

Richard was already seated, glancing at some paperwork, while on his phone. He was dressed in a very smart blue blazer with an open neck shirt, quite informal for him. He had his right ankle resting on his left knee, with papers in his right hand and a phone in the left, leaning back engrossed in his work. He had his back to them, but as they approached he turned; with his head still down, he looked up above the top of his glasses, and smiled a hello.

'Ah Eleanor, so glad you could join me.'

Richard said as he abruptly finished his call to concentrate on his guest. He stood as he slipped off his glasses. He didn't extend his hand, and Eleanor saw this in a positive light, she was one of the team, and you don't shake the boss's hand every time he requests a meeting, even if it is for dinner. She noticed that as he removed his glasses, he handed them to a man to his right, who had already gathered up the paperwork, and silently slipped back into the shadows.

They were seated at a very large table placed right in the centre of the terrace. As Eleanor took her seat she saw Victoria on the next table, Eleanor smiled, Victoria returned it, and at the same time blew a kiss and raised her crossed fingers for good luck. She was sitting on a table with Dr Blake Gibson, the man who had ignored Eleanor at Le Sous-sol; he was staring at Eleanor again, so she simply ignored him.

'I hope it's not too chilly?' Richard said. 'It's still a little early in the year to be sitting out on the terrace, but I thought we could at least have an aperitif here, and then retire to main dining room.' He spoke with a well-educated accent, clear and confident. His suggestion was perfectly acceptable to Eleanor.

'I love the view of the Casino, and all the fast cars,' she replied.

'If you like gambling, and fast cars you are a girl after my own heart.'

They both noticed the Formula 1 racing driver, David Coulthard; several people had recognised him, and he was signing autographs. Being stopped in the street seemed to be a price he was happy to pay for his fame, and he didn't appear to resent being approached.

She looked at the menu, and there were at least four starters that she liked the sound of. Richard had a way of making people feel comfortable, and he complimented her on her dress, which was gratefully accepted. He had his elbows on the table with his hands linked to make a bridge where his chin sat. Eleanor unconsciously replicated his body language, and relaxed. Before she sat down she had butterflies in her stomach, she was never usually nervous, but this felt like an important occasion, but within minutes of chatting she felt comfortable, and her nerves settled.

The table to their left had three men, and one lady with open laptops; they were all members of Richard's team, and clearly were all still working throughout dinner. Eleanor wondered why they would be out on the terrace, until one of them came over to Richard, asked a couple of questions, and then went off to act upon his instruction. Clearly, Richard wanted them close, and they had him there to answer questions as they arose. Richard returned his attention to Eleanor, they ordered, and he got straight to business.

'Now let's talk about my thinking.' Richard said as he leaned back, his arm on the back of his chair. 'I am here to look at a substantial investment. The gentlemen we are seeing are French, and I will introduce you as my PA. They speak perfectly good English, or so I am led to believe, so I want you to be listening to any French they speak. I've been in meetings before when I would have loved to know what they were saying.'

Eleanor said, 'so I will be your spy in the camp?' The bread was served, a task that required three people, two with a large silver tray each, with various options, and one with tongs to serve.

Richard replied, 'in a buying or investing situation, let's just say . . . I want to take the opportunity to stack the cards in my favour. Also, I have business interests in France and Spain, and I want you to communicate in their mother tongue. English is spoken almost everywhere I do business, but I think it is ignorant of me to always expect them to speak my language.'

Throughout dinner they talked more in depth about her role, as seen from his perspective. He spoke about his expectations, but his request was a simple one, be available as needed, and he would say specifically what he required of her on that particular task. It was straight forward, she could relax, and enjoy the evening. For early spring it was still remarkably warm, and they were able to remain on the terrace for dessert. Richard introduced her to Yquem, he told her it was one of the premier dessert wines of the world.

'Yquem is from Bordeaux, in Sauternes, and the area is actually susceptible to attack by "noble rot" and it is that, that makes it taste so good.' Richard said. 'Listen to me lecturing. I'm sorry, I go on sometimes, tell me when I do.' She would normally say, if asked, that she disliked sweet wine, but this was different. This particular bottle of golden nectar, was a nineteen twenty one.

'I can assure you that this is the single best year for Yquem ever,' and who was she to disagree, as it tasted divine.

'I hope you don't mind me asking, but whose decision was it to approach me in the first place, and what made you choose me?' She gathered her hair with her left hand from the right hand side, and put it behind her left shoulder as she leaned towards Richard.

'I spoke to Janice in HR, and after we had both seen your feature in Country Life, celebrating your exam results. As I'm sure you know, we went to the same school, and we both thought it was a natural fit.

What you may not know is, I read your father's book, "Effective Communication" and I applied a lot of his techniques to my business.'

She was surprised, and flattered, and thanked him, adding, 'that's amazing, what a small world.'

'I am sure you have read it. It really helped me as a confident young man going alone in the big wide world of business, and everything he said, I still routinely practice today.'

Eleanor had a hunch that Richard knew of her father, and she didn't know why. They chatted generally for a while, and Eleanor found him easy company. Richard recalled the dedication in her father's book. A wonderful, poignant message to his wife, and daughters.

Prompting him to ask, 'how is your sister?'

'Emily is fine thank you. Do you know she lives in America?'

'Yes I was aware. I get a profile summary from our HR department on all employees, and it was covered in that.'

Eleanor said, 'that sounds ominous. I'd like to see what it said.'

'It's all from information in the public domain, probably off your Facebook account I would imagine.'

Until now, it never occurred to Eleanor just how much a public profile could influence her professional life. She only imagined friends looking at Facebook and made a mental note to check it after dinner to see if it sat well with the business image that she wanted to portray. They each had another after dinner drink and chatted about their school days, the various teachers they both knew and so on.

'Emily is working, and living in Washington now.'

Richard asked, 'do you know that W.I.B.C Head Office is in Washington?'

Eleanor said, 'yes. It was covered in my interview. I was told that I would be working mainly in Europe, but that I may have to travel with you to Washington.' It was an added bonus, and she hoped to spend some time there in the future.

'I am due to go soon, I'm not taking the whole team, but you can come with me if you like and have a working holiday so you can see Emily?'

'That's very kind, thank you.'

Richard asked, 'do you get on well, I know sisters can clash sometimes especially if one feels like the other gets all of the attention.'

Eleanor replied, 'oh God no. We have always got on. I honestly can't remember a single argument. She is nearly three years older than me, and according to my Mother, right from the day I arrived, Emily called me her best friend. She is very bright, and did fantastic in all of her exams, but I never felt pressure to compete. I think we both have our strengths, and hers is definitely academia, where mine is communication and languages.'

Richard asked, 'what is she in Washington for?'

'She is the Chairperson of a Committee formed specifically to produce a government report.' Eleanor crossed her arms across her body, and held her bare arms, she was just starting to notice the drop in temperature.

He asked, 'what's the subject?'

'Water. It's all about the amount of fresh water, and the planet's ability to support a growing population. That's probably a real dumbed down summary, but I think that is the gist of it.'

Richard said, 'that is such an amazing coincidence. I am involved with a company building Dams.' He talked at length about his concerns. She was surprised that he seemed both knowledgeable, and concerned. She thought, "Maybe wealth allows people to think altruistically".

'It's a finite resource,' he claimed.

Eleanor said, 'she'd love talking to you. Get her started on the subject, and she could talk for hours. I always thought that rain would just constantly recycle.'

Richard asked Eleanor to pass on an important message to Emily. 'It is absolutely imperative that she covers rationing. I have a document I would like her to read and it goes into great detail about the need to ration usage in the West to assist areas such as North Africa. If I email it to you would you promise to give her a copy? If she has any doubts about the authenticity of the data I am happy to meet with her, and talk about it.'

He was clearly very passionate about the subject and Eleanor promised to forward it straight to Emily. He even asked Eleanor to shake on it, and as they shook hands she said, 'I assure you I will make sure she knows how you feel, and I will get the report to her.'

They talked some more of the past, and that their lives should cross again at this juncture. They both had plenty of examples of the way lives cross. How you could meet someone for the first time and find strange connections such as parents working for the same business, friends of one are neighbours of the other and the seemingly endless interconnection.

'What is that called, the "Chaos' theory". I'm possibly mixing my metaphors but all the same, the fact that this happens no one would deny,' Richard said.

She replied, 'as they say, it's a small world.'

Chapter 21

The evening was drawing to a close, and Eleanor had made it through the first meeting with her new boss. Just before retiring for the night Richard asked her, 'So you like the F1 Grand Prix racing?'

'I absolutely love it, and this is my favourite track. I never miss the Monaco race.' Eleanor replied as he wrapped her cerise silk stole over her shoulders.

Richard said, 'Would you like to go around the circuit?'

She accepted, but hadn't realised he literally meant here, and now. There was a selection of cars to choose from to go round the track in. He had with him a black Pagani Zonda Huayra, with its beautiful low set nose, and its bubble cabin set forward, complete with its signature four exhaust pipes in a chrome circle. Also, in Richard's collection was a fully restored Ferrari California, nineteen fifty eight original in red, that belonged to Enzo Ferrari himself, a man Richard admired.

Richard collected pieces of living history, and many of his cars had famous previous owners. These included a nineteen forty seven Rolls Royce Silver Shadow, which belonged to Mr Royce. A gold, nineteen seventy three Cadillac Fleetwood, that had belonged to Elvis. One that Richard didn't have, but was on his wish list was Adolph Hitler's car, currently owned by the Formula One supremo, Bernie Ecclestone. As they approached the Ferrari, there was a driver waiting at the car, with the keys. From the terrace Eleanor had seen this chap standing by the car but hadn't given it much thought; now she realised he had been waiting there all night, just in case their boss decided to take the car out. Richard took the keys, and threw them to Eleanor.

'You can drive.'

'What!! What if I crash?'

'All of my team are insured automatically for any car in the fleet. Just enjoy it. It's only a car, we can always have it repaired.'

She didn't know if he was joking or not, she couldn't tell. But she wasn't exaggerating, she really did love fast cars, so she slid into the driver's seat, slipped off her high heels and put them on the back seat, leaving her free to drive in stocking feet. Aware that her skirt was riding up a little she did her best to pull it down, she held each side, and pulled as she wiggled her backside to allow the skirt to come towards her knees. So Richard, being a gentleman, diverted his gaze. She adjusted the seat, and was ready to go.

Eleanor almost stalled, she would have found that most embarrassing, but thankfully she dipped the clutch just in time. Despite the shaky start she soon got the hang of it. She was soon going through the tunnel, and the engine noise was so loud as it bounced off the walls, it really added to the overall sensation. Forgetting herself, she quite unconsciously screamed.

'WOOOOOOW!! It's amazing! I love it!'

To be heard above the engine noise, Richard had to shout, as they had the roof down. They passed the waterfront, just before the swimming pool complex and Richard yelled. 'THIS IS WHERE WE WATCH THE RACE,' Richard had to shout to be heard as he pointed to the waterfront where he moored his yacht, 'You can come with us this year.'

She put her foot down up the hill back to Casino Square. Eleanor had always been very competitive, and she liked to win. Being behind the wheel of the car made her feel empowered, and she drove with absolute confidence. Richard was impressed that she handled the car so well; she knew how to control the power without wheel spinning or sliding. She pulled up, back in the space she had left minutes ago, and she had a grin from ear to ear. As they stepped out of the car, and back into the chilly night air, Richard turned to Eleanor.

'I'm going to the casino for an hour if you want to join me?'

Eleanor had actually never been to a casino and really would love to accept his offer, but she wondered if he was just being polite.

Richard said, 'Victoria is coming too.'

'Okay great thank you. Shall I run and get my passport?'

Richard said, 'you won't need your passport, they know me. Of course I don't mind, if I did I wouldn't have asked. Come on, I'm feeling lucky.'

Victoria was coming towards them with her catwalk model

saunter, and giggling. She had obviously been drinking. Victoria took Richards left arm, he offered his right to Eleanor, and she happily took it. The casino building itself, was built in the classic Beaux Arts style, and was amazingly plush. They walked straight in. The staff was more or less bowing as they said good evening. It was absolutely heaving, and Eleanor thought she could people watch here all night. There was a bustling atmosphere of nervous excitement, and an undercurrent of noisy chatter. The international clientele came together with this one guilty pleasure. As Eleanor looked around she could see many young attractive girls on the arms of older assumedly wealthy men.

The minimum bet in the high rollers area was ten thousand Euros a hand, and you played against the house. A pit boss had already placed thirty, hundred thousand Euro chips at Richard's playing position. Always at the seat known as "Third Base", so he could see what cards had been dealt before making his decision. It was also hard for Eleanor to get used to the invisible crew that sorted everything before Richard's arrival. It had been an impromptu invite for Eleanor to join him, and yet she was catered for without any obvious communication.

'I hope it's not too presumptuous, our waitress has served the Yquem that you so enjoyed over diner.' Richard said to Eleanor.

'No not at all. Thank you . . . very kind.' Richard passed Victoria, and Eleanor one chip each.

Eleanor politely declined saying, she couldn't possibly take a hundred thousand to bet, but Richard insisted.

'This is the deal,' he said. 'If you win, you pay me back my stake plus half of your winnings. That's what I do with all of the girls.' Richard took his seat, and indicated to Eleanor her place to his right and said, 'If we all play, it actually increases my chance of winning.'

Eleanor accepted, after all there was no point refusing a man like Richard. She did as Victoria had, and turned her one hundred chip into ten, thousand Euro chips. There were two other players at this table, one Arabic, and the other spoke English to the croupier with a broad Russian accent. The Russian was biting down on an unlit big fat Cuban, Cohiba Esplendido cigar. His fingers were adorned with large diamonds, and he was immaculately dressed. This stocky man had one boot on his stool, and one on the floor, as he leaned on the table. This hand was in play before Mr Weiss' party were ready. Both the Arab, and the Russian had played twenty thousand Euros a hand, and the house beat both players.

Weiss placed a hundred thousand chip to buy a hand. The Arab gathered up his chips, his body language spoke volumes, he was bent over, and looking dejected as he walked away grumbling about the bad night he was having. The Russian didn't need to change his bet as he was playing against the house, but he did anyway, and matched Weiss, while the girls played one each of their chips.

Eleanor looked at her hand, and asked Weiss, 'what should I do, play or fold?' as she raised the corner of her cards to display her hand.

'You should definitely play, you have a pair, plus ace high, that's good.'

Players' advising each other of tactics during a game was not allowed but Weiss was well known to the casino, nothing was said. He always tipped extremely well wherever he went, and this tended to sharpen one's customer service. Suddenly the background noise rose as a crowd had gathered around one of the roulette tables. Eleanor could see the electronic display showing the previous twenty numbers, and the last seven were black, and the money on the table was backing an eighth. Some people factor in the law of averages, and that would suggest a red was destined, but this casino crowd chased the run, no money was on red, it was all on black, and from the cheer that went up Eleanor assumed it was yet another black. She returned her attention to their game. Victoria folded her first hand while the other three bet.

'Well done. That's a full house.' Richard said. Eleanor had no idea what she had won.

'Yeah, brilliant,' was her response.

'Yu hade miy hond. Bwut ai wun tu zo ollz vell. Cungratchulation.' The Russian said.

The dealer paid out nine to one for a full house, increasing Eleanor's total to one hundred and fifty thousand in a matter of minutes, so she paid Richard his stake back and half of her winnings, as agreed.

'Now this I could get used to,' Eleanor said, with a wide grin.

They played on for about an hour. They say luck favours the brave, and the girls were up. It would have been more, but on a whim on the way out Eleanor put two thousand on number eighteen on a turn of the roulette wheel, and lost, only to see the eighteen come up as the very next number. Eleanor did the best of all, after paying back Richard's stake she left with forty thousand.

Eleanor couldn't believe how much fun it was to gamble. The adrenaline rush was amazing when she won. She could see how easily gambling for some could become an addiction, but she would certainly go again, she thought to herself, *after all I don't have an addictive personality*. She said goodnight to Richard on the way out.

'That was a fantastic night by any stretch of the imagination.'

Chapter 22

Emily was working for a government quango called "AQWA" Access to Quality Water for All, a comprehensive study for the US government. It was commissioned by the Senate, and Emily reported directly to Senator, Harvey Kugel. AQWA was to study the effects of the population growth on fresh water supplies worldwide.

She was engrossed in the project, and had been emailing Eleanor two and three times a day on the subject. Both of the sisters had found their ideal jobs. Emily had always championed environmental causes, and she believed that sustainable levels of fresh water for an ever expanding population was the one subject that tended to be overlooked, and she felt that it needed to be taken more seriously. No news programs were even talking about it, compared to "Climate change". Emily hadn't seen a single feature on the potential for a serious lack of water to serve a growing population, despite all of her, and countless others work suggesting it was almost inevitable.

Emily was sitting at her desk surrounded by a mountain of paperwork, thick files in stacks three feet high. She was working on twenty or so files at the same time, at least three were open, and their contents spread in front of her computer keyboard. She put her glasses on her head, and took a Skype call off a tipsy sounding Eleanor. She told Emily all about Richard, and the fact that he had asked about her and her work with the AQWA. Eleanor asked how the study was going.

'Really good. At last the powers that be are taking this serious. I have been given a grant to complete a comprehensive research paper on behalf of the government,' Emily said.

'That's great news. Have you met the president yet?' Eleanor asked not expecting a yes, but the reply was less light-hearted.

'No, not yet, but I have been to the White House. In fact I have been twice already, and I am there again next week.'

Emily was looking at the small image of herself rather than the large one of Eleanor on the Skype screen, and thought how tired she looked. She put her glasses on, and turned her focus back to Eleanor.

'The only issue is the Senator who is in charge of the project, he doesn't seem to value my opinion; I don't like him. He really does have little man syndrome.'

Despite being pessimistic, Emily never moaned about anybody, other than herself, so this was completely out of character. She started out liking everyone, until they proved unworthy of her trust. Eleanor was surprised by the venom in her voice. This chap must have seriously unnerved Emily.

'Well at least they are taking your concerns seriously.' Eleanor's face kept disappearing, as she took off her shoes. But she came back to the screen and looked at Emily to tell her what her new boss had said. 'Richard asked me to pass on an essential message, and a report. He said "You must cover rationing". He said tell her it's "absolutely essential". He also asked me to email you a report that he said proved categorically that immediate rationing is a necessity, I have literally just received it, and forwarded it to you. Also look at his email to me too where he says that you have permission to quote it as a source.'

'That's a surprise, he must have read my mind. To be honest I wasn't going to do anything on rationing in this report as I thought it would be dismissed out of hand. So all of our work has been focused on the population reaching 11 billion, and what the total amount of people the planet can support. But for rationing now, we have no independent evidence on which to comment so this could prove very useful. Let me read it through, and if the evidence is irrefutable, I would be willing to quote it. Tell him I can't promise to include it until I, or my team review the contents. But I will promise to give it the time it deserves.'

'I will let him know, thanks. He said that you need to make the government talk about the issue.'

'Tell him thank you. He may have given me the courage of my convictions; it could be the push we need to cover immediate rationing.'

Emily had been talking about the worldwide water issues for three or four years now. She was aware some American States were already running into issues. Eleanor was always a good listener, especially where Emily was concerned. However, she wasn't really in the mood tonight, and when she had passed on Richard's comments, she was only half listening. Chipping in here and there, but her sister hadn't noticed. She tuned back in when the conversation veered back to Emily's boss.

'He is slimy, this Senator Harvey Kugel. I have a gut feeling that I need to tread carefully around him ... thankfully he is away this week.'

'He sounds like a James Bond villain,' Eleanor responded, as she flopped on the bed, onto a very soft black mink throw.

'Look at the end of the day, it will be on the Government's agenda at last, and it will be a much bigger issue than one man. See him as a stepping stone to get this subject where you need it to be.' Emily could always rely on her sister to find the right words of comfort. Eleanor was right this was much bigger than Senator Kugel. 'You know what he did yesterday, he actually pinched my bottom. Can you believe that? Oh he really gives me the creeps.'

Eleanor said, 'don't stay in a room alone with him, and next time he tries it on, tell him you will report him for sexual harassment.'

Emily said, 'I will. I can deal with a little creep like him don't worry, I'm just sounding off.'

Eleanor wasn't convinced by her bravado. It had been such a long time since Emily had had a boyfriend, or at least one the family had been introduced to. She has always been a bit insecure. She was romantically linked to a work colleague a couple of years ago, a rather masculine older lady. But Emily never mentioned her, and Eleanor was too polite to bring it up. Emily would talk about her in her own time.

Emily said, 'Richard is right you know. I am certain that we will have to ration the water, it's the only way to make sure everyone will get a fair share.'

Eleanor said, 'I'll let him know that you are doing it. He will be pleased. When are you off?'

'I'm going to Africa tomorrow, so I may be out of contact for a day or two.' Emily said. She sounded very matter of fact. 'There is a proposed dam that we need to report on as part of this overall project. I'll email you as soon as I can with an update and my local contact details.' The sisters said goodnight, and promised to catch up soon. If their father could see them now he would be very proud. Emily knew her father would have approved of the work she was doing, if only she had a better boss.

Senator Harvey Kugel was easy to dislike, and his five years of service to date, hadn't changed that. His office was almost as big as his ego, adorned with pictures of himself, with a variety of famous faces. Before taking residence, he had a raised platform installed along the window wall, it was built specifically to house the Senator's desk. Kugel wasn't that tall, and this elevated area gave him the height that he felt he deserved. After suffering meningitis at the age of two he had never developed as fast as his school friends, and . . . to him at least, his height was always an issue. Not knowing this Emily only saw the egotism.

The Senator ran his office with a big stick approach, never choosing to dangle a carrot. You did what you were told, period. His thick mop of hair was fashioned like Elvis Presley, it also gave him an additional inch or so that he longed for. Despite his hair being white his thick bushy eyebrows were black, and never trimmed.

Surprisingly, the general public liked him and this was down to the duality of his personality. He had a public persona of a silver spooned politician who had never done a real day's work in his life, however he championed popular causes, this self-serving Senator would often turn up towards the end of a successful project to bask in the glory, claiming more responsibility than he deserved.

He was a heavy smoker, looked to be in his mid-forties rather than his actual age of mid-thirties, and his wife said he drank too much, always neat Jack Daniels. He has even started to have a glass with his breakfast, and when he does she could tell just from his eyes, which already stood out anyway, as each is a different colour. All the wisdom available on healthy living was largely ignored by Senator Harvey Kugel.

Harvey was from a long line of political heavy weights on his Mother's side, and in old money he would be seen as "Upper Class". Call it what you will, it meant one thing, he was destined to have both money and power, however short or tall he was, and he treated everyone around him as inferiors. Emily detested working for the man, if it wasn't for the importance of the project she probably would have quit long ago.

Chapter 23

Eleanor was in the Business Suite of the Hotel Du Paris with Richard, waiting for Victoria to join them with their guests. The first thing he asked her came as a bit of a surprise.

'What did Emily say about the report?'

Eleanor replied, 'she emailed me this morning, and said they like it a lot, and are almost certain to use it.' Richard looked very relieved.

He said, 'great, right, let's focus on this meeting. This is quite important to my long term plans, I will explain why, if we do a deal. '

Apparently, Richard had this Business Suite on permanent lease, including all of the facilities, and he kept documents related to his European interests here in a safe, which was also on a long term lease. This was Eleanor's first task as a translator, they were meeting two Frenchmen from a company called Nanostem Technologie SARL, and Eleanor was to sit, and listen when they spoke privately in French, note it down on her iPad. She and Richard both had an app that allowed him to see exactly what she typed. Eleanor set this up before their guests came in, this way Richard would instantly see her translations. Victoria knocked, and entered while Eleanor stood to greet the two young men.

'Good morning I am Eleanor Myers. I am here to take the minutes of the meeting.'

'Good Morning Mademoiselle, I am Philippe Chevalier and this is my business partner Mathieu Duval.'

'Pleased to meet you,' Mathieu said as he shook her hand.

'Right gentlemen, can I offer you a coffee?' Richard stood as he said this, leaning forward with his hands on the glass table top, and waited for them to come to him to shake hands.

'Cafe Au Lait, s'il vous plaît M. Weiss'. Philippe responded in a smooth, rolling, French accent.

'Richard please,' Weiss replied.

Weiss looked in control, and very sure of himself. They spent the next five minutes or so on what appeared to Richard to be an appropriate amount of sociability. The Frenchmen were not intimidated by him, but they still felt the pressure of presenting their business to someone who could make such a significant difference. The money alone would really help, but the credibility was of equal importance. Richard was quick to get down to business.

'Right I've read the prospectus, and now I want to hear in your own words . . .' He put down his pen and leaned forward. 'Tell me about your unique product?'

The mood changed slightly, but perceptively. It was getting serious, the tension increased for the two Frenchmen. Philippe cleared his throat, and said to his business partner, *Je vais prendre la tête si ce est ok*. He spoke French, just as Richard had predicted he might. Looking like she was doing no more than taking the minutes of the meeting, Eleanor keyed the translation into her iPad: "I will take the lead if that's ok", so Richard could see on his screen exactly what Philippe had just said. This translation already indicated to Richard who the key decision maker was. Philippe cleared his throat and began his presentation.

'Utilising the very latest Nanotechnology, we have created a product that we call "Nano Stem Cells"; we use the mnemonic NSC,' he paused, unsure if he had chosen the right term. After checking with Mathieu if it was the correct English term, he continued, 'no sorry, the acronym, I always confuse those two words. They are the smallest code-able transmitters available in the world today. Each NSC mimics a "Pluripotent Cell", in other words they are able to be any aspect of the whole that they become part of, hence the name. Our research facility-'

Richard cut him short in what was meant to be Philippe's background to their product. Richard was leaning back in his chair, his left hand on his iPad, and his right hand gripped his Monte Blanc Rolling Stones special, hovering over a writing pad. All that was on the paper so far were doodles, squares, and lots of them. Richard looked directly at both Frenchmen.

'Listen, I have all that . . . cut to the chase; I want to know in simple terms what you have to sell, and who your target market is? Tell me about the product, not the science, what people will actually do with this invention of yours.' In his enthusiasm, Richard thumped the table with his left palm as he said, 'HOW!' bang, 'WILL I GET!' bang, 'A RETURN!' bang, 'ON MY INVESTMENT,' bang! Mathieu quickly looked to Phillippe then turned to Richard.

'When we began to work on Nanostem's, our original desire was to help people to sing. There are endless talent shows worldwide these days, and with our NSC's a performer will be able to dramatically increase their vocal performance.' Mathieu added. 'When our Venture Capital investors got involved they encouraged us to also focus on the medical side. We believe that NSC's could also help people with speech impediments, from let's say Stroke victims to someone with a stutter.'

'So how do people use it and how does it work?' Richard asked.

Philippe replied, 'the application is in a spray form. It is currently available in aerosol cans. When the spray makes contact with the surface of the inside of the mouth, it sends a signal back to ask for its coordinates, and operating instructions. Each NSC, is then given its location destination, based on 3D mapping of the inside of the user's mouth, or for that matter whatever image is scanned.'

Philippe now became animated, talking with his hands. 'Each one is sent to the nearest available location to its landing area. The dimensions of each individual NSC is only ten nanometres, that is ten thousand-millionths of a meter in length, despite the size, each one has what is best described as an ultra-miniature computer.'

Eleanor asked, 'so it is only you say, ten nanometres and yet it contains enough information to communicate with a technology to receive a location? How does it then travel to that location?'

Richard hadn't said she couldn't get involved, and it was pure curiosity that led to her question. It was also valid, and Richard was interested in the answer. He seemed happy that she was becoming involved.

Philippe said, 'to your first question Eleanor, yes it can communicate, but it doesn't contain anything, the computer is in the body or skin of the NSC. To answer your second question, it can also move. Despite its minute size, it is multifunctional. The way they squeeze together forms a . . . '

Philippe hesitated, and turned to Mathieu, *Comment dit-on hexagonal*. Eleanor, forgetting herself, very nearly answered Philippe question. She translated for Richard but hadn't really needed to as it became obvious. Mathieu replied 'Hexagonal' and everyone laughed. Philippe continued.

'Sorry it's more or less the same, anyway they form a hexagon, and once they are in place, they link together like a jigsaw, and then the movement mechanism changes slightly. Each NSC surrenders their individual movement to the greater wave type movement. The best way to describe it is like a second skin around the whole of the inside of the user's mouth and down into their throat. Once in place, it forms what we have termed, "Intelligent Material" and it works almost like a muscle. In reality, the user's own muscles are being assisted or prompted to create a different shape.'

Richard put down his pen and leaned forward to ask, 'how long does it last?' Eleanor could tell that Richard was very interested.

Philippe said, 'how long does the NSC's last once in situ? . . . They are permanent . . . They are permanent, and never break down, so once in place they stay in place.'

Eleanor asked, 'what about eating?'

Philippe replied, 'no problem whatsoever. Normal food can be consumed, there are a couple of items to avoid, particularly pomegranate juice, for some reason, but we are close to a solution to this minor issue.'

Weiss was now focused on securing a deal, he loved it. The presentation from the two Frenchmen was detailed, and professional and their confidence grew as the meeting progressed. They comfortably answered every question put to them. 'So you see this as a way to improve someone's singing?'

Philippe answered, 'that is certainly one application for this product. What we are able to do, is record a voice while modulating, and map the movements of certain key sounds, such as ahhhhhhh for example. We can then programme the NSC's to move the muscles inside the mouth to mirror that of the singer they wish to emulate.' Philippe realised that Richard had noticed him wringing his hands, and so to consciously avoid this, he leant on the table towards Richard and his left hand gripped his right arm at the wrist.

He continued, 'despite the word used in a song, a lot of singers will simply make the sounds on those long notes. Imagine taking all of the key measurements of Andrea Bocelli singing and programming that pattern, in theory his voice could be mimicked. Our system analyses all aspects of sound, we create the shape in many pictorial forms on a computer screen, and by recreating the exact same pattern, we can reproduce the sound.' He made a wavy line with his index finger.

Richard asked, 'are you saying that anyone could sing like whichever singer they chose to emulate?'

'Yes and no.' Mathieu said as he took the floor. 'You would first of all have to have the general physical characteristics of the singer you wished to sound like.'

Richard said, 'so tell me about the commercial aspects that you have identified?'

Mathieu was dressed in a smart suit, and he looked like a duck out of water. It was clear that, the shirt and tie were not his normal attire. However, when it came to sales, and marketing it was Mathieu's turn to impress.

'The NSC's are expensive to produce, but when we can increase production, the cost will keep coming down.' Victoria had poured more coffees without asking, and placed them discretely, not affecting the flow. Mathieu continued, 'We see three main products, the first a cheap aerosol can available to all, with this product, the main income stream will be from the software to control the NSC's. Once sprayed into place, they only work with the software, and we have a monthly subscription model.'

Mathieu paused, expecting a question that never came, and so pushed on. 'The second application we have in mind is a completely bespoke service for professionals with full mapping. The third income stream we envisage is the speech impediment market.' Mathieu was intuitive and picked up on the fact that Richard favoured the potential medical applications, and so he was improvising and changed his rehearsed pitch accordingly.

Mathieu continued, 'we also want to have the medical usage licences... but we still haven't modelled the income from this area. From our initial trials, we are convinced that our NSC's can be adapted to be used throughout the cardiovascular system.'

Mathieu didn't know that this was exactly why Richard was interested. It was an impressive presentation, and Richard was almost certainly going to get involved. In a negotiation of this magnitude Richard had done all of his homework, and he was 90% certain before he met them today that it was a deal he wanted to do. The concluding factor was how good the men behind the product were, and he was thus far impressed with them. The serious business of the numbers was now under close scrutiny by Richard's team, so he invited his guests to join him for lunch; it would give his accountant's time to rework some numbers he wanted, before making an offer.

It was their first time at the Hotel Du Paris for the two Frenchmen, and they couldn't stop effusing about the quality of the wine and food. Eleanor happily chatted away over lunch helping to lighten the mood, she noticed that Richard hadn't touched the wine, but made sure his guests were drinking throughout. Richard constantly indicated to a waiter to fill up their glasses; it had also been pre-arranged that their wine glasses were to be filled beyond the third of the way up the glass that would normally be poured.

Mathieu said to Eleanor, 'that was the best white wine I have ever tasted. I should be ashamed that I as a Frenchman have never heard of Monsieur Pierre Vincent, and the Domaine de la Vougeraie perfect Corton-Charlemagne 2011.'

After lunch they returned to the office to begin price negotiations. Mathieu held the door for Eleanor, but immediately a member of staff took over, and smiled an apology that she hadn't got there sooner. Eleanor walked back into the office with Mathieu, followed by Richard with Philippe. Richard started to put a comprehensive offer to the French men, and Philippe quickly responded 'Please bear in mind that the product is ready to go and the interest is so great that we are-' Richard interrupted Philippe's response.

'No need to defend the valuation. I don't blame you for putting it together in this way, but I am going to make you an alternative offer. I want to buy eighty percent of the company.' Richard broke down his offer, and explained how it would take out the Venture Capitalists, and leave Philippe and Mathieu with a substantial preference shareholding. 'Gentlemen, do we have a deal?' With this, Richard fell silent.

The two entrepreneurs were caught by surprise at such a generous offer. They were hoping to get either Mr Weiss personally or his bank to back them, but this offer was like a lottery win after years of building their business without taking a great deal of income, this would be life changing, but they had sufficient decorum to hold this in.

'May I first of all thank you for your offer. Would you mind if we confer?' Philippe asked.

Richard gave his approval, and just as he predicted, the Frenchmen didn't think to excuse themselves to have a private conversation, they just spoke to each other in French. Eleanor relayed what they said instantly, so Richard had his translation. They were both happy to the do the deal that Richard had proposed, but agreed that they shouldn't just take his offer as they would look too keen, so instead they decided that Philippe should ask for the offer to be increased to ten million Euros each.

Armed with this translation Richard said. 'Gentlemen I am not prepared to change my offer.'

They didn't confer again. Philippe put out his hand and said. 'We accept your terms Richard. Thank you for believing in us.' Mathieu added his thanks, and shook Richard's hand. The deal was done.

Chapter 24

Emily Myers did call Dr David Prost after they met at the University, and today she arrived for a one to one session. She regularly had this stress that kept bothering her, but today she felt good, and wondered if she should be there at all. But on balance, even though she felt her issues were in the past, she would still like to see what he had to say.

Dr David Prost looked like a young Jeff Bridges, but what was more disconcerting, he actually sounded like him too. He had completely lost any sign of an English accent, and anyone that heard him now assumed he was American by birth. There was no doubt, even without saying anything, that he had a real presence. When Emily arrived at his surgery she was very upbeat, and cheerful. After greeting her, he led Emily to his consultation room.

There were large comfy sofas arranged in a horseshoe configuration, Emily sat on the right hand side of the middle sofa with Dr Prost on the sofa to her left. She had slipped off her shoes, and tucked her feet under her. The room was bright and airy; the colour theme, blue, many different shades of blue. The patio door was ajar and the sun was seeping through the light cotton blinds. Dr Prost had read that blue is often seen as a cold colour, but through trial and error, he discovered that it helped his clients to talk; he had no rational idea why, he just knew it was so.

She began by telling David all about her role in AQWA, and how excited she was. She was off to Africa tomorrow on a vital research project to do with a report she was compiling for AQWA. Prost kept asking questions to try, and establish what issues she wanted to discuss, but she kept assuring him that she had issues as a child, but she was fine now. He thought her body language told a different story.

David asked Emily, 'now let's talk about this assignment, and your trip to Africa. Are you feeling anxious about the outcome of this project?'

'Not at all, I feel really good.'

Emily was talking fast when she said, 'finally I have the White House listening, and they have commissioned this report. I have all of the facts, now all I need to do is pull them together in such a fashion that will highlight the undeniable situation. They will have to do something!'

David asked her, 'how would you feel if no action was taken after you complete this task? Bear in mind Governments have budgetary constraints to take into account regardless of the issue placed before them.'

'They have approved the budget for the report, and it will show the deficit that we face, and all of the possible solutions. They will simply have to act, 'she replied.

She was passionate, particularly about this pet cause, which in turn had led to her being busy. David had found that if a person that suffers anxiety is fully occupied, they feel less stressed. But he was concerned that her excitement was based on the report she was preparing leading to a solution. He wondered how this would affect her if no action was taken, however it wasn't his job to dampen her spirits.

David said, 'at the PTSD course you said that you were suffering stress, you related it particularly to people suffering in war zones, and an obsession to watching World War 2 programs. But today you seem to be suggesting that this is not the case?'

Emily said, 'I suppose it is fair to say that stress is sometimes an issue for me, I do get days when I can't get the sadness to lift. I think I was born to fret.'

He was pleased that she was starting to open up to him, he made a note to talk to her about herself deprecating at a future date. For now he talked about NLP, Neuro Linguistic Programming, and the way a practitioner could look at behavioural patterns learned through experience, and how they can be changed. He said he had a lot of success when linking this with hypnotherapy.

David said, 'I would like to try this approach, would that be okay with you?'

She thought he meant at some point in the future, but he meant here and now. She thought about it, and concluded that she had nothing to lose, so she accepted. Once Emily was in a hypnotic state,

David started to give her unconscious mind instruction. He didn't have a script when he did this, but focused on uplifting coping strategies. She began to cough, she had swallowed her own saliva, and her gag reflex was activated, but she stayed under. She started to speak, David thought that it was unusual that while under hypnosis that someone should speak who hadn't been asked a question.

She began talking about a war, and how frightened she was. David heard this, and was intrigued. So he prompted her, and she continued to claim that she was actually in the war. He probed to find out which war she was talking about, and it became clear that she believed she was in the Second World War. He had little experience in regression, it wasn't something he used hypnotherapy for, he only used the treatment for stress relief.

He brought her gently to the surface, and she yawned, and stretched like she had just had an 8 hour sleep. David decided to not mention the talk about War, as he wanted to research such behaviour before drawing any conclusions. So instead he focused on his original diagnosis.

'I would like to prescribe some Diazepam for you to keep with you on the trip. They are for self-medicating. If you start to get stressed I want you to take one fifty milligram dose to stop your body going through the symptoms of fight or flight.'

He explained what this meant, to put her mind at rest. David was leaning forward, his forearms on his thighs, keeping eye contact with Emily. By being in her personal space like this, he commanded her full attention. He was close enough for Emily to catch the fresh smell of his breath; as a man that used his words to help his patience he made sure there was no distraction, and so he was always very aware of his dental hygiene.

'It's great to see you so positive, and you look really well, but I am just a little concerned that you do too much, and start to put your body through stress, you may start getting the same sensations you had as a young girl.'

She was disappointed in this prescription because she felt so well. She had been on and off tablets since her father had died, and felt that she didn't need them now. However she totally trusted David as her family had trusted his father before him, so she would do as advised, and take the tablets if necessary. It was quite comforting to have a fellow Brit to speak to, for that natural affinity everyone has with someone that comes from their home town.

'So I don't have to take them if I feel okay?'

David replied, 'that's right; you have them just in case. You see happy stress, and sad stress is the same, it produces adrenalin. If you are working really hard and to a deadline. You may well start to feel those sensations you had as a child, or the more recent worries over war time.' He put his hand on her arm, to comfort her.

David said, 'I want to avoid that if we can. You see the lack of dopamine in your brain is the root cause of depression, and that can be depleted very quickly. Don't think it through too much, it's just a precaution.' He concluded.

The traffic outside was noisier than usual, and they could hear several horns blaring. It is a busy metropolis, and like anyone who lives in a city, it was a background noise that David grew to largely ignore. He always thought, *this much noise in a quiet village would have everyone out to see what all the fuss was about*, but here it was routine. David has one of those hypnotic voices, once he had their ear, most of his patients tended to relax and forget about the outside world. Such was his character that people naturally relaxed around him without knowing why.

David thought it would be better if she had less of a stressful task ahead of her, but it wasn't his place to suggest a client's employment. Knowing Emily, and her family as he did, he was aware that Emily always seemed to need a drama in her life. Maybe not on a conscious level, but somewhere in her subconscious, she seemed to attract a tense environment, on the verge of being out of control. David didn't know if she was aware of this but at least she promised to take her medication if the stress was getting hold of her. She would get the prescription filled, and take the tablets if she needed to.

They hugged before she left. It was a closeness that was the natural domain of a healer. Dr Prost was a medical man, and as such, he had a scientific approach to most of his work. But he still knew that there was more to life than could be viewed under a microscope, and by accepting this it helped him to help his patients, and who was he to argue with positive results.

'I remember your Mom hugging me when I was a patient of your Dads, it's the only real memory I have of the time he was treating me. How strange that after all these years that you are treating me too . . . what with us both being in Washington, what's the chance of that happening?'

Just before she left, David's business partner popped in to say hello. 'Hi my name is Silvio, or Sil.' He said, while giving his all-conquering smile.

Emily shook his hand. 'Nice to meet you. I'm sorry I can't stay for a chat.'

Silvio said, 'David told me about your trip to Africa . . . I hope it goes well.'

With that Emily left. As they parted Prost felt Emily's fragility. He was concerned for her, and he hoped she would keep her promise.

∞

'She is very attractive, I insist that you make sure I am here next time you treat her.' David's business partner had an eye for the girls, and didn't struggle to charm them. David shook his head.

'Don't mix business, and pleasure, she is a patient of ours, and it's against our Hippocratic Oath.'

'No my friend, she is your patient not mine.'

With this Silvio went to his desk to catch up on paperwork. David had to smile; Silvio was always the same, ever since they met. David rented a room in a private house near their University campus. Not knowing who he would be sharing with. David arrived first, and took the best room, the one with the best view was damp, the two large rooms at the front of the house had a strange smell, so he chose the box room, the only one with a wardrobe, even though it had a broken door. When Silvio arrived he did so with his ever present flair.

'I have arrange'ead to take the Presidencial Suite, can you tell me which one it is?'

Silvio laughed aloud at his own joke, as he always laughed at his own jokes. He always showed his big white smile. David thought they looked dazzling white because of his Spanish olive skin colour. David had visited the area on a number of occasions, and already knew the cheaper places for students to shop.

'I will show you around, I know it like the back of my hand' David said.

'What does this mean?' Silvio asked.

'It is a common saying that indicates that you know something really well,' David replied.

Silvio said, 'I would have to say, I know it like the back of my left hand, because I don't think I would recognise my right.'

David was ready to laugh at what he was sure was a gag, but as Silvio didn't laugh at all, he didn't know if he was joking or not. As they had only just met, David didn't like to ask, but as time unfolded David got used to Silvio's sense of humour, and would refer to his business partner as the funniest guy I have ever met.

It turned out that they were sharing with two girls who would spend the next two years arguing over Silvio, who seemed to alternate between the two, leaving David wondering *what's wrong with me*? Silvio spoke English well, only struggling with pronunciation on words ending 'ed', and others that were commonly hard for Spanish speakers to get their tongues around. But he told David that he wasn't great at reading, and writing English and yet he had come to America to do his physiology degree. When they started work, the extent of the syllabus left Silvio wondering why he believed he could do this. But he learned fast, and by the end of the first six months, his English was as good as anyone's.

David had a dry sense of humour, and usually delivered his funny lines without laughing, and that didn't translate well into Spanish. They laughed a lot, David in particular was always snickering. But Silvio soon stopped having to translate to understand, and was thinking in English, he soon completely understood David, and they were known around the campus as Laurel and Hardy.

Their University life was stereotypical, they drank too much, some of the time and worked too little some of the time, but after two years they came away with good Degrees and the best of friends. They each preferred separate subjects, one reason, not a formulated proposal or any sort of strategic decision, but more a back of the mind, "What if", should they not compete, moreover, if they looked at Doctorates in complementary specializations, this would open up the opportunity to work together.

Shortly after graduating, David's father wanted to take early retirement on health grounds, and David took over his practice. Within a matter of weeks, fate intervened, and Silvio had an inheritance, and used this to buy into the established business, boosting David senior's pension, thereby allowing him the ill health retirement he needed.

They made great business partners; David kept his eye on the margins, while Silvio used his personality to attract clients. It wouldn't be a bad thing if Silvio did get close to Emily. David still considered the Myers close family friends, and there was always the possibility that he might renew his friendship with Eleanor, for who he still held a torch.

Chapter 25

Eleanor arrived in Spain, landing at Malaga Airport, and while travelling along the coast road, she reflected on the memories of childhood again. The A7 from the airport traversed west along the mountainside with its panoramic view of the sea, so very familiar to her. What felt like a strange coincidence, Marbella was the Myers' family summer retreat, and it was also one of Richard's haunts. She thought, maybe it wasn't such a big surprise as Val D'isere and Marbella were two very popular locations. Eleanor was heading straight to Puerto Banus to meet Richard on his yacht, she knew she was there when she saw the statue of Jose Banus looking out to sea.

In the week since the Monaco deal she hadn't needed to attend any meetings. Richard had been in the United Kingdom where her expertise was not required. She was on full pay whether she worked or not, that was her contractual position, however her own work ethic made her feel uncomfortable. She couldn't relax, and accept that she was value for money to Richard at the best of times, but while not working it was more acute. Richard spoke to her briefly after the Nanostem Technologie deal, and all he had said was, 'Well done.'

It was still spring, but the weather in Spain was perfect. It was warm without being too hot. The sky was a beautiful cloudless deep blue that made Eleanor think how beautiful this planet really was. The Port was busy for this time of year, but the crowd was very different to the one that Eleanor recalled, as a child on a summer holidays. She noticed that in the spring there were a lot of men chatting to women plying their trade. She walked right past, quite fascinated as she made her way to Richards yacht.

The captain saw her before she saw him, he was a fifty two year old Dutch Captain sporting a deep tan, and the leathery skin of a man who had spent years in the sun, and most of them out at sea. He was dressed in smart white pleated shorts, and a brilliant white short sleeve shirt, with brown leather Deck Shoes. He looked great for his age. He still had a full head of blond hair with no grey in sight, and all his own teeth, that were as white as the shirt. He was waiting to greet Eleanor at the bottom of the gang plank. After introducing himself, he escorted her onto the yacht, and showed her through to Richard's office on board. When she entered Richard rose from his desk.

'Eleanor, how nice to see you again.' He extended his hand to shake and got straight down to business. 'I am so pleased with the way we handled the Nanostem Technology negotiations. You were instrumental in securing the right deal. What I didn't tell you is that my team put a value on the business of twice the price that I paid, and I would have happily agreed to twenty million each, rather than jeopardise the deal, but it's thanks to your translation that I saved ten million Euros.'

Eleanor said, 'well I can hardly take the credit, it was the reason you employed me in the first place. But I must say I am really pleased with the way it worked out. Does this mean I keep my job?' She laughed.

Richard said, 'don't you worry . . . you are earmarked for a long term position.'

She recalled her conversation with the pilot, and remembered that full time was literally that. She was also aware that if she wasn't required, there was plenty of down time, so if she was offered full time today she would jump at the chance. He handed her a copy of a BAC's, a same day bank transfer for fifty thousand Euros made out to her account.

'I have a little bonus for you, for the great result.'

Eleanor said, 'there is really no need, you already pay me very well.' She looked down at the piece of paper astonished. 'But I am very very grateful, and hope I can be of assistance again.'

Weiss didn't get the response he had expected, so he tried to pick up on what the issue could be, he was quite naturally intuitive. He recognised the fact that Eleanor held herself with a lot of confidence without having to try too hard. Today she was simply, but elegantly dressed in a light cotton white dress, that matched her retro fashion restyled hair, a.k.a. 1960's Jackie Kennedy look. Her expression was stoical, but there was something in her body language that suggested to Richard that she was slightly uncomfortable.

'If I am doing well out of a deal, I reward those involved in its success. I do this for all of the staff, so don't feel it comes with strings attached.'

He got it right, as he often did, and when Richard said this it put her mind at ease, she was clearly feeling a little over paid, and wondering at what price. But concluded that she was simply in the right place at the right time, and there was no doubt that the money Richard threw at his staff created loyalty. He commanded your full attention, and paid well for that commitment, so she would relax, and make the most of this opportunity. She gratefully accepted the bonus. Richard nodded, and further explained the purchase of Nanostem.

'The technology we acquired was a strategic purchase. I have a UK business, RW Pharmaceutical PLC, and we have been working on a very similar product for the medical sector. Don't laugh as I am not the first rich man to attempt to do this, but I am looking to extend my life. If we can get the NSC's to work inside the veins, I believe we could extend life. Can you imagine the market for a longer life? ' As he said this a shadow descended on the room, as a yacht docked in the adjoining slip.

'You have met my surgeon Dr Blake Gibson, he is the MD of this company. I always call him my personal surgeon, but in reality he has never done any surgery on me, it just sounds good. He is a miserable man at the best of times, but he is okay when you get to know him. I will tell you about him some day.'

Weiss went to the window to look at the craft pulling alongside their starboard side. The very large buoys were in place to protect the side of his yacht, but Weiss was still looking to make sure there was no coming together of the two large boats. Without turning he continued.

'Basically I believe that RW Pharmaceutical will monetise much faster if we integrate Nanostem. Basically I intend to float RW Pharmaceutical PLC, and the purchase of Nanostem will help achieve the price point I am looking for.'

The other yacht was still reversing into its position; the captain was sounding his horn. The noise was very loud, and reverberated around Richard's office. Eleanor wondered why the bigger the vehicles, the louder the horn. Were yacht captains usually deaf? At the same time Richard said, 'There is always some bastard with a bigger yacht.' He moved from behind his desk, and gestured to Eleanor to join him for a coffee on the Weather Deck.

Richard continued, 'at RW Pharmaceutical's research facility in Oxford the team are working on, amongst other projects, the health of arteries, and their work is focusing on strengthening the inner wall of veins, potentially applying this to heart valves. Philippe's teardrop material, and unique application technique is the missing link. My team were raving about the Nanostem Technology prior to the meeting, and I was going to buy it, it was all down to how cheap I could get it.'

There were two crew members with fresh towels, and large glasses of Evian with ice, and a slice of lemon. They walked around the table offering the refreshment. Richard took a glass, as did Eleanor, as he continued, 'for Nanostem to focus on Karaoke was an error of judgement. It turns out that they are keen amateur musicians, and they have a modest studio. Initially they were looking for a solution to improve the vocal performances for the recording purposes. They really didn't see the bigger picture.'

He wrapped the towel around his neck, and held each end in clenched fists and continued, 'Medically... they haven't really contemplated the comprehensive uses beyond anything to do with the throat, and even that was through the venture capitalist insistence. When Mathieu touched on a "Speech impediment cure" I thought they had got wise to my interests, but even if they did, they have no sense of the phenomenal potential.'

Richard lectured without any input from Eleanor, for her part, she was very attentive as she was genuinely fascinated. He was clearly very excited about the project, and was enthusiastic as he spoke. His team in the UK had advanced the project over the last three years, and it was his team that had alerted Richard to the material that Nanostem had designed. The first thoughts were to imitate the design, but the patents were comprehensive, hence the takeover became the preferred option. It was the right decision because in the short space of time since the deal was struck, the UK team had already been able to confirm that the medical uses that they had purchased it for, were working exactly as expected. As the product had already been approved to be used in a medical capacity, it would be on the market in months, not years.

Richard said, 'More water, or would you like a coffee?' Eleanor had coffee. She sat on one of the heavily cushioned swivel chairs. As Richard poured the coffee he said, 'I asked you to come as I will need you in a series of meetings in Gibraltar.' When the yacht captain saw him pour his own coffee, he gave two crew members a look that made it clear they hadn't performed their job very well. Eleanor saw this play out and was mildly amused, how important is it that the owner of a yacht pours his own coffee, after all, it was already laid out ready. He handed her a cup and continued, 'there will be several meetings I would like you to attend. Some on behalf of the bank.'

Richard cross charged the bank for all of Eleanor's work. Her contract was with Weiss & Associates, and he invoiced the bank for her time, as he did with all of his staff, all with a considerable profit margin for himself. 'Most of the attendees speak English, and they are all working for me in one capacity or another, however I have several documents that will be in both Spanish, and English and there will inevitably be some amendments, there always is. Now rather than have any delay, they will be amended as agreed on the day . . . It should be straightforward.'

The wake from the docking yacht caused small waves that slapped the hull, they could be heard but not felt, the yacht didn't pitched at all, Eleanor thought, it must have good stabilisers, either that or it was just too large for such a small wake to effect it. 'Will they know I can translate?' Eleanor asked.

'Yes they are all being paid by my company to work for me. Correction, I really should say, either me personally or my bank,' Richard spoke of the bank as his own personal property, it did carry his name; however it was a public company, and anything but his personally. 'One of the attendees is a banker that acts as my Trustee. I have a complex structure in place to maximise tax efficiency; it's basically a series of Trusts; several of which are based in Gibraltar, I am resident in Gibraltar for personal tax purposes.' This allowed Weiss to legitimately only pay one hundred thousand pounds sterling per annum tax on his worldwide income.

The coffee was hot, but that didn't stop Richard downing his quickly, a young lady refilled his cup before he had a chance to do it himself. He said, 'The trust laws are, amongst the best in the world, and I often need someone to front a deal. Anonymity can also play a part for various reasons, usually around the negotiations. To do a single purchase on a very large scale actually affects the price; if word gets out that I am buying, the share value will rise. But don't worry about the technical aspects, as far as your role is concerned, all I need you to do is to read both sets of documents over the next two days, and make sure you are happy with the translations.'

They continued to chat for an hour or so, Richard had at least three more coffees while he told Eleanor more about his business empire. She knew he was a very highly motivated, single minded man, but what was most fascinating to Eleanor, was that he already seemed focused on his next deal. She wondered at what point he would be satiated.

'What part will Dr Gibson play in the new company?' she asked.

Richard said, 'I'm not sure yet, I may move him from there altogether as I think Philippe will be the Managing Director, and Mathieu Technical Director as they are such a strong team. Blake pisses everyone off anyway.' Richard hardly ever swore, even the more mild words tended to not form part of his vocabulary, Eleanor took this slip as a sign that he was relaxed around her.

'So what is his story, you said you would tell me all about him?'

'I think he is talented, but he got struck off.' When he didn't follow up, Eleanor thought that he probably didn't want to talk about him, but after a couple of minutes he said, 'he made a name for himself in the boob job boom in the late eighties, early nineties. I met him as an investor. As lap dancing was booming . . . not that I have ever been interested in that.' Rather than her think he was being a prude he added, 'when you are paying someone to remove their clothes it's no longer sexy for me. I'm not against it, it just does nothing for me'. She sat just listening.

Richard said, 'I digress, anyway, the business had a demand for girls with decent boobs, and one side-line industry was a gap in the market that Gibson wanted to fill with his "New U" clinics, and he needed a few million to get the business off the ground.' Richard sat up, and faced Eleanor as he continued. 'He had this new silicone implant that was much cheaper to manufacture, and Gibson wanted to open "New U" stores all across the USA. He went from competent confidence to absolute arrogance in a matter of months. I made two further investments before the first complaint.' Richard looked down, and to the right as he recalled the time in question. 'An implant leaked, and caused septicaemia. Gibson tried to assure me it was a one off, but I wanted out. So Gibson bought me out, at a discounted value I might add.'

Weiss had already had his investment back threefold in dividends. 'It was the beginning of the end of "New U". The implants were failing, and a high court judge ruled that "New U" was responsible. As the claims built up, the share price went down. Gibson cut corners, used inferior products and he lost the company, with his reputation severely damaged. The "General Medical Council" deemed him personally culpable, and he lost his licence.' Richard shook his head, recalling how obvious it was to leave the sinking ship, while Gibson ploughed on.

'He still says, "I've lost millions", but I say to him, "You started with nothing, and you now have money. What's the problem?", but all he can focus on is that I had quadrupled my investment, and he had more or less lost 90% of his, and he fixated on what he had lost rather than what he was left with.' Richard stopped talking as he had more or less covered everything that had happened. Eleanor broke the silence with her question. 'So he didn't really care about his patients?'

Richard replied, 'not really, if I'm honest. I didn't know that at the start otherwise I wouldn't have invested. I said to him after it collapsed, "You shouldn't have used cheap implants", he started to defend the implants, trying to justify to me, why he used the material he did.' He leaned back again, and completed his tale.

'I told him that he is a talented, and skillful doctor, and he said something like, "I didn't realise how much I would miss being a surgeon". But it was the power, he liked having someones life in his hands. I promised him I would get a licence sorted out, and some work. But there are plenty of opportunities that don't need a license, and from that day on Dr. Blake Gibson worked for Richard Weiss Pharmaceuticals full time, and I appointed him to the Board. He has done a good job, but as I say, he rubs people up the wrong way.' They could hear talking as someone arrived.

'He was abused as a kid, and it seems to me that he gets a kick out of other people's pain. We had a discussion once about when are "you", still "You". So if I remove your arm that doesn't affect the sense of self, the "you". How many things could we remove or swap in a transplant. Kidneys, heart, and so on, and still that sense of self remain. Are we just our minds?'

Eleanor said, 'I take it you had been drinking.'

They both laughed, he said, 'Exactly, just a semi drunk, what if. But Blake got really into it, explaining to me how to do it. So he can be a bit weird, even with me, but at the end of the day, I fund him, so he does whatever I ask, and he totally worships me, so I would trust him to work on me,' Richard said. 'Now then, let's stop talking business. Rainbird is here, how do you fancy doing some yoga?'

After a pleasant afternoon doing yoga with Rainbird, Eleanor joined Richard, Victoria, and three of Richards's contacts for dinner around the pool. After dinner, Richard played the drums in his band. The friends he had invited were all musicians, and they had a great night playing old Rolling Stones songs together. Eleanor thought they were actually quite good.

Chapter 26

Eleanor spent the next two days on the yacht. On the first afternoon she saw Gibson fishing on the back deck. As always he was alone, and chain smoking. He caught a really big Conger Eel, and she saw him keep smacking its head on the edge of the deck. As he killed the fish, he looked over at Eleanor with a look of contempt, and while he had her gaze, he spat over the side of the yacht, turned his back on Eleanor, and walked off. It left Eleanor wondering if it was her he didn't like. She certainly wouldn't like to be alone with him on the yacht, he was definitely weird.

The night before the Gibraltar meetings she transferred with Victoria to a hotel in Marbella, as Richard had a completely confidential meeting. As they left the vessel they could see that this guest really was a VVIP who wanted to conduct the meeting in complete secrecy. The gang plank had been covered with an awning; it created an entrance from the roadside, straight to the yacht. The front of this tunnel was splayed out on the roadside, this way the person arriving by car could transfer in complete privacy.

Even Victoria didn't know who Richard was meeting. The person was in Richard's dairy as BBRW, which Victoria said meant, "Booked by Richard Weiss". These occasional BBRW entries took priority over any other meetings, and they were the only ones that Victoria didn't book herself, but she never questioned her boss. There had been several over the years, and Victoria had never been involved in any of them. Rumour had it that it was either a member of the Saudi Royal family, or a famous musician, but this had never been confirmed.

Eleanor travelled with Victoria across to Gibraltar, on the Wednesday morning for a series of meetings. Richard was already in Gibraltar, the yacht had a berth there too. Before the first meeting started, Eleanor was able to tell Richard that the documents were all fine, and they were translated correctly. Slight interpretations could be pointed out, but they were more to do with presentation rather than accuracy, and she didn't want to appear unnecessarily pedantic. After coffee, Richard chaired the first meeting. He opened by saying, 'Good morning everyone, can I take it you all have the agenda for the next two days?'

Everyone confirmed they had. Also, each attendee had a complete set of all of the documents under discussion. There were eleven lever arch files of documents in each bundle. In the meeting were three external bankers, two accountants, two lawyers on behalf of Richard Weiss, and three trustees from the Harris & Tarling Trust Corporation based in Gibraltar. Richard had Victoria to his left, and Eleanor on his right. He was sat in a chair with a large back, reminiscent of those on the "Voice".

Richard said, 'my primary objective is to set up the Trusts for my new project. I am ready to do a very large transaction, and my anonymity is required.' He looked right in the eyes of everyone round the table one at a time. When he focused on each of them, most found his piercing gaze intimidating, and they lowered their gaze as he continued, 'I am weeks away from doing this deal, and I intend to use this opportunity to do the gearing exercise we have previously discussed.'

Richard had been quietly working away on the Tambura project for years. Initially his UK property agents had told him how cheap land was in Africa and when he went out there on a reconnaissance some eight years ago, he instantly saw an opportunity. In this particular area, the land came with water, lots of it, and as the land owner he would have control of the water usage. He surreptitiously went about buying whatever he could in the region. It had to be done in various corporate names so no one got alerted to his game plan. So eight years on, and he had almost complete control of the area.

Eleanor was fascinated by the meeting. It wasn't boring as Richard had warned. She couldn't profess to keep up with the technical aspects, but she got a feel for the general principles being discussed. She could only admire Richard, who seemed to fully understand the technical aspects from the legal, accounting, banking, and Trust perspective. Everyone else professed to only understand their own specialist area, and by and large they didn't cross over to the other professions.

From what she could make out, Richard was undertaking to invest twenty four billion Dollars on behalf of W.I.B.C into the Tambura Trust. This first Trust was investing in a second Trust, and in turn, this Trust was purchasing shares in W.I.B.C. After this transaction had taken place, W.I.B.C would then invest a further twenty four billion Dollars into the Tambura Trust. The transactions were only on paper, so there didn't need to be a physical exchange of any kind.

The signing ceremony had a strict running order, and happened consecutively. Each had to be in sequence as it would be impossible for Trust two to invest money it hadn't yet received, and so on. Therefore, each company's documentation had different times on the meeting minutes. One of the accountants called this a Round Robin. Once one of the accountants yawned, it passed around the room. It wasn't boredom, it was just getting exhausting, spending hours poring over documents. The monotony didn't seem to reach Richard, he looked tireless.

'Would it be possible to take a lunch break please Richard?' Jesus, the Spanish banker, enquired.

Richard replied, 'I would much rather work straight through.' However, it was clear to Richard that they needed a break. He leant back in his chair with his hands behind his neck, with his eyes looking up at the ceiling. Richard posed the question, 'are you all ok to eat while we continue to work?' The way he asked, he only wanted one answer, so they had a working lunch.

Eleanor heard the banker ask Richard about the potential conflict of interest. 'Can you act for the bank, and in some capacity for the Trust?' It hadn't occurred to Eleanor until the banker voiced this opinion, but it seemed the question was soon satisfied. Despite the workload Richard looked as fresh by the end of the long day as he had in the morning. He couldn't persuade everyone to do a really late night to get the task finished as they said mistakes could be made if they didn't take a break, so the meeting was adjourned until the morning.

It had been a good day so far, and Richard was on a high and on good form. He asked Victoria, 'Would you, and Eleanor join me for dinner on the yacht?' Eleanor knew that the question was asked of

Victoria as she was the one who had booked everything, and she accepted on behalf of them both. Once around the dining table Richard said, 'I bet today was really boring?'

Eleanor said, 'no, actually I really enjoyed it. I was fascinated by the subject, and I think I followed it quite well'. Victoria was less interested, but was equally more than happy with the day. Eleanor couldn't believe that while they were chatting, sitting around the table on the lower deck, a small audience had gathered, and literally stood there watching them. All they were doing was toasting the day with a glass of champagne, and yet the crowd were transfixed. Richard took it in his stride, but Eleanor felt a little bit on show. She couldn't imagine why on earth people would want to be looking at her, even if she was sitting on a large Yacht.

'From what I could gather, you agreed to invest twenty odd billion today. I'm still fairly new so I am not used to numbers like this'. Eleanor said.

Richard replied, 'I have never done a deal like this before. It is my single biggest deal ever. What we did today is known as gearing, all high street banks do it. My whole business life has been leading to this point. The deal is done, tomorrow is simply a formality. Everyone will make the necessary amendments agreed over the course of the day, and I will be signing my life away tomorrow.' While talking, he was doing a drum roll on his practice pads, while playing he continued, 'the next stage will be to raise funds by utilising the Trust assets as collateral for land acquisition. It's known as OPiuM, Other People's Money, and is quite common. When done correctly, perfectly legal. The overall transactions will make me one of the richest men in the world.' He stopped drumming when he said this through clenched teeth, and punched his fist into the air.

She hadn't known Richard for long, but she noticed that he rarely let his hair down. He had a glass or two of wine, but so far, never more, sometimes encouraging others to drink while he didn't. Eleanor thought this was down to wanting to remain in control, but she was pleased to see that tonight he seemed more relaxed, and was having a good drink.

He said, 'have you read anything about "loss aversion"?' Eleanor hadn't, so Richard gave her a brief summary. 'Basically humans are hot wired to avoid loss. Our decisions are influenced by this "loss aversion" without us even knowing it. There have been some fantastic papers on the subject, and it is almost like our survival instinct.' He stood stretching his spine, head right back, utilizing his yoga knowledge.

Richard continued, 'the biggest, and most important decisions we will ever make, are influenced by this. I completely believe this to be true, and I take it into account on every investment decision I make. I am convinced that this is one of the reasons I have been so successful.' His enthusiasm was contagious, and all on-board were enjoying themselves. At the end of another enjoyable evening, Eleanor was expecting to transfer to the hotel in Marbella, but she was pleasantly surprised that she was back on board the yacht, and all of her belongings had already been transferred from the hotel. They went to bed late, but Eleanor still woke refreshed, and ready to start another long day around the board table.

As they were all fresh and most of the discussions had already taken place, the morning went fast. When it came to the signing there were some bank documents that were in English, and Spanish, and Eleanor had to approve the amendments. There were a couple of mistakes that she highlighted, and the amends were promptly corrected, and printed for the signing ceremony. Two of the partners from Philip James accountants, both called Mark, were the first to comment on the signing.

'We have separated the roles for the completion of the deal. I will be working for you Richard, and Mark will be working for W.I.B.C.' It was Mark Evans who stood to say this, and he acknowledged Mark Francis to his right. They were both bald, both wore dark rimmed glasses and they both, wore cheap shoes.

He went on to say, 'we have created a Chinese wall, and satisfied our compliance department that there will be no conflict of interest.' Eleanor had no idea what a Chinese wall meant, but she followed the principal. From what she could gather, it allowed one advisory company to work on both sides of a deal for two parties that had some connection. As they were representing different legal entities it was the conflicts of interest that were the critical point. She Googled the meaning, and read, "On each side of the imaginary Chinese wall, sits an adviser, and it is their individual integrity that avoids the conflict".

The room was full of talented professionals, and who was she to question the technical elements. Eleanor could see why accountants had a reputation for being a bit steady Eddie boring types, but she had seen the fee schedule as part of the paperwork bundle, and as they were working on a percentage of the deal value, they were making a small fortune out of this one transaction. So she thought there is a lot to be said for a steady Eddie type after all.

The lawyer stood, and said, 'from our perspective, this issue was dealt with right from the start, I had a conference with my partner at five am this morning, and I can confirm that both sides of the transaction are ready to complete.' It was largely ignored, but both Marks looked a little uncomfortable. Mark Francis was stroking his head, conscious of the few hairs he had left, sticking up, and he was doing his best to plaster them in place. Richard saw this, and made a mental note to not shake hands with him.

The forty year old single malt whiskey they were all enjoying wouldn't improve Marks bad breath either. Eleanor thought it was quite noticeable that here in Gibraltar, alcoholic drinks were served in meetings. Richard, and the girls didn't indulge. This whole setup was to bring together all of Richard's land in Tambura. He had big plans for the water there, and this deal was one of the last jigsaw pieces of his grand plan.

The final task saw Andrew Harris pass a Bearer Share Certificate to Richard; they shook hands as the last document changed hands. He handed this straight to Victoria, and said, 'you know where this goes.' At the end of the day, Richard looked very pleased. It was clear that everyone in the room was happy too. Eleanor's first few weeks had been quite incredible. With her salary, casino win and bonus, she had doubled her life savings in the first month, and she considered herself fortunate. She concluded that when things start to go well, everything seems inspired, and it all spirals upwards, and it feels like you can do no wrong. She'd look forward to the challenges that the future would bring, if it was her time to shine, she would make the most of it, of that she was certain.

Book 3

Chapter 27

In the three months since the Nanostem deal, Eleanor was permanently based in France. While there she had translated all of the Nanostem literature from French into English. The technical documents were a challenge, particularly the issues around the scientific terms, most of which were universal, but they were very specific to the medical profession, and were certainly not terms that she knew. Richard had given them a tight deadline, and Eleanor was pleased that she had just completed her final task on time, a translation of the Nanostem website, thanks to excellent technical support off Mathieu.

Weiss had decided to merge RW Pharmaceutical PLC with Nanostem Technologie. Both sides of the merger were very pleased with this decision as the synergies were clear for all to see. A Mergers, and Acquisition team were collating the essential documents relating to corporate governance, Technological Patents, and accounting. The overriding goal was to prepare the merged entity for a NYSE stock market flotation. Institutional investors had responded very positively to the announcement, and advanced commitments had put the value at somewhere in the region of four billion seven hundred and fifty million dollars. The press were calling the merger a "Match made in Heaven". New Scientist went further, and claimed that, "in the science of vascular regeneration, this is a potential game changer".

Weiss was set to take a personal profit of three billion dollars. He wasn't the first, and he wouldn't be the last Chairman to make Billions from a flotation, but this was one of the fastest on record, from original setup of Richard Weiss Pharmaceuticals PLC to full market flotation in just three years. This had further added to his reputation as an extraordinary entrepreneurial businessman. No one at RWP or Nanostem begrudged Richard this windfall as he had issued shares to all of his team, and there was no obligation on him to do that, so it was seen by all as a generous bonus. That meant, despite the very long hours, and the hard work, everyone had an excellent attitude, and got the job done on schedule.

Eleanor was amazed at how many deals Richard was involved in. While she worked on Nanostem, he had done an additional five deals to her knowledge. The way he did this was to encourage inventors to put forward a business plan for their product, and if he liked it, he would fund it. Despite not needing Eleanor's translation skills, Richard had still sent some info to Eleanor for her gut instinct. Eleanor had never been in business, and couldn't see what she could add to help him make a decision. But when she put this to him, he said he gathered opinions about products from his staff, to get a variety of views, so she just commented as requested. She was really enjoying her role, and loved the variety. She could see a rosy future for herself working with Richard.

∞

Richard was invited to attend a conference in Washington DC, an exclusive affair with several influential bankers, and senior politicians. There were several items on the agenda. The three main issues being, "Global Recovery", the "Trade Deficit", and the "Interest Rate". Richard kept his promise, and invited Eleanor to join him. She would only need to attend two meetings with Richard, and then she could have an extended break with her sister. As W.I.B.C Headquarters was based in Washington, there was every chance that they would work from here for the rest of the summer.

Eleanor moved in with her sister. As soon as she arrived, it was the week that the bad press started. Emily hit the headlines, it was in most daily newspapers. She was constantly featured on CNN, and NBC News, and there wasn't a single news item that took her side. Who would have known that there were so many "Water Experts" to be called upon to give their opinion? They were all focused on "water rationing" which Emily's report had quoted from the source that Richard Weiss had provided as a possible solution for fairer water distribution. Rather than stimulating a healthy debate, it had become the single focus of the witch hunt.

The TV interviews that Emily gave hadn't helped. She came across as anything but an expert. The interviewers, claiming to be playing "Devil's Advocate", put preposterous questions to her, and she was ridiculed. The low point was Emily crying, and shouting on a live news programme "the West is using forty times more water than Africa, and I can't see why we shouldn't use less, we could make it equal for everyone".

The ensuing panic caused sales of bottled water to shoot up, and supermarket shelves were quickly emptied, they couldn't keep up with demand. It got even worse when the majority of concern switched to the lack of water in the USA. It would be political suicide, to not find a solution to the shortfall, which without any hard evidence was becoming a larger deficit daily. Other countries were following the story but it was the USA where the subject had become political. Emily's report was not used as a basis for political discussion, despite being commissioned by the government.

The Hoover Dam got a lot of coverage, as it was now common knowledge that the reserves there, were getting lower, and lower. With a hundred billion dollars of new build property in the pipeline, prices would be decimated unless a solution was found. The conspiracy theorists were jumping on the bandwagon, stating, "If global warming is true, and the planet's oceans were growing, how could we be short of water?"

The arguments would run on, and something would have to be done. Emily seemed close to a nervous breakdown. Dr David Prost thought that her confidence was little more than a thin veneer, and underneath she was very vulnerable, and this event was showing that he was right. He also had something that he needed to discuss. When Prost knew that Eleanor was in town, he suggested that they should all meet for dinner, and so a date was set. From a professional stance, he wanted Eleanor there for Emily's sake, but he did feel very apprehensive on a personal level. Would she still feel about him as he felt about her? Well he wouldn't have too long to find out.

Chapter 28

There were some thirty or so people in attendance at the meeting hosted by the "Federal Reserve". Eleanor was with Richard when he introduced himself to Senator Harvey Kugel, who didn't even acknowledge Eleanor, she had already formed an opinion from what Emily had said.

After a few pleasantries with the Senator, Richard excused himself, and found his place next to Victoria with Eleanor seated on his left. Eleanor found the politics completely boring, and the meeting dragged. The banking community had lurched from one compliance breach to another. Miss selling, Libor fixing, huge fines, and massive losses, but W.I.B.C had no such issues. Richard with his normal aplomb seemed to captivate his audience. They were his peers but, due to his reputation, they all seemed to give his arguments more weight. As far as bankers bonuses were concerned, Richard's were better than most, but as he constantly delivered a market leading dividend yield, he avoided the spotlight.

Eleanor was grateful to Richard for bringing her to Washington, and giving her the time off to be with Emily, but in this meeting, she felt a little superfluous. Victoria took the minutes as Richard didn't trust the official versions the FR would distribute. When the main meeting broke up Eleanor had to mingle. Richard asked her to get personal mobile numbers from as many of the attendees as she could. She went around with Victoria; the task was easy as they stood out, two attractive women in a room full of middle aged men.

They had about 25 cards between them, more or less everyone, so they sat, and had a drink together catching up on the last couple of months. Richard hadn't spent much time in France, he was jetting around the world on business deals, and Victoria had travelled with him. Richard was heavily invested in land, and property, and had been on the acquisition trail. He had spent multi-millions in Africa to add to his huge tracts of land he already owned. In investment circles there was a rumour that he had purchased a mining company with new technology, and he was interested in land rich with gold, and diamonds, but Victoria had seen the pre-sale documentation, and according to the particulars, the land he had just acquired was of no interest to other mining companies as there wasn't a known seam from samples taken. Many mining CEO's were watching closely.

Very few knew of his grand plan, all other investors had not considered the possibilities. But Weiss had a plan that he had now turned his full attention to. Victoria told Eleanor more of what she knew about Tambura, and Richard's water deal.

The drink flowed, and the girls relaxed, and started giggling over some of the D.I.S antics. No matter how long the gap between seeing each other, Eleanor, and Victoria were always very comfortable in each other's company. Richard was standing at the bar with Senator Harvey Kugel, deep in conversation.

Kugel played a key role in the USA banking sector as he was the Chairman of the Board of the Federal Reserve, F.R, whose primary task was to maintain economic stability in the USA and control inflation, usually through adjusting the base rate. Kugel explained this as "The price that banks pay for liquidity, and this balancing act affects a Nation's disposable income". Kugel was known for his sound bites, and another constantly re-quoted bit was, "too much disposable income can lead to inflation; not enough can lead to recession. The very system is prone to boom and bust."

The Chairman's position became available after the outgoing Chairman resigned under public pressure for heads to roll for the general mess the economy was in. Some said Kugel had been instrumental in turning the economy around after the global turmoil of two thousand and eight, by implementing changes that allowed for recovery, and in turn, securing himself the Chairmanship, others said he was just in the right place at the right time.

Either way, he was always taken serious when he gave his opinion, in reality, few people were able to work the system as well as Senator Harvey Kugel. He had sat on the board of the FR ever since his appointment as a Senator, and as the Chairman he wielded a lot of power.

He was able to completely influence all key decisions of the Board, making him one of the most powerful men in the USA. A position gained, that does not need a public election to hold. Kugel was unpopular in the FR amongst many staff as his general demeanour was unpleasant. He was arrogant, ignorant, controlling and rather pompous. However, no one would deny that he had a certain flair for economic strategy, and he was Emily's 'stepping stone' to forcing the government to recognise the water accessibility issue.

Victoria whispered, 'I've seen that chap on Richards's yacht at one of the BBRW meetings.'

Eleanor replied, 'it can't be. I was with Richard when he introduced himself.'

Victoria said, 'it definitely is. I was on the way off the yacht one day as he walked on. I smiled and said good morning, and he just looked through me, and snarled. He's really creepy.'

Eleanor said, 'are you absolutely sure . . . my sister worked for the Senator, I know it would have definitely come up.'

'Absolutely. I am one hundred percent certain.'

It left Eleanor speechless. She couldn't quite get her head around it. Something was not right, tonight wasn't the right time, but as soon as she saw Richard, she would ask, *How long had he known Kugel*?

Chapter 29

'What name please?' the waitress asked.

Eleanor said, 'Prost. A table for three in the name of Dr. Prost.'

'Ah . . . David. He is one of our favourite regulars. Follow me please, I am Gabby, and I will be your server tonight.' As they walked across the busy restaurant Eleanor saw David at the table, and waved. He waved back as he stood up to greet them. *My first love,* he wrote on his wall, after she recently accepted his friend request on Facebook. When David saw her profile picture, he had to look long, and hard at it to see the girl he once knew. After all she was only seventeen when they had to break up. As she crossed the room David thought, *wow . . . she had got even better with age.*

They followed the waitress in single file with Emily, in front of Eleanor. 'Emily Hi'

After David had greeted Emily, he turned to look at his old flame, she stood, very demure, her coat buttoned to her neck, with a floppy fashionable beret, her right leg crossed over her left with her hands down crossed in front of her, holding the long handles of her handbag. David saw all of this in complete clarity, and etched it into his memory. He stood with his arms at his side, hands out with the palms up in that "Look at you", pose reserved for use when someone greets a long lost friend. It seemed like minutes to Eleanor, but it was only seconds that they both stood, soaking up as much information with their eyes, as they could.

She never even stopped to wonder if he was single, she had already decided that if he was married, they would still be friends anyway. The smiles, the joy, the overload of emotions, and then the warning of the tears that came from the lips as they gave away how she was really feeling. When David saw this, to his surprise, as he hadn't cried since his mother's funeral, he welled up too. They equally closed the physical divide as she jumped into his arms, and he held her close, her feet four inches off the ground.

Gabby looked at Emily and mouthed, 'I will come back'. David became aware of Eleanor's chest against his, and thought, *she didn't have those last time we met.* Although they had never consummated their relationship, there had been lots of heavy petting. Things in him were stirring, and so before it became obvious, he put her down. This was definitely not the time or place.

It wasn't just Emily that could see there was still chemistry between them, the owner, Marco, came over to see who all the fuss was over, and asked, 'Hey Doc, who is this beauty? Welcome, welcome.'

David said, 'Eleanor this is Marco.' the flamboyant owner kissed her left cheek, right cheek, and left again.

'Mama Mia.' Marco was Italian American, but he tended to ham it up a little in the restaurant, he was almost a parody of the happy Italian restaurateur. David thought it was the best Italian in Washington.

Marco said, 'call me Geppetto, everybody does.' The muffled noise of the restaurant rumbled in the background.

Marco saw Emily, and said to her 'oh, I'm so sorry,' and he repeated his greeting ritual. Parody or not, he was genuinely popular with all of his customers. The sisters were more than happy to fall in line, and call him Geppetto, but David continued with Marco, as he explained, 'we are all originally from England, and our families were great friends'. David was only 18 when his parents moved to Washington, and he was devastated to have to leave Eleanor.

Gabby walked past, 'this is my beautiful wife.' Geppetto told the sisters. 'She only works here to keep her eye on me.'

Marco winked at Emily as he said this. Gabby took no notice, she was usually the butt of Marco's jokes, but she had no complaints, they both knew it worked well, as they were busy all night every night.

Without asking, Marco pulled up a fourth chair to join his guests, he spoke Italian to his wife. You didn't need to understand Italian to recognise the tone of her reply, it suggested that he was giving her a job to do, while he sat down to drink. But it was a tag team that simply worked, and they both willingly played their part. A bottle of Prosecco came, and Marco said, 'ladies, please have an aperitif on the house. Do you like Champagne?' The sisters both thanked him as they accepted his kind offer. David had sat many a night with Marco, it was one of the reasons he didn't call him Geppetto, they had become good friends. Marco said, 'this is Italian champagne . . . from my home town on the Amalfi coast. It is the best Prosecco you can get.'

David noticed that Emily looked better than she did last time they met, and he wondered if she had taken the tablets, or if it was Eleanor's calming influence. Antipasto came, all sorted by Marco. David couldn't have planned it better if he tried. It was a great start to his reunion with Eleanor.

With a "Front of House" instinct, almost akin to mind-reading, Marco sensed the time to leave his guests to it. He excused himself promising to return. They looked at the menus before David got to say his piece, in the background they heard laughter, and 'Call me Geppetto, everybody does'. David recommended the saltimbocca, 'if you are ok with veal?' he added.

Over the meal David was able to talk about his recent discovery. 'Emily, after your consultation you mentioned my mother hugging you when you were first treated by my father. It stuck in my mind for days, and I couldn't think why, but then it occurred to me. My Mother died in nineteen eighty nine, and your father was still alive then. Something didn't stack up, so I have arranged to have all of our old files retrieved out of storage. I have also requested some audio tapes to follow. Can you remember much about your time with my father?'

Emily said, 'no not really. Dad died, and I was devastated. I was only eight, so I buried most of it . . . way into the back of my mind'. Eleanor listening to the conversation could sense a revelation coming, and was relieved to be here to lend her support.

David said, 'you first came to see my father when you were aged five.' Emily sat open mouthed, this was completely unexpected as she had no recollection whatsoever. 'From what I can gather, there was an incident at school. There is no easy way to put this . . . you had a boy, possibly two, sexually assault you. They, or he, were only around two years older, so it never went any further.'

'Did they,' Eleanor paused, not sure how to phrase the question, 'did they actually have sex?' She hadn't any need to feel uncomfortable, this is exactly what David wanted, to get everything out in the open.

He answered, 'from what I have seen so far, no. I want to know if I should go through everything, or would you prefer that I leave it alone?'

'What is the best thing to do?' Eleanor asked.

David said, 'well it is not as cut, and dried as you may think. Some schools of thought are that very old mental scars are best left alone, and the practitioner should concentrate on current issue. Others feel, without the "holistic" approach you can't really truly heal a patient.'

'And which side of the fence are you on?' Eleanor pushed.

He replied, 'fair question. If I am honest, I would prefer to fully understand what happened then, and to see what impact it had on Emily.' He looked at them both in turn, doing his best to not favour either with his gaze. 'I would then be able to advise, but I ultimately work for Emily. There are three potential issues, the current horrendous press, the passing of your father, and the issue, aged five. They are not linked, but they have all had their impact.'

'I want to see the files.' Emily said. 'Can I have the files ... would that be ok?' She had responded in a different way to how David predicted. She seemed pleased to have this information.

'Of course you can. They are your files ... shall I ...' Prost didn't get to finish his sentence, Emily talked across him.

'I want them all. I knew there was something causing these bouts of stress, and those files hold the key.' Prost was less convinced, but was pleased to get this response. He felt that she was clutching at this as a reason for the way her life had turned out, but he didn't want to curb her enthusiasm, any positives may help. Eleanor too, seemed really pleased that this may be the answer to Emily's issues.

Emily said, 'I want the files, and the tapes. I've always had a feeling that I had unresolved issues. Ellie will you help me please?' Emily was the only person who occasionally called Eleanor Ellie.

Eleanor replied, 'of course I will. I'm here for you!' They talked through the logistics of getting the files delivered, and agreed to meet up in two weeks' time, at David's practice. Eleanor would go too, and they would talk openly about the findings. Eleanor had one more meeting at work to attend, and then she would have the next three weeks to dedicate to the task.

∞

With the main issue discussed, they were able to relax, and enjoy the rest of the evening. There was music playing in the background all night, but after all of the main meals had been served Marco played guitar, and sang, accompanied by his friend on mandolin, and backing vocals. They started with Volare, and got the crowd singing along with the Dean Martin version, with mainly English lyrics. Eleanor wasn't expecting what happened next, Marco said, 'this song is for the beautiful Eleanor,' he started playing, and singing "Stuck on you" by Lionel Richie. Eleanor looked at David, eyes wide, and said, 'you remembered.' It was their song as teenagers.

David said, 'what was it that your mom used to say . . . If it's meant to be, you will be together when the time is right.' He had the last word on the subject, 'let's hope it's our time at last.'

Chapter 30

The two boxes contained files full of notes, letters, and summarised transcripts of the salient points of the actual therapy sessions. The only thing missing were the tapes. David had warned them that they were old reel to reel tapes that had to be stored in a moisture free environment, stored by the same company but in a different location, so they would follow in due course. For David to retrieve the tapes he had to obtain permission off Elizabeth Myers, she had emailed, apologising unnecessarily to Emily for not ever bringing it up, defending her position not to drag up the past.

In her email she wrote, 'it was traumatic at the time, but she seemed better, and then she was ill again, and it just got buried in history. I feel a fool for not thinking to say sooner.' She ended by giving her permission. Emily completely understood, and hoped her mother could understand her own need for closure.

The sisters individual approach to assimilate the information contained in the boxes was completely different, but at the same time complementary. Emily was regimented, and wanted everything military fashion. She created a timeline that they could both work with, showing each part of the process documented, and arranged in date order. Where Eleanor's method was more freestyle, surrounding herself with dozens of post-it notes, and as she whittled those down into categories, she transferred them to a mind map on a flip-chart.

'We always worked well together as kids too,' Eleanor said. There was something about the task that was bringing the best out of Emily. She was energised as they pieced together what had happened. She was going about the task in a detached fashion, as if she were studying an event that happened to someone else. Over a coffee break she said to Eleanor.

'I know that when I understand what happened, I will be able to put it to bed once, and for all, and I will be able to go forward with a clear mind.' Within four days they had an understanding of the event itself, but without the tapes it was sterile, and lacked clarity. They really needed to hear those recordings.

Eleanor said, 'is any of it coming back to you?' As she asked this, the phone on Emily's desk rang, she didn't answer it, explained to Eleanor.

'It's David on the landline, you may want to take it instead.' Caller display showed his number, so Emily got out of her seat so that Eleanor could take his call. . .

As Eleanor put the phone down, Emily asked, 'what did he say?'

'He said he has the tapes, and we should go to his place so that we can listen to them together.'

'There is the missing piece of the jigsaw on those tapes.' Eleanor hoped her sister was right.

Chapter 31

Eleanor arrived early for her meeting with Richard at W.I.B.C headquarters. This was to be her last meeting before her summer holiday. She intended to pose the question of Senator Kugel to Richard, even if it jeopardised her job. After reflecting on the possibility of Weiss using her, she had concluded that it was feasible, but it was hard to believe, and so she concluded, it was unlikely. She just hoped that Victoria was mistaken.

For now her mind was on her work, in attendance were seven dignitaries from the French Government. No doubt the meeting could have taken place while Weiss, and his team were in France, but one of Richard's business practices was to, *make the customer travel to you, and the probability of a deal is increased.*

Richard said, 'morning Eleanor, today I want to get a "Heads of Terms" agreed on a deal, and I want you to mingle with our guests at every available opportunity. Translate, at your discretion, anything I say that they don't understand. Use the Comms App again if there is something that I should know, but the chance of getting lucky again is unlikely.' Richard was looking through paperwork as he spoke. 'These guys are diplomats, they will be well versed in negotiating. So speak French to them, I think that will help to demonstrate we have made an effort to make them feel welcome.'

Victoria asked, 'are you happy with the place settings? I switched the Foreign Secretary facing you to the Minister of State.'

'Yes perfect.' Any deal that Weiss was involved in, he would utilise any available intelligence to increase his chance of success. Whenever there was more than one person in the meeting, he would have the attendee most likely to be the decision maker in the chair opposite his. In the Boardroom, they sat around a modern rectangular Board Table with Weiss, and his team on one side, and the clients/guests on the other. Eleanor didn't need to pose the question of Kugel, she had her answer when the Senator arrived for the meeting, and his place setting was at Richard's right hand side.

Richard said, 'bonjour Madam, and Messieurs, and welcome to W.I.B.C headquarters. I am afraid that is the extent of my French.' The room reacted appropriately to his comment. They were all relaxed, and in good spirits.

'If there is anything we cover today that needs to be translated, I have Eleanor on hand.' Richards offer met with approval. Richard found that Government meetings had a different emphasis, as the delegates were not spending their own money, and it may come down to how good the customer felt. 'I would also like to thank Senator Harvey Kugel for putting both parties together.'

After Richard's introduction, the French delegates each took turns to introduce themselves, and state what office they held. They outlined certain protocols that they needed to follow, and the parameters of the meeting, confirming that they had the authority to complete a transaction. It left Richard's team without doubt that this party represented the French Government, and had the autonomy to conclude a deal.

Despite being experienced negotiators, they were showing their hand early, and Richard clearly had the upper hand. Within an hour, all of the formalities were out of the way, and it was time to get down to business. 'We, the French Government, wish to purchase 100 billion litres of your water. We would like to agree to a price that includes delivery, and any foreign duty.' The Minister of State continued, 'we are here to complete the deal if we can agree the purchase price'.

Richard said, 'thank you Mr Cherrie. I have issued specific Terms and Conditions that are not negotiable.' Richard had his copy open as he spoke. 'Can you confirm that you find them acceptable?'

Cherrie glanced down at his notes, and responded, 'to complete the purchase you require a non-refundable deposit, and confirmation that we do not require an environmental report or access to reports from any other country. I believe these are the specific terms that you are referring to?' He pushed his glasses further up the bridge of his nose, 'and yes we find them acceptable.'

'Thank you Mr Cherrie, and may I thank you all. I am very pleased that we have a platform acceptable to both sides to do business, and I thank you for "cutting to the chase".' This term was translated by Eleanor as the bemused French dignitaries weren't sure of the Americanism.

'Mr Weiss, you misunderstand. We wish to conclude the purchase today.' Cherrie wanted to agree the deal straight away. 'We are here to reach terms, and agree the timing for payment, etc. I would like to make an offer of one hundred million dollars.'

Richard replied, 'I am afraid that will not be possible at this stage. We have other interested parties, and I need to explore all possibilities prior to making my final decision.' There was a little confusion at this statement. The French delegates were under the illusion that a deal was there to be done.

'Can I suggest we take a short break for both parties to . . .' Richard was interrupted.

'You are a clever negotiator Mr Weiss.' Cherrie was the only one on the French side speaking. 'What is the expression the "take away close", I think you call it. Tempt customers, and then tell them they can't buy so the price increases.' Cherrie took his glasses off, and was pointing them at Richard as he spoke.

Richard said, 'not at all sir. I am not in a position to conclude a deal with you today, however I am pleased that my Terms have met with your approval. What I will agree to today is to sign a comprehensive "Heads of Agreement subject to contract".'

'Mr Weiss, I can increase our offer to a maximum of 150 million dollars. I assure you this is the absolute maximum that we are prepared to pay.'

Richard replied, 'I appreciate your candour Mr Cherrie, and I accept that your price is fair, but I am not in a position to complete the sale today.'

Kugel, who had sat silent until now, said, 'why don't we take a quick recess?' Richard face gave nothing away. He accepted Kugel's suggestion, and the French delegates were shown into a meeting room with coffee ready, and waiting. Richard remained in the boardroom. The French party knew the game, and saw this as a rehearsed play, and they were certain that the deal would conclude once the meeting was reconvened. In the boardroom Kugel said, 'Richard come on, I need this. My ten percent is a lot of money, and remember it is my public office that got the French around the table in the first place.'

Richard was adamant, 'we are not selling,' and the exchange quickly became heated. Eleanor, and Victoria were still in the room, and Richard was clearly uncomfortable talking in front of them.

'Look I want this. Let's just get our money out now,' Kugel demanded, 'you don't know how many meetings, and bribes it has taken me to put the deal together in Tambura.' Richards face reddened, and for a while he lost his normal composure. This was a side of his character that Eleanor had never seen. Victoria was equally taken aback by his sudden switch to an angry riposte. Kugel was the only one in the room that wasn't surprised. It was a side of Richard that he was familiar with.

'Our money! What the FUCK are you talking about? It's MY money and MY decision,' Richard said. Spit could be seen flying from his mouth, some hit Kugel, who wiped at his face. Not really backing down, but only just about fighting corner.

'Don't forget that I created the opportunity with the Tambura Government in the first place. Listen, you are making a mistake. Intelligence suggests that between thirty thousand, and ninety thousand people could die. If the public knew this, they would be against the USA making a purchase.' It had been Richard's plan all along to create a water shortage scare allowing him to charge a premium price for the water under his control. But after having the initial inspiration, he had left Kugel to flex his political muscle, and bring the right deals to the table. But Kugel was funded by Weiss right through the project, and Richard had the ultimate say whether Kugel liked it or not.

Richard said, 'why do you think we are here today! It's an insurance policy. The French are prepared to do a deal without any regard to the environmental impact. I want to use today's Heads of Terms in my negotiations with our government, because the capacity with the French is a fraction of the USA.'

Kugel said, 'the more water we sell the larger the impact, and it is the death rate increase that concerns me. It goes from ninety thousand to potentially hundreds of thousands.'

Richard was getting angry, and said, 'I couldn't give a toss how many of them die, and neither do you . . . you hypocrite.' They were so emotionally charged that the fact that this conversation was taking place in front of the girls seemed to escape the attention of either man. 'Everyone knows that most of Africa is overpopulated in the first place. We will be doing the country a favour,' Richard said. Eleanor noticed that his eyes looked darker when he was angry, they looked soulless. She had a feeling that she had seen those eyes before.

Kugel said, 'that is not my point. The more water we sell, the higher the collateral damage. It's all gone completely to plan, and I don't want to blow it now.'

The conversation was interrupted by a telephone call, Richard raised his voice, 'tell them they need to book an appointment.' Richard slammed down the phone, and looked a little flustered. The phone went again, Richard picked up, and this time sat listening, shaking his head. In the lobby were four inspectors from the Banking Regulator, and four police officers with an arrest warrant for "Richard Christopher Weiss".

As Richard stormed out, Harvey sat back in his chair, the flair of Weiss temper brought back some of Kugel's childhood memories. He had been schooled at various Boarding Schools from a young age, Harvey, found he and others like him, had one thing common, bullying. He was bullied ruthlessly from a young age, but it wasn't long before he in turn bullied others. In his mind's eye, Harvey started to fashion his character as a moody, in-control man who was just about to enact revenge on his tormentors. In his school days his general demeanour was such that he seemed almost normalized to giving, and receiving pain.

The other painful childhood memories that shaped the man were the three catholic priests, who had found the perfect profession in which to act out their paedophilia. When his mind went back to those days, he fixated on a day when two priests held Harvey down while one of the Brothers raped him. But the cause of most of the nightmare was down to the embarrassing fact that on that occasion, even though they repulsed him, he had an erection.

As an adult, he could never rationalise this as he had no thoughts of same sex relationships. The ultimate control, that was different, he enjoyed dominating women in the bedroom, and anyone and everyone outside of it. He was certain that his past had influenced this. But he internalized all of his demons, and he had no appetite to talk through any issue with a psychiatrist. He wasn't comfortable with much of his youth, but he concluded that his past had shaped his character today.

Kugel was a ruthless, ambitious man who liked to get his own way. He had few friends and lots of enemies. He was a complex character, and even his own family felt a little intimidated at times. His marriage produced two boys, and despite his personal experience of boarding school, he still sent his own children to follow in his footsteps. His wife had not been keen; Harvey didn't find it easy to express his feeling, particularly with his children and he said, "I'm not having some young man under my roof being full of testosterone, marking his territory in my house," and Mrs Kugel didn't want to go up against tradition. If it was good enough for Harvey she accepted it as her boy's fate, she concluded, "it had done Harvey no harm".

Chapter 32

Emily sat on a chair in David Prost's consulting room, with the leg support up, and the head rest lowered. David was happy to have Eleanor in attendance. From the old files, it was clear that the five year old Emily never talked about the boy or boys specifically. Therefore David recommended regression therapy to allow Emily to go back to the incident, and relive the experience to establish what happened, and hopefully put the past to bed once and for all. David had given Emily fifty milligrams of Diazepam, and asked her to relax, and lie quietly for ten minutes before the session began, while Eleanor gave David an update on the last four days.

'I feel such a bloody fool,' Eleanor said. 'I was convinced that I had a valuable skill, and I was headhunted by Weiss. What kind of ego do I have that I was so flattered, but I was played like a fool.'

'Are you certain that Weiss used you, or could it be a coincidence?' David replied. Emily closed her eyes, oblivious to the other two in the room, initially she could hear their conversation, but now it was way in the background, she was drifting off to sleep.

Eleanor said, 'It was a setup from the start, and I don't know why I didn't see it. I thought I was a well-rounded, intelligent woman with a little street savvy thrown in for good measure. But I am just an egotistical twat. Excuse my French.'

David said, 'ok . . . so do you want to talk about it?'

'Not for my sake but for Em's. It is all part of this spate of bad press. It started with Emily getting her assignment. She had to do this whole water report on the future availability of fresh water, and look at a whole raft of data.'

David said, 'yes I know all about it, we discussed it here. I was concerned there may be a setback if Emily's suggestions were ignored.'

Eleanor said, 'well she got the job first . . . to cut a long story short, from what I can make of it, Weiss employed me to make sure I got Emily to read, and use a document on water rationing. He gave me a detailed report that seemed to be legitimate, and went on to me about how essential it was. I know if I hadn't told Em what he said, and given her his report, she wouldn't have even covered it.'

'Ok let's say that is true. Why? What was his motivation?' David was shaking his head, not to disagree, it was just an unconscious reaction to this incredulous notion.

Eleanor replied, 'this is the worst part. He owns lakes, and dams in Africa. He used us to create a water scare, and its spreading. It's the biggest news story, and who will come to the rescue? Weiss. He intends to sell water to the Government, and I fell for it. I helped him secure a deal, nothing to do with water, and I thought how clever he was selecting me, but it helped him convince me that it was all about my skill.'

David said, 'do you have any proof or are you making assumptions? I am on your side, do not take what I am saying the wrong way, but it seems like a movie script?'

'Yes, well sort of, I have a copy of the trust documents on my lap top. I should have seen it a mile off. He set up a Trust in Gibraltar called the "Tambura Trust" where did Emily go in Africa . . . Tambura.'

David said, 'did you know she was going to Tambura?'

Eleanor replied, 'I take your point, she may have just said Africa. Anyway, he is working with Kugel. Senator Harvey Kugel, that slime ball! Kugel sets up government meetings, and brings in Weiss. Kugel also commissioned the report that Emily did, and he set her up for a fall. He also set up the deal with the government in Africa for Weiss to buy land. Kugel makes it happen, and Weiss funds it. For his trouble Weiss pays Kugel a percentage of the profits. They have been working on it for years, Victoria said there are some forty separate deals that are linked to the Tambura Trust. So he purchased the land with his bank lending him the money, and he placed the land in a Trust. He then personally borrowed to own a lot of the trust himself. I am not quite sure of the steps, but it was some sort of gearing, he called it. I even worked on the trust set up without any knowledge whatsoever that it was all part of this long game Weiss had been playing.'

David said, 'that is incredible. I have never heard anything like this. Extraordinary.'

Eleanor said, 'It gets worse. He met with the French government just to get them to agree to buy the water without the appropriate environmental checks. It is this agreement he is going to use to do the deal with the USA. Demonstrating, that if another country will do it, so should America. With Kugel on the inside supporting the purchase. But the main reason I resigned, is because people are going to die, and he couldn't care less.'

'Really. You heard him say as much?' David asked.

Eleanor replied, 'yes! him and Kugel. I think that France, not having that much requirement, creates less collateral damage, his words not mine. But it could be catastrophic if the USA buys. They would be literally moving huge amounts of fresh water from one continent to another. It's just ridiculous. It was always to control water. With the general public panicking, and Kugel working on the inside, lakes, rivers, and the underground sources are all under Richard's control, and I helped him set Emily up.'

'I think he is going to pull it off too, but if he doesn't he will dispose of his stock in smaller shipments. He paid next to nothing for this land as all of the mining companies know that this particular area is not commercially viable. It's hard to get your head around just how long he has been planning all of this. Am I rambling on . . . sorry.'

'Don't apologise. You need to get it off your chest and it may help me treat Emily.' David got fresh orange juice for Eleanor, and she sat back to let David do his job. He dimmed the lights, and began. Emily was relaxed, and comfortable. The diazepam had helped, but there was also a calm atmosphere in David's consultation room.

David's voice always had a hypnotic tone, but when he utilised hypnotherapy or regression techniques, it took on a whole new timbre. He spoke very slowly and extended certain words, turning sleep into sleeeeeep. He started to hypnotise Emily.

'Take a deep breath in through your nose, and exhale slowly through your mouth, I want you to let go of all your pent up energy.' Emily had already shut her eyes. 'I want you to keep focused on my voice as you gradually fall to sleep.' She did as he asked, but was starting to suppress a cough. 'Take another deep breath in through your nose . . . hold it, now gradually breath out, and this time let go of any tension.' The urged to cough passed. 'You are becoming tired, very tired . . . you may want to sleep . . .' He emphasised certain words.

Prost called this, talking to the unconscious mind. This part of the therapy could not be rushed. Those that believe in hypnotherapy succumb without resistance, while some people subconsciously fight against his instructions. As he had successfully used hypnotherapy on Emily, he believed she was a good candidate for regression, he was right, and within fifteen minutes, she was ready to go back in time.

'Emily, I want you to travel back with me. You are twenty one, and you have just earned your degree. Can you remember?' Silence, she made no reply. 'Emily, can you remember?' Eleanor thought that Emily would come out of her trance to answer, but she didn't. Her closed eyelids started to quiver as she replied. 'Yes.'

David continued, 'it was a very happy time, and you did so well with your distinction.' In gradual steps he took Emily back through the years, one or two years at a time. He didn't dwell in, and around her eighth birthday, he took her right back to age five, right to her first day at school. It was always simple questions he asked as he hypnotised patients. He didn't linger on the way down, so he could spend more time at the relevant point in history. He took her past the incident to the start of her school life, and stayed around there until he was certain that Emily really had regressed. One or two of the answers Emily gave, Eleanor was able to confirm as true, with a nod of the head, or a raising of the eyebrows in David's direction.

He now brought Emily gently forward to that fateful day, right to the time of the event. The files recorded that it was in the school grounds at the 11 a.m. recess. 'Emily. Can you tell me where you are, and what you are doing?'

Emily said, 'I'm playing with Katie.'

Eleanor whispered, 'it was her best friend at school.'

David continued, 'what are you playing?'

'We are playing with a ball . . . we are playing catch.'

'Where are you Emily?'

'I am in the playground.' He gently coaxed her forward. 'Katie threw the ball over the fence. It was an accident.' Her voice sounding like that of an adult, imitating a child.

'Now keep moving forward, and tell me what happens?' They were getting tantalisingly close to the unknown aspects of the assault. David was on tenterhooks as he gently probed.

Emily said, 'Katie wants to play horses with the other girls, but I don't want to play their silly game.'

David asked, 'what are you doing now?'

Emily answered, 'I want to get the ball, but we aren't allowed through the fence because of the pond, but we know how to get through. The girls don't go, but the boys do.'

David asked, 'are you going through to the pond?'

'Yes. I can see the ball, it is only a little way, I will go quickly, and get it and come straight back.' Emily stopped talking. David wondered if they would get any further. What she said so far was well documented. It was what happened next that they were searching for. Just as he thought he had lost contact with the five year old, she spoke again. To Eleanor it was decidedly eerie, as it was Emily's adult voice talking just like a shy five year old girl.

Emily said, 'the boy is there, and he just pulled up my dress. The boys do this. "Stop it! You!".'

David said, 'did he stop when you told him to?'

'I am holding the end of my dress, he is a bigger, and he is doing it again.' She paused.

David asked, 'did he talk to you?'

'Yes, he said he wants to see my pants. I am scared he is from the big class, and they don't play games like this with us.' She had gone quiet again.

David waited, and then asked, 'what is happening now?'

Emily screamed, it sounded like a girl's scream. She continued in a stressed, frantic voice as the scene played out in her mind. 'He has got my arms. He is pulling at my clothes, they've ripped.'

She was crying, and very upset, still her eyes were closed as she lay in David's comfy chair. Even though the thirty one year old Emily was safe, Eleanor felt like running to, and embracing the five year old talking to them now.

'He let go of my one arm so he can pull my clothes off. I have twisted out of his arms.' She was breathing very fast as if she was running. 'I am back at the fence but the other boy is blocking the way. He has his arms, and legs spread out blocking the hole.'

She switched between past, and present tense. 'When I couldn't get past, the other one grabbed me, and threw me to the ground. The other boy is telling him what to do. He stood up, my face is covered in dirt, and my nose is bleeding. I have hurt my knee. I am up, and I am running towards the pond. They haven't come after me, and I am hiding by the edge of the pond. I don't want to get my new shoes wet, mommy will be mad.'

Emily needed no more prompting as she was reliving the scene second by second. It was worse than any of the file notes, and more painful to listen to. For the first time she confirmed that there were two boys.

'I want them to go, and leave me alone!!!' Emily started crying in David's chair. 'They are still by the fence, and laughing at me. They are throwing stones. Owww!! One just hit me right on my side, and it really hurts.' She held her side.

Emily continued without prompting, 'more hit me, and they didn't hurt as much but I think they are going to hit my head, so I need to get away from them. There is a narrow ledge past the water, they keep laughing at me, I need to walk on the ledge to get away, and get to the other side of the pool so the stones can't reach me . . . I looked back to see if they were gone, and ahhhhhhhhhh!' Emily's final scream was blood curdling. She came rapidly back to consciousness. David preferred to bring clients back gradually, but he wasn't aware of any adverse effect for coming out so fast.

Emily said, 'it was him! It was Kugel! I saw him. He had those David Bowie eyes, you know, each a different colour. It was definitely him, I know it was.'

Thankfully Emily didn't seem the worse for the experience, in fact the truth revealed, gave her strength. Most patients in regression therapy learn about the past by listening to the recordings of the session when they return to full consciousness, but Emily retained a large portion of what she had revealed. 'It was definitely him!' She said.

'Really! That's not possible, surely.' Eleanor said, 'David is that possible?'

David replied, 'well our lives do seem so intricately intertwined, you never know. The good news is, I can find out.'

'How!' Eleanor asked.

David replied, 'when the school called all of the parents about the incident, they all agreed to see the same therapist. It is common in an event like this, especially with young children, to see one practitioner, to allow the complete picture to emerge. It doesn't always happen because families usually side with their own child, and tend to want a biased view that fits with their own child's version of events.'

Eleanor sat open mouthed.

David continued, 'this boy's mother contacted your parents, and wanted to work together on a solution. Apparently quite a well to do, influential family, but by all accounts, the boy's mother was appalled at what her son had done. She agreed to Philip's request for them both to see my father.' David told them about a teacher who heard the commotion, and ran over to see what was going on, he saw one boy climbing back through the fence. The school actually instigated the investigation particularly as Emily went underwater, but this they knew from the file notes.

David said, 'when first questioned, he mentioned another boy, but in subsequent consultations, he denied their being anyone else involved. My father always believed there were two boys, but there was no proof. Emily, you only mentioned the water, and your side never really came out. So I have the files on this boy.'

'So will you let us have the files?' Emily asked.

David said, 'I will not be able to do that because of client confidentiality, but I will check the name for you. Each file only refers to the one patient, so that they retain a level of privacy. But I can certainly find the name.'

'David please! We need to know. If this is Kugel, we need to know, we need to see the files, and listen to the recordings.' He looked on the verge of agreeing to the request. After all it was his father that was the therapist at the time. 'Listen if the boy is Kugel I . . .' He paused. It was clear he was torn. Every doctor these days was aware of the ability to get sued, and with old sex offender crimes constantly making the news this could blow up in his face. That said, these were his friends, and if the tormentor was Kugel, maybe they should know.

David said, 'listen, let's compromise. If it is not Kugel then you can't have the files. Bear in mind you have seen a complete list of pupils, and I think if Kugel's name was there, you would have seen it.'

'We weren't looking for his name, but we did go through the list very methodically, and I agree, I think we would have seen it.' Eleanor said.

Emily said, 'it was him. I know for sure. It was him. I just looked him, right in his different coloured eyes. It's not just that, they are dead eyes, there is no emotion in them, then, and now. It was him.'

David's dad had dementia, and he wouldn't be able to recall any conversations. So David decided to take a chance, and blame it on his Father if it ever came out. After all, he was sure it may resolve mental issues, but wouldn't result in a prosecution. David made up his mind, and said, 'ok listen, I will send you the files. Find out what you need to know, and then return them to me. Please don't copy them, my career is at stake.' It was agreed. He would retrieve them from storage and FedEx them the next day.

'Listen, I know what's coming. Richard Weiss is the other boy.' Eleanor said.

Emily said, 'yes! Yes, of course he is, Ellie you're absolutely right!'

Eleanor said, 'we knew Richard was at our school, but I bet they both were.'

The girls completely agreed, and were already convinced without any evidence. Call it intuition, they felt that their lives had crossed in the past, and had crossed again today. David was more sceptical, and intended to undertake research to prove it either way. He had visited Disney Resort in Florida, and met an old next door neighbour he hadn't seen for years, and damned if the very next day at Sea World, he was sat next to an old school friend. Sometimes fate seems to play a part in people's lives, and he thought the girls might be right. After they left, David went through his extensive library. A collection started by his Father that David had added to. He remembered a fascinating book on the subject of lives intertwining. David didn't give it much credence at the time, but something was telling him that he must find it and read it again . . . it was called, "Soul Mechanic".'

Chapter 33

Victoria, and Eleanor were alone in Emily's apartment. They sat together, each with a large glass of white wine. Victoria's tears started more or less straight away. She didn't have to say that it was over Richard, Eleanor knew it would be. Victoria had no family, she was an only child of an only child, and her mother had passed away, three years ago. She was in her sixteenth year with Weiss, and had long since even attempted to have a life outside of work. Eleanor passed her a box of tissues, and gave her a hug. Close up, the bruise, concealed with foundation, was visible, confirming Eleanor's suspicion.

Victoria considered Eleanor a true friend that she could confide in, but she was unsure if Eleanor knew just how much she needed her. After all Victoria really had very few people in her life, and Eleanor was quite the opposite, and had friends, and family reaching back over the course of her life. But Victoria had to rely on their friendship as she was in need of a friend tonight more than ever before.

Eleanor asked, 'what on earth happened?'

Victoria replied, 'I'm being stupid.' She was drying her tears, looking in a compact mirror to wipe her mascara, and then continued. 'When I was in Africa with Richard I crossed the line, and had a personal relationship with him.'

Eleanor said, 'you know what they say, "it takes two to tango".'

Victoria said, 'I started it. I have known him professionally for over fifteen years, I have worked for him personally for twelve, but because you were all in France, there was only me, Rainbird, Mike Morgan, and Richard. Rainbird had to go home for personal reasons, and Michael took her to the airport. We were sitting around the hotel pool, and for the first time ever I noticed him look at me. Foolishly I said "Do you find me attractive?" '

Eleanor asked, 'why was that foolish? What did he say?'

'He said "Of course", and I said, "I have never seen you with a partner in all the time I have worked for you". He told me that he never mixed business with pleasure as it will never be the same afterwards. He was right on that one.'

Eleanor asked, 'so you ended up in bed?'

'Yes . . . It was perfect. He was so romantic on the night, and we both woke up in my bed. He didn't say anything the next day or the rest of the trip. From then on we were never alone together, he either had a meeting or Michael was there.'

Eleanor said, 'have you talked since you got back?'

Victoria replied, 'it's worse than that. On the day he was arrested, he was released on bail. Actually, he came back just after you walked out. I didn't tell him you had resigned. I didn't get the chance. He was vile, and so angry. I've never know him raise his voice before. He kicked his office door. He then punched that full length mirror in his office, and cut his hand. His eyes were so . . . . so . . . cold. He changed that day.'

Eleanor asked, 'how did you get the bruise?'

Victoria reached for her mirror again. She thought she had hidden the mark on her left cheek. 'I can't tell you it all, honestly, it's too embarrassing.'

'Don't be silly. You can tell me anything, it won't go any further, I promise you.' Victoria had another flood of tears. They embraced again, Eleanor felt so sorry for her that she cried too. Victoria had no intention of talking about the main issue when she arrived, but she came to realise that in Eleanor she had a true friend, and as they no longer worked together, it would be easier to confide in her.

Victoria said, 'no one was in his office, he was banging, and shouting, I didn't even know if he was actually on the telephone or just shouting to himself. The "Securities and Exchange Commission" had stopped the RWP floatation, and I think this was part of it. It's as if it had been building up, and he just snapped, and the bad side of his character came out. After about an hour it had calmed down . . . so I knocked, and put my head around the door. He told me to come in, and lock the door. I went over to him, and put my arms around him. He responded gently at first, but then he just attacked me.'

Victoria was coming to the point in her tale that was the hardest to say. Eleanor just sat next to her holding her hand. She didn't ask her anything, she would tell her if she wanted to, in her own time. Victoria said, 'it started out as fairly aggressive sex. I was concerned about the noise, and didn't want to do anything. He bent me over the desk, and clawed at my clothes, ripping them off. I was turned on at first, but then he got much too rough. I said no, he was hurting, but he didn't listen. He pinned me down. He had both arms behind my back.'

More tears. Another break in the monologue. 'Oh God I can't believe I'm telling you this, it's so embarrassing.' She took her time, Eleanor was a good listener. 'He held my head down. Literally, this bruise is from his office desk. I know couples can have fairly aggressive sex when the mood takes, but this was different, he was totally dominating me. I've never done it like that, and I didn't want to do it. At least not like that. I'm not being a prude, but he forced himself, and it was painful. And the people outside must have heard him.' Victoria buried her face in her hands, sobbing, and hiding her embarrassment.

Victoria said, 'it was horrid. When he had had his orgasm I thought he would calm down. Like a fool I was even prepared to forgive him.' Having almost told her tale, she started to sound stronger as she dabbed at her eyes with another tissue from the almost empty box, and continued. 'In a way I was glad he wanted me again, and I thought I would be able to talk to him about how I didn't like it like that. I went to put my arms around him, and he pushed me really hard, and I went flying . . . clothes around my ankles, my face killing me, my rear end bleeding, and well you know.' She didn't need to get graphic, it wasn't difficult to fill in the gaps.

'I've never felt so disgusted with myself ever. I really did like Richard a lot. But this side of his character I despise . . .' A big deep breath in, she placed her palms at her temples, there were no more tears. 'I don't know what to do.' Victoria had been telling her tale for the last forty minutes while Eleanor sat quietly. She had not made eye contact while she said what she had to say. Victoria looked better for talking.

Eleanor said, 'you are going to have to leave him.'

Victoria said, 'I can't . . . I don't have a life outside of my job. I've never had time for a proper boyfriend as I'm always at work. '

Eleanor knew Victoria didn't have many family members, but she hadn't realise she had none at all. Eleanor asked, 'do you have money or do you need some?' Ever since she met Victoria, Eleanor had always liked her, but tonight she realised that her friend, who had always been strong, confident, and in control, tonight was vulnerable, weak, and alone.

Victoria replied, 'oh no I've made plenty of money. It's . . . it's just . . . it's my whole life.'

Eleanor said, 'he will do it again. You know that don't you?'

Victoria replied, 'I can't. I've got to sort it out. This is one bad day after twelve fantastic years. It's my fault.'

Eleanor said, 'don't say that, it's not at all. That was rape.'

Victoria said, 'look, I didn't stop him. I just think he likes it rough, and I don't.'

'You know why I've left,' Eleanor said, 'he doesn't care if people die. That is not a nice man. You have to get out.'

Victoria said, 'I can't. I'll stay, and I will stop it from ever happening again. The water deal too. I know this is not the man I know.'

Eleanor knew that it was pointless saying anymore. 'I love you, and I am here for you Victoria. Our relationship is very important to me.' As far as Victoria was concerned, this was the most important thing to her. To know she had someone outside her work that cared about her.

Victoria said, 'I really love you too, you are like the sister I never had.'

Eleanor warmed a nice vegetarian pasta dish for dinner, and insisted that Victoria stay the night. 'I have a big enough bed, and spare PJ's.' she said.

Victoria said, 'Richard is making an announcement on TV tomorrow. I don't know what he is going to say. I usually type everything for him but he didn't want me to, he has written something long hand.'

Eleanor asked, 'what do you think he is going to announce?'

Victoria said, 'I don't know. Most people think he is going to sue the SEC.' Victoria felt so much better for talking, and agreed to stay over so they would both watch Richard on the news in the morning.

Chapter 34

They were in front of the TV at 10 am, the proposed time of Richard's announcement. 'Good Morning, and welcome to "The Washington News" this Friday the 5th August. Here are today's headlines, Richard Weiss of W.I.B.C. was arrested yesterday, but later released on bail. In an official statement, W.I.B.C, stated that Mr Weiss was released without charge, and the allegations were completely false, and without foundation. Weiss was under investigation for allegedly utilising bank funds as security for personal investments.'

Due to sanctions placed on Weiss by the Financial Services regulator, he had to suspend the flotation of his Pharmaceutical businesses, RWP. Victoria said, 'he will be absolutely livid.' The girls were in the sitting room at Emily's, not moving from the TV absolutely mesmerised. As The Washington News went to an ad break, Eleanor switched channels, they were all leading with this, they stayed with CNN for their take on the arrest.

The newsreader said, 'in an interview earlier today, Miss Salmon, chief press officer for the SEC, The Securities & Exchange Commission issued a statement saying, "we are completely satisfied, and have been given the reassurances required to support the investments made by Mr Weiss". She went on to confirm, that five senior Board Members of the SEC had resigned as a result of the wrongful arrest. It was accepted that they didn't have sufficient evidence to take this case forward, and they acted inappropriately, and disproportionately.

When asked why they did act so aggressively, Miss Salmon defended the principal rather than this particular arrest. She said, 'after the likes of Bernard Madoff, they had become more sensitive to the potential for wrongdoing of this nature. But on this occasion they had got it completely wrong, and had issued a sincere apology to Mr Weiss.'

In Emily's apartment the girls talked about what he would say, guessing he will sue them.

'We can go live to our Washington correspondent, Max Wannamaker, outside W.I.B.C headquarters. Max, what is the latest on this fiasco surrounding Mr Weiss?'

'Morning Katie, I am here live outside the offices of W.I.B.C where we are expecting an appearance from Mr Weiss himself, to make a personal statement. Four hundred million dollars were wiped off the share price on the news of his arrest, but those shares today opened up on the price prior to the arrest.'

'Can you speculate for us Max; what do we expect Mr Weiss to say today?'

'Well Katie, what I can tell you is Mr Weiss is expected to sue the Securities & Exchange Commission for compensation. To date he has not said a word, he claimed from the start that he would be exonerated, and only then would he make a public statement. The whole affair may have cost him hundreds of Millions, and who would blame him if he did take a law suit. Some people are calling him the Teflon man, as nothing ever sticks.'

∞

Inside W.I.B.C, Weiss watched CNN while editing his announcement. He didn't use the banks PR gurus or any of his usual entourage to prepare for this task, he sat alone. He wanted to get the tone of this, just so. His right hand was bandaged, but otherwise he looked his impeccable self. In front of his new full length mirror, he adjusted the knot on his tie, and looked closely at his face. He removed an eyelash from his right cheek, and was ready to face the cameras.

He was a little nervous as he walked outside, and to the podium and it wasn't like him. Dozens of cameras flashed, this was headline news. There were lots of microphones from the various news feeds. He looked very confident when he stood before them, and any sense of nervous anticipation disappeared.

'Good Morning America, my name is Richard Weiss, and I represent the shareholders of Weiss Investment Banking Corporation, a bank of the utmost integrity with a long history of providing a first class service to our clients while achieving a healthy return to our shareholders . . . As you are aware, I was questioned in relation to a potential regulatory breech, and after a comprehensive investigation, my name, and reputation. . .'

He paused while he glanced at his notes to gather his thoughts. As he raised his head, he didn't focus on anyone in the crowd, but instead looked right into the camera. 'W.I.B.C, and my business interests have been cleared of any wrongdoing.' He didn't appear to blink. The girls watching had to briefly avert their gaze. It was like he was in the room talking to them.

He continued, 'after complete cooperation throughout, I have been completely absolved. I would like to announce that, against the advice of my legal team, I will not be pursuing the SEC for compensation. The reason for this decision is, I am a complete advocate of our excellent supervisory system, and I know that they were only doing their job, so I will continue to support our regulatory framework.' He knew he was coming across well, but thought he was potentially doing too well, he decided to switch on the charm, and the rest of his delivery sounded humble.

'I would like to take this opportunity to thank our investors for their continued support. My proposed flotation of RW Pharmaceuticals can, and will now go ahead as originally proposed.'

'Mr Weiss . . . Max Wanamaker CNN, can you confirm that you stand to make a personal fortune of three billion dollars?'

Richard replied, 'I have long since had enough money for personal needs, and I would make more money if I held on to the company. RW Pharmaceuticals will revolutionise modern medicine. The reason for the flotation is to put the business in the hands of a team that are far more capable of taking the business forward than I am. We genuinely feel that we are going to change the world of medicine. I can assure you that the share price will dramatically increase. Now please excuse me, I have five days of work to catch up on. Thank you.'

He didn't wait for questions, microphones were being thrust in his direction, but he had said all he wanted to say. After a slight wave, and a nod of the head, he turned his back on them all, and walked back into his office. The girls still watching saw his usual confident gait. It was a walk that any good actor would be proud of. He disappeared back into W.I.B.C Headquarters.

Wanamaker said, 'Well Katie, the speculation around Weiss was how much compensation he would be paid, and as you have just heard, in a surprise move, Weiss announced that he will not be pursuing a claim. I bet there will be a sigh of relief at the SEC Headquarters today. This is Max Wanamaker for CNN.'

Katie said, 'thank you Max. Well did I just see a feature from our sponsors, ha ha ha. Still good news as you say Max.'

When Richard returned to the office he went straight into a Board meeting to discuss his TV appearance, he received a standing ovation for his performance. He took his place at the head of the table, and each of the Board in turn said something complimentary. Only one of them had anything negative to add, he said, 'the compensation could have been substantial, and most people would have sued.' Most in the room knew better than to go up against Weiss, and they cowered, wanting it known that this was not their view, but Weiss kept his composure when he replied.

'I'm not most people. In life you have to choose your battles. If I went up against the system, they would never stop looking for retribution. It is far better to play their game. Today was about our shareholders, and all those that are lining up to invest in RWP. I suggest that you all increase your W.I.B.C shareholding gentlemen. We all have luck, and misfortunes come our way, it is how we respond to the situation that determines the outcome.' With that he walked out.

By the time they got back to their desks, they had already missed the spike in the share price. Weiss anticipated the response to his speech, and had set a sale of his shares in motion before he had said a word, and he now had the money needed for his RWP Flotation. When he was alone, Weiss went back to his full length mirror. He got within an inch, and looked hard at himself. He looked deep into his own eyes. If anybody could see his face now, they wouldn't want to argue with him. The way he felt today, woe betide the person who stood in his way.

He had agreed to not press charges if the people behind the arrest resigned. This was agreed as long as he didn't make the agreement public knowledge, and he was fine with that. It was the result he wanted, he didn't need anyone to know to make him feel good about it. Something had come out of this challenging week, and Weiss had come to terms with a side of his character that he had until now, kept suppressed. He had won again. He would always win. But he now accepted that he also liked to see others lose. A latent aggression had been awakened.

Chapter 35

Victoria went back to work after promising Eleanor she would put an end to the personal relationship, and return to strictly business. She also agreed to leave if anything else happened. An advantage of her returning, she would keep the sisters up to speed on Weiss' water negotiations. Not that they knew what to do to stop him, but they hoped to at least try. She also promised to leave immediately if there was a chance of a repeat of the aggression. She was going to leave even if he didn't try to have rough sex. If he turned again, she would just leave.

Emily returned to the flat, and said to Eleanor, 'right! Let's do this', as the sisters set about the box of files. There were three children whose first names began with "H" but none of them had the surname Kugel, and they started to doubt their earlier conclusion. Emily was so sure before, but maybe Kugel was a figment of her imagination, seeing his face instead of the boy that did it. Possibly she had just got spooked and they had jumped to a premature conclusion. They both instinctively felt her original claim to be true, but without evidence they simply must have been mistaken.

It was quite a leap of faith to imagine the scenario they had arrived at, but for them it was put to bed when the new box arrived, and the boy was called Harvey Taylor, which in itself was a coincidence to match the first name, but it wasn't Kugel. After previously going through the process, they now had a routine. Some of the files could be ignored as they covered the formal documentation of the facts. They knew how to get to the heart of the information that they wanted.

One of the things that stood out, Taylor had said that it was another boy that told him to do it. He attended eight therapy sessions in total with Prost senior, and was asked each time about for the name of the other boy, but he always denied his existence. Prost's notes came to the conclusion that the lad was either threatened or bribed to not disclose the other culprit. He later went further to state that Taylor was not exhibiting any sense of fear, so a bribe was more likely. Prost summarised the boy as cold, calculating, and manipulative, quite an unusual character profile for an eight year old. It was also noted "After all said and done, this was an eight year old boy harassing a five year old girl". The trauma of the water dramatically increased the severity, and had turned the incident into a far more serious situation.

These file notes were never written for the purpose they were now being used. The girls were looking at it as if it were forensic evidence gathered at a murder scene. This was an incident that required the doctor to try, and make sure there were no long term issues that couldn't be dealt with. There was obviously a desire from all parties to understand the incident, and to make sure lessons could be learned in order to avoid anything like it happening again.

The more that Emily knew, the stronger she became. It almost felt like the adult Emily could help the child she once was. Something else had occurred to her throughout the process, the five year old had felt guilty, looking back from today she wondered why. Maybe it was being through the fence in the first place or possibly for not standing up for herself. The more she reflected on it the more she thought it was down to the sexual nature of the incident, as if in some way she was complicit, and she was being naughty, and rude. One thing was absolutely certain. She knew now, unreservedly, that there was no need to ever have felt guilty . . . For several nights she had dreamt of holding the little girl she once was. It was a strange dream, and one that she would try interpreting, but whatever it meant, she continued getting stronger.

They focused so heavily on their review of the notes that the sisters missed a call from David. He left a voicemail, when they were taking a break Emily pressed play. 'Right, girls, I have the tapes, you need to come to the practice straight away, I have some information that I will save until you get here.' The message ended, and the sisters looked at each other. They didn't have to say anything, they could hear it in his voice, he had important news, and it sounded like good news too. Within 5 minutes they had left to get straight to David's place.

They buzzed the intercom, 'come straight up.' They walked in, and

David said, 'you might want to sit down for this.' His face looked like it was Christmas, and he had the best gift ever. 'I have a patient who is a forensic detective that comes in occasionally, usually when he has been working on a particularly gruesome murder.' The girls hadn't even taken off their coats, 'he did some digging for me, and you were absolutely right. It was Kugel.'

For some reason, they were all really pleased, and it was hard to say why. David thought, *maybe knowledge is power*, maybe it felt good just to confirm that they were not mad suggesting it in the first place, but if they really stopped to ask why they were happy, it was because this was somehow important. Emily summed up the feeling when she said, 'God knows why something from twenty six years ago could be so relevant today, but still something tells me it is.'

David told them what he knew. 'He was christened Harvey Taylor, his father is Edward Taylor, a scientist, and inventor. Edward married Christine Kugel, and she took her husband's name. When they had Harvey, their only child, he had the family name too. Christine was, or is, they are still alive, very wealthy.'

David explained, 'apparently, Edward could work anywhere in the world, so they moved to England for Harvey to be schooled there. After the incident they moved back to America, and changed their surnames. They took Christine's maiden name, she was after all from a very wealthy, and influential family, thereby rewriting Harvey's past. You can find everything on the family on Google, but history before the incident doesn't seem to exist.' They spent the next hour or so looking on line, searching Kugel and his family, and then they turned to the tapes.

∞

The tapes were old fashioned ones on spools, so David had borrowed a reel to reel player. Each tape started with an introduction from Dr Prost Senior, and it was so striking that David sounded exactly the same as his father, apart from the American accent. It was tempting to fast forward as the technique was the same that David had used on

Emily, a slow decent for a deeper relaxation, and a better result. They listened to her tape first, 'Emily, do you want to tell me your favourite colour?'

Prost senior began with small talk to get his patients talking. Emily on tape sounded sad, and a little frightened. The feelings of trepidation to the listeners soon passed, and they got into detached listening to glean whatever they could. It came to an end after an hour, and they had learned nothing new. There was twenty hours of tapes, so they decided to listen to Emily, and Kugel chronologically, to get a sense of the whole process. It was going to take a long time if they listened to them being hypnotised every time, so they decided to fast forward after all, to hear just the questions, and answers.

The first tape of Kugel contained nothing of interest. David Senior had spoken to Kugel at length before trying hypnosis. Even hypnotised he was sticking to his version of events, namely that he was the only boy, and he was only playing.

David senior on tape asked, 'why did you throw the stones Harvey?'

Harvey replied, 'I was throwing them into the water, it was an accident. She was playing too.' This was typical of the questions, and answers provided. There wasn't really anything so far that wasn't noted in the files. Each tape took about thirty minutes even when attempting to pick up just the essential elements. Each tape started the same, there was also a preamble before his patients arrived, stating who was attending, the date, time, and purpose, but there was a different message that Prost recorded on the third session with Kugel.

David senior said, 'I am today working with Harvey Taylor, and it is my professional opinion that the hypnosis is not working as I would like. This young man is strong willed, and despite him showing the signs of being hypnotised, the information he provides is, in my opinion, what he wants me to hear. I think that he has convinced himself that his version of events is true. I am therefore going to try regression. I want to take him back to the day, and get him to relive the event.'

The noise of the tape turning off, and then on again was followed by the familiar pattern. Prost senior said, 'I want you to travel back for me. Listen to me, and we will travel back together. Come with me now . . . I am taking you back.' You could hear mumbling from the boy. It was strange, guttural, deeper than his eight years should have produced, not a man's voice exactly, more like a boy trying to imitate a man.

'That's German!' Emily said. They listened on, and there was more of the same, but the actual words were not clear.

'Can you understand German Eleanor?' David asked.

Eleanor replied, 'yes, at a basic level.' She put her elbows on her knees, and leaned forward. 'I completely agree, it does sound German, I just can't quite make out what he is saying.' The tape ran on, and Dr Prost Senior was summing up, so they immediately put on the next tape. They listened to the opening preamble first, Prost senior started with his objectives of the session he was about to record.

'I wish to further explore regression, as the last session created a rather unusual situation. Taylor spoke in a strange voice that was almost certainly German. I didn't pursue this at the time as I had to make further enquiries as to his background. The mother's maiden name is Christine Kugel, and the name led me to the thought that German was spoken in the family. It turns out that this is not the case, and so I intend to see what I can find out, what this boy does have on his mind?'

They fast forwarded eighteen minutes, the standard time it took David senior to complete his talk into the hypnosis. Once under, he regressed Harvey again, and asked his questions.

Prost senior asked the question, 'sprechen sie Deutch?'

Harvey replied, 'ja.'

Prost asked another, 'do you also speak English?'

Harvey replied, 'yes.' mumbled a little, but clear enough.

Prost senior said, 'what is your name?'

Harvey said, 'I am Reichsfuhrer Heinrich Himmler of the Schutzstaffel.'

Prost senior said, 'I want you to use the whole of your mind. Can you access Harvey, and Heinrich?' No answer straight away, so he asked the question again, this time the boy replied.

'Yes.'

Prost asked, 'are you Heinrich, or are you Harvey?'

'I am Harvey, and I am Heinrich.'

Prost senior asked, 'do you remember Emily Heinrich?'

Harvey replied, 'no.'

The tape continued, 'Harvey I want you to bring to the front of your mind Emily. Heinrich do you know this young lady?'

'No.' The boy started to mumble again. Prost senior tried to take him down again but he was no longer regressed or relaxed enough to talk. Once the session was over, Prost senior summarised, 'That was quite remarkable. I have heard of this but I have never had a patient ever recall a name from a past life, or at least, to believe in a past life. It was a famous name, and I can't rule out some form of false memory. I will do the same with Emily to see if there is in some way a connection.'

As they listened to the tapes, they sat in complete silence. It was extraordinary. They went straight to the next tape, and fast forwarded until they came to the question, 'can you tell me your name?' Silence, he tried again. 'Can you tell me your name?'

Emily replied, 'my name is Alicia.'

Chapter 36

Weiss hadn't slept well, since the TV appearance, and was having very graphic, realistic dreams. He had changed, he didn't know if it was the endless pressure he placed upon himself by constantly doing high stake deals, or if it was something else, but he felt fundamentally different. He still had charm when required, but the staff in particular had seen this angrier man. Victoria had returned to work, and nothing was said about the incident. He was angry with other people, but managed to avoid being nasty to her.

The RWP flotation sold even better than anticipated, and the uplift in value put squarely on the shoulders of Richards TV appearance. His personal profit on this single transaction ended up at three billion two hundred and thirty million dollars. His share transaction travelled from Gibraltar to Cyprus, on to the Isle of Man, then through Jersey to its final destination, tax free in Monaco. This arrangement was perfectly legal, and was designed in such a way that the funds were not accessible in any jurisdiction should there be a foreclosure, bankruptcy or lawsuit against Weiss. Richard was happy to be one of the richest, and be able to retain access to his assets while no one else could ever touch them.

Philippe, Mathieu, and the team were all in New York for the flotation, and everyone was ecstatic, that it was such a success. The celebrations were likely to go on late into the evening, Weiss had in effect sold out, so he would no longer be working with this team, and he was able to excuse himself. All but one of D.I.S were given the night off to enjoy the celebrations, so Richard went back to his hotel alone. The deal for him was in cash rather than in shares, and it should have felt more rewarding but Weiss was not as satisfied as he should have been. The more deals he did, the more he wanted to do, and the less satiated he became.

Sitting alone in his hotel suite, he found himself in front of the mirror again, not just to comb his hair or to shave, but to look into his own eyes. He could see the change, and he liked it. He always had the ability to manipulate, and get the best out of a deal, but he had always been even handed, and fair. The new harder edge, he liked, and he intended to make the most of it. He wanted to destroy any competition. He decided that Victoria was too valuable to lose, and he would not let her get close again, but when he thought about the day he dominated Victoria in his office, he liked it.

Rainbird was the only person who didn't have the night off. He had kept up his yoga, and massage routine, but did little else with her recently. She had foretold of the arrest, and release without charge, and she said all along the RWP would float, she said all this well before he even purchased Nanostem. So he decided it was time to take her psychic ability more seriously. When she arrived they kissed on each cheek, something he rarely encouraged with staff, but had long since accepted with Rainbird.

Richard said, 'I want to accept your offer to work with me on a spiritual level. I resisted because I always thought that it didn't sit well with my business mind.'

'Richard, darrling please don't see it like that. You will be even better at business.'

Richard said, 'whenever we meditate in yoga, I feel that I will end up like the "Nowhere Man" of the Beatles song, sitting in the lotus position not wanting to go to work ever again. This wouldn't suit me.'

Rainbird replied, 'I can help you to see the real you. You can fulfil your life's destiny if you really know who you are. I can help you Richard, you know this.'

Richard said, 'ok listen. I am ready. Help me.' For the first time ever, Rainbird could see he was finally prepared to let down his guard, and not just physical, his mental strength meant he usually blocked her out. She did a little preparation to create the right space to work in. She had joss sticks, a singing bowl that she played, and Buddhist chanting on in the background to help Richard relax. She then used her tarot cards. She turned cards but said nothing. Richard really was relaxed, they had worked together for years, and she was the closest he came to having a friend.

'Tell me what is on your mind. You look like you are not sleeping?' She said.

Richard said, 'I'm not. I feel different . . . I keep losing my temper.'

Rainbird replied, 'Don't worry, everyone knows it is not like you darrrling. No one will judge you on days when they have worked with you for years.'

He said, 'that is not my concern. I like it . . . and that's the problem. Sometimes I feel perfectly normal, and I look at Victoria, and question myself, how could I have been mean to her, the rest of the time I really couldn't care less.'

Rainbird said, 'it's fine to be selfish for a while . . . to think of yourself.' He closed his eyes, and let his chin fall towards his chest.

Richard replied, 'I am not making my point. I actually like it. I like being nasty, and I do not care!' He didn't know if it was something she had said or done, but he needed to lie down. He lay his head on a cushion, and put his feet on the arm of the sofa.

Rainbird said, 'tell me about your dreams?' He had to consider his answer. He took a deep breath and replied, 'I want to be in complete command. I almost feel God like. I wake up, and question why I was thinking that way. Within an hour or so, I lean towards the bad guy again.'

Rainbird said, 'the cards are showing aggression. Not based on anger, aggression by decision. Please shuffle the cards for me.' When he had done as she asked, she put them on the table in front of them, and asked him to split the pack in two, and choose one of the piles. She got him to repeat the exercise with the chosen half. 'If I didn't know you darrrling, I would make my excuses, and leave.'

Richard pleaded, 'tell me what you see, I need to know.'

'I have the greatest respect for you Richard, and you have only ever been generous, that is why I don't understand what I am seeing here.'

'Rainbird . . .' He waited but she hesitated. 'Just tell me what you see?'

Rainbird replied, 'I see power . . . power at all costs. Complete domination.'

Richard said, 'if that was all you can see you wouldn't make your excuses, and leave. Tell me the truth. What do you see?' She paused, clearly torn, should she tell him. She looked up, looked him in the eye.

'Evil' He actually smirked when she said it, 'I see Evil, Richard, or the devil. It's not good.' She put the cards down, and hoped to be done for the night. Richard sat up, and emptied his Brandy in one. She began to feel very uncomfortable around him.

'Tell me Rainbird. How come this is coming out in me now?'

'Darrrling,' even though she was quite emotional, she couldn't help use her common expression, it had become such a part of her, 'you are a soul experiencing life. You and I, everyone, we have all been here before. You may have unfinished business from a past life. Maybe something or someone from a past life has triggered these emotions.' Rainbird went on to explain her philosophy. How a soul will need to experience a whole spectrum of emotions. She expected him to be dismissive about the concept but he wasn't. She said, 'you have been here before, we all have.'

Richard said, 'so tell me about my past life?' Before she replied she had more preparation, mainly in her own mind, taking herself into an almost trance like state. It was important that she grounded herself first, and create adequate protection blocking out any unwanted negative energy. She asked Richard to supplicate his hands, 'like we do in Yoga, the dumb waiter pose,' she said as she took hold of his hands in hers.

She tensed up, it wasn't subtle, but Weiss couldn't interpret the body language. He felt a great wave of tiredness engulf him, and he drifted, he didn't know for how long, but he made himself jump when he snored, and he forced himself back into full consciousness. He opened his eyes, and opened them wide towards her indicating that he wanted her to continue.

'You are not alone. You have travelled with Mr Kugel, and Dr Gibson from your last life. Kugel was . . .' she paused, eyes closed. She now knew who they all were in their past lives. She was short of breath, and looked quite disturbed at her discovery. She wondered if she should tell him, but what difference would it make if he did know.

Richard pushed her to reveal what she knew, and with a feeling that she had no choice but to tell him she said, 'Harvey Kugel, and Dr Blake Gibson were in the Second World War with you. Kugel was Heinrich Himmler, Gibson was Dr Mengele, and you . . . you were Adolph Hitler.'

Chapter 37

David arranged for the sisters to come to see him today as he wanted to hypnotise Eleanor. He had also decided that he should also be regressed, and he wanted Silvio to do this with the girls in the room. Ideally he would encourage them all to follow suit to pursue a theory he had been reading about. He had no idea what he would uncover, but he could see no downside, and in the back of his mind it would be nice if Silvio, and Emily were in a relationship. They were both single, and he saw it as a great opportunity for a close group of friends.

David was really drawn to this idea, and he didn't really know why, he hoped the book he had recently read hadn't made him see a connection that wasn't really there. He knew it wasn't just to have friends around him, he had always been fine in his own company. He told himself that he hoped he wasn't just being selfish, but he didn't think he was, there was definitely more to it than that. He felt having Emily in their fold, was almost meant to be.

When the girls arrived David, and Eleanor embraced, holding on to each other as if their lives depended on it. He fixed coffee, and sat with the girls in his consultation room. 'You said you have something you want to discuss?' Emily said.

David replied, 'yes . . . I have had this book for years, it's called "Soul Mechanic", or more accurately, "How to be a Soul Mechanic", and I read it again this week. In fact David had reread it cover to cover three times since he dusted it off, constantly selecting the most relevant sections. 'I have used this book in the past, and there are techniques described that I have found useful.'

'Is it about regression?' Emily asked.

'No, not per se. It is more esoteric than I normally prescribe to, but I am becoming more intrigued about the information we have on this connection with Kugel.'

'Can I read it?' Emily asked.

'I'd like to read it too?' Eleanor added.

David said, 'of course you can. Basically . . . this book is about the soul, for the sake of this conversation, let's assume that having a soul is accepted.' David was torn between the known, and provable facts versus a spiritual outlook requiring faith.

David continued, 'this book states that souls travel in groups. The fact that two people could be connected in a past life, this book says, that it is always that way. We travel in groups good, and bad alike. An enemy today could be an enemy from the past or for that matter, will play a part in our future lives.'

They continuing discussing the possibility of soul groups, but the sisters needed no convincing. They were prepared to accept it wholeheartedly without even reading about it for themselves. David said, 'Sil is going to regress me. I want to find out if it is true. Have we been together in a past life?' Because of David's experience when he regressed Emily, he completely believed that she had been here before. When David first asked Silvio to regress him to a past life, he laughed, he thought David was joking, and said, 'come on David, you are a doctor, you can't seriously believe that you have been reincarnated?'

David assured him that it was a serious request, and so today David would regress Eleanor to gather as much knowledge as possible to create further questions for David's session, and then Silvio would regress David, who in turn wanted to regress Silvio, but so far he had refused saying, 'I haven't got used to this life yet. I don't want to find out I have other ones to worry about.' Silvio had a home visit today, and wouldn't be staying for Eleanor's regression, but he was fully committed to try, and regress David when he returned. Once he agreed David gently encouraged Silvio to also be regressed, and all he got was, 'maybe. Let's see.'

David had rehearsed the conversation in his mind as he had mistakenly thought he may have a harder task selling the principal to the girls. He should have known they would be receptive. 'I've always thought there's more to this life than we know about, but I'm basically thick, so what do I know,' Emily said.

'I am not religious, as such, but I feel the same too.' Eleanor added. So everyone agreed that the possibility of a past life together, should be looked into through further regression. David stressed again that there wasn't really a downside, as there were no known physical side effects. So Eleanor lay down, ready for her turn in the hot seat.

Most people that want to be hypnotised can be, but some people go under deeply quite quickly, and within minutes David was able to ask, 'can you tell me your name?'

Eleanor replied, 'my name is Sophie.'

David asked, 'Sophie where do you live?'

Eleanor replied, 'I live in Alsace, in a village called Rittershoffen.'

David came back with, 'are you married?'

Eleanor said, 'yes I am, but my husband died in the war.'

David asked, 'do you have any children?'

Eleanor answered, 'yes I have a five year old daughter, Alicia.' David spent at least 10 minutes in the company of Sophie asking all about her life. She told of the day she had seen both Hitler, and Himmler. Even though it was 75 years ago, and a different life, the fear she had felt at the time she was able to embrace today, and impart to leave the listener in no doubt about the gravity of the occasion.

After the session they listened back to the recording, and they were all completely stunned. So they now had a full picture of Sophie, and Alicia. They also now knew about a third person from their past life, Hans. On tape, Sophie had described him as a friend that was of very special significance in her life. Eleanor said that she really hoped that Hans would turn out to be David. Even though it would also be his preferred outcome, David said, 'let's not jump to any conclusion, and end up disappointed.'

Eleanor crossed her fingers, and was completely convinced this would be true. She didn't have to wait too long. As David took his turn, they were able to confirm that he was indeed Hans in their past life together. Interestingly, they both could access information from both lives while regressed, albeit it was not so easy to decipher what was useful information.

'Why isn't this common knowledge?' Eleanor said, 'if soul groups travel together how come there aren't more reported cases?'

Emily replied, 'could it be that our situation was different as the bad guy in our soul story was Hitler?'

Emily continued to feel stronger through the process, and started to believe that she would never have to suffer again, it was like an instant cure. As a young girl she had been attacked, and the perpetrator had previously caused her harm, it all made sense to her, why she had been stressed in the first place. 'I just knew!'

The girls' acceptance was based on faith, a simple belief that they could have lived before. David urged caution, and more study before jumping to conclusions, but the girls both were convinced they were all part of the same soul group. Eleanor said, 'you can't ignore the fact that we just heard you say you were Hans.'

David said, 'I am excited as you with the prospect, but without any evidence it is not sensible to just accept reincarnation, and we should look into the subject.' They weren't really listening so David said, 'ok leave it to me to do some research, and I will find out all I can. Who knows, I remain sceptical although it is very persuasive on the face of it, but I certainly want to study it more.' The first thing he intended to do was to go through the history books, Register of Births, and other official documents to see if the people they were referring to in regression actually existed.

The girls didn't need much more evidence, they were going with the regression concept as a fact. But they said nothing else, and they left David to do his research. Just as the sisters were about to leave David asked Eleanor, 'could I take you to dinner this weekend?' She happily accepted.

Chapter 38

The water deal in Tambura had given Weiss the realisation of just how easy it was to control people's lives. It was his decision, and his alone if those people down river of his Dam's would have his water. Without it they die, the control made him feel powerful, it was extraordinary, and he originally only did it for the money, the side effect was the life in his hands.

Weiss ordered books, CD's, and anything else he could get his hands on to learn all he could about Hitler. He even started buying Hitler memorabilia, he found the extent of the items available was quite incredible, and in a matter of weeks he had quite a collection. Handwritten letters, signatures on books with personal dedications. Weapons purporting to have belonged to Hitler, were at the top of his list, and his most treasured possession in this collection was a handgun, handmade for Hitler. Weiss held it in his right hand, and found it a perfect fit. He started to think that there were physical similarities that weren't obvious at first, such as boot size, chest size, hair colour, and his list went on.

He spent a lot more time in front of the mirror, obsessed with his own eyes. He was sure they had become darker, no longer a deep brown, almost black. It may have been a trick of the light, but still, there was a difference. They looked soulless even to Weiss who never blinked while looking, even though he could stand there lost for several minutes at a time.

He started to refer to his "Glorious past", to anyone that would listen to him. He had discharged the handgun in his office, more than once. The change was noticeable with all of D.I.S, but they had known him for so long, no one was particularly concerned. Rumours were rife, but they were so farfetched, and out of character that no one really believed them, but since firing his gun, not many were prepared to knock, and enter.

He was standing there in the mirror, and a name came to him, "Vlad Tepes", he had a thought that there was a longer line of connection to other powerful military leaders. He wished he had Rainbird here to ask her. He decided it was possible that he had been around as other dictators, even though the thought was intoxicating, he decided it wasn't of any value to him. But Hitler, and Weiss, that was a team he would back. He knew he was at the pinnacle of his mental power, and was looking forward to the up and coming months. His word of the day popped into his head, *Revenge*.

Chapter 39

Eleanor arrived early for her date with David, only to find he was even earlier, and already sitting at the bar with Marco. They were both nervous, and therefore thankful of Marco's company, at least for the first drink. Marco had sat at the bar many a night with David, sometimes three or four times a week, and it was a friendship based on mutual respect for each other.

Eleanor said, 'I was really worried about tonight.'

David replied, 'me too, I can't believe it, but I was ready about four hours ago, and sitting there trying to rehearse what we would talk about.'

Marco was less thick skinned than David gave him credit for, and told them both that the bar area was required, and he needed to show them to the table. Marco went off to get his chef to create something special off menu. So Eleanor, and David were finally alone, sitting across from each other on what seemed like an important date to both of them.

'Do you remember when I took you to dinner?' He was talking about the day he had passed his driving test at the age of 17, and he took Eleanor to a restaurant.

Eleanor said, 'of course, it was my first actual date. I felt so grown up.' They soon relaxed, and were talking about the past. They were both recalling various occasions, theme park trips, birthday parties, and lots of other memories of their teenage years together. David asked about Eleanor's best friend from back then, and she said that she is still in regular contact with Susy, and in fact she was Godmother to both of her children.

David said, 'do you remember when I bought you a ring? I said something like, this is a friendship ring, and one day you can give it back, and upgrade it to a wedding ring. It sounds childish now, but it felt important to me then.'

Eleanor surprised David when she said, 'I still have it, I used to wear it on my little finger as it didn't fit any other.' They both laughed when he confessed he knew nothing of ring sizes at the time. 'I stopped wearing it when it got too tight, but I put it in a box of various trinkets from childhood. I always intended to hold you to it,' she laughed.

She told David that she had every card, letter, and poem that he ever wrote, she saved them all. He was amazed that for over seventeen years or more she had kept all the things that he had given her. Before tonight, he wondered if she would have fond memories as he did, but this was better than he could have hoped for.

Eleanor said, 'I used to think you were a bit camp when you read poetry to me,' she giggled out loud, 'well I didn't even know any poets, and I certainly didn't know any teenagers that were into poetry, but you were so sweet, I didn't want to say anything.'

David felt a little twinge of embarrassment for the pretentious teenager that he must have seemed to her until she added, 'I totally get it now. You made poetry accessible to me, and when I was mature enough to be swept along by poetry, I understood, and it made me miss you even more. I would read Shelley, "Mary Dear, come to me soon, I am not well whilst you art far" and think of you reading it to me.'

They inevitably talked about other partners, and why they were still single. David said, 'I don't want to put you off by coming on too strong, but I never met anyone that I loved as much as I loved you, and I am not sure I ever will. I may well be recalling the past through rose tinted glasses, but I don't think that is the case. I just always felt we were meant to be together.'

Eleanor said, 'I still remember the start of my attempt at a poem, "why are you leaving me", it went, I thought you loved me, I thought you wanted me, I thought you needed me, so why are you leaving me.' She was really pleased when he continued with verse two. It was becoming obvious that the feelings they had for each other had never really gone away for either of them.

Marco produced an amazing dinner, and they had a wonderful night. David being a gentleman, asked to escort her home, but he didn't ask her back to his apartment that first night. They had said a lot, and both knew this wouldn't be the last date. When he kissed her goodnight it was a long lingering gentle kiss. A loving kiss that they both felt said more than all of the words. As she walked towards her door, David said, 'can I call you tomorrow?'

'You had better,' she smiled.

Chapter 40

David took it upon himself to know as much as he could on the subject of reincarnation, and for over three weeks he had spent every waking hour on this one pursuit. He read everything he could get his hands on, and he had interviewed therapists who specialised in the subject. The regression therapists all believed in what they were doing, but David thought that some were certainly more impressive than others. It was clear that there was an abundance of information on the subject, so when choosing which to review, he decided to avoid those which leant towards a religious agenda. He instead looked at scientific studies, and again there was a wealth of material.

David was also fortunate that the writer of the original book that took him down this path, "Be Your Own Soul Mechanic", agreed to meet, and to be interviewed. David was surprised that the writer was a scientist, and she had based all of her work on children that talk of past lives without any prompting or regression. She had even traced the people that these children claimed to have been in past lives, and noted physical links to those past lives. Some had birthmarks that matched injuries received in a previous existence. So she was very much coming at the subject from the same standpoint as David.

He had several documents to go through, and they included the birth certificates he had requested. He satisfied himself that the people that had been talked about in the regression sessions really had existed. He wanted to trace everything he could on them, to see when they died, and try to establish a link between deaths, and reincarnation dates. But all of his research was leading to the conclusion that reincarnation seemed to stand up to close scrutiny.

He hadn't seen any patients as he was completely immersed in the research. Silvio had supported him too, for which David was very grateful. In fact it was Silvio who had suggested doing more regression sessions, so far he had only regressed David and was still resisting David regressing him. For David, it wasn't just what these sessions revealed, it also seemed to open the floodgates of information from past lives.

David sat, writing in his journal. Almost daily, he recalled more of his life as Hans, and that of the other participants in Rittershoffen, of what he now called his "Soul Group". His opening pages talked about the way the information came to him, and even though he wrote, "Recalled", he put it in brackets, as this wasn't quite right. It was much more like a bulk download that he could access just like any other memories once complete. More often than not, this happened during the night. So each morning, for a few days now, he wrote notes of the latest chapter of their past lives.

He also continued to read on the subject, and he thought he found something that might apply specifically to him. Out of the soul groups that travel together, some individuals are said to be there in a wider capacity, and he felt this to be his destiny. Dr David Prost was the Guardian Angel of his Soul Group. With everything he was remembering, he now accepted this without any question or doubt. But what it all actually meant, still eluded him.

The deaths of Sophie, and Alicia started to play heavy on his mind, even though it was something he couldn't change, but he felt it served as a reminder to keep them safe in this life. He hadn't gained any psychic ability at all, more of a knowing. So he concluded this knowledge had been gifted to him so he could be the girl's protector. He thought of it a little like a parental role, and a need to keep his family safe. It also felt predetermined. He found that his role would be the same in all future lives, and it may not even be in this life, that he will serve his true purpose.

He read the last section back several times, and thought, *what is the point in knowing that*. He questioned keeping a journal at all, saying to himself, 'what good would it do.' But he couldn't help it, he felt drawn to documenting everything, come what may. He even contemplated how he could make all of this available to his next life, to steal a march on Weiss. But so far had drawn a blank, he was still young, he would try, and find a way. To do that he would need to see if there was a pattern to the reincarnation, but he was getting ahead of himself, so he continued with his writing.

He wrote about the group, and tried to piece together who they all had been, and how they had fared in Rittershoffen. He wanted to have a full picture before he shared what he had learned with the group, as he thought he had more questions than answers at this stage. But he also started to work on a theory, and he wasn't sure where or how it was connected to his past life memories.

The scope of his theory was about the development of a soul, and an end to the constant cycle of souls inhabiting a physical body of a life on earth. When it came to real genius, such as that displayed by Einstein, and other giants of his ilk, David had these under the heading "Guardian Angels", and sub heading of "Old Souls". He was forming a hypothesis, that by coming back time, and time again, and managing to retain some access to their past life knowledge, they became geniuses.

As well as "Old Souls" as a subheading, he had, "Good Souls". Jesus, and Mother Teresa as his examples of such souls. Again he thought they were Guardian Angels, which had existed for a sufficient amount time to have gathered the capacity of what David called, "Pure Love".

Under this he wrote, and underlined four times, *we are only hurting ourselves, and we will come back again, and again until we stop, and inequality is the ultimate reason that we hurt each other.* On the following page he wrote, *It wasn't the fact that some people were rich, but that the poor who often have literally nothing to lose causes the lack of harmony. No matter how the difference is framed, religion being a main example, it is still a group of people with nothing that becomes the disenfranchised.* He hadn't any other thoughts or comments on this, it was just another line that felt true to him, but what it meant, and how, or if, he could do anything about it, had as yet to come into focus.

Continuing his categorization of different types of souls, he had a completely separate one from Good Souls, for music. He noted that musical souls had already transcended the physical, and their role was different to other souls. Although why, and how again hadn't come to him yet, but his notes so far suggested that people who had music in them vibrated at a different speed to other souls. This was written without great analysis as he would have almost certainly not written it as something that he knew or believed, but something ethereal, and just out of reach. He made a note to talk to someone about it. He wasn't sure he would ever get to the bottom of any of these theories, but he felt better for writing them down.

His most random group of words were capitalized, and he had drawn a circle around them. A GATHERING IS DUE. He left this isolated, and turned the page to continue what he said was the opposite side of "Good Souls", and he simply wrote "Evil Souls". He crossed it through, and searched for another word. He went online, and looked at synonyms of evil, but nothing else was quite right. So many movies had this theme, "Good vs Evil", and he concluded this was probably an overworked imagination rehashing old Disney stories, but he could think of no other alternative at this stage.

David continued with his research, and documenting everything that came to him, whether it seemed relevant or not. He had a line written in the margin of his journal, it simply said, *the shares are in a safe in a hotel*. This meant nothing to him, but he thought he would ask Eleanor if it rang any bells with her. Eleanor put a coffee on his desk, and sat back in front of her screen where she working. He decided to leave his journal for now, and come back to it later with fresh eyes.

∞

Eleanor knew David had done lots of research, but she was less interested in the subject generally, and was more interested in how it affected them. She was keen to know more about their history. Eleanor asked David, 'How far back in history have we been together?'

He opened his journal again, and wrote "How far back", as a reminder to come back to that question. 'I think we were together before the War, how many times I don't know yet,' he replied.

Eleanor had no response for this. She now knew that their relationship stretched back decades if not centuries. She had already more or less moved in with David, throughout the three weeks he had been studying reincarnation. She had been going backwards, and forwards to get her clothes from Emily's, and one day David said, 'why don't you stay here while you are in Washington?' So she moved in.

As Eleanor was only visiting the USA, they hadn't discussed or even thought about the future, but it simply made sense as they had hardly been apart since that first date. So as it was temporary, it didn't seem to be such a big step. They both found it incredible that they had been together nearly eighty years ago when love had first blossomed, and again as teenagers, when once again they had a longing for each other that had never been satiated.

Tonight, for the first time, David asked her to sleep in his bed. They undressed in the dark, and slipped under the quilt. They were lying in bed, both naked, and Eleanor said, 'do you remember when I said "I don't know if I love you". We were at my house, and no one was at home, and you really wanted to go all of the way.' He carried on kissing her.

'It wasn't true, I did love you, I just didn't want to have sex, I wasn't ready. I was worried what my mom would think, and for some reason I knew that she would know.'

He didn't reply, she was lying on her back on the left of the bed, and he was propped up on his left forearm stroking her hair. He knew she just wanted to get it off her chest, and took his time, he moved to nibble her ear.

'You know what that does to me,' she said through whispered breath. 'You did that to me then, and it was so hard to stop myself. Were you angry with me?'

He was a gentleman then as well as now, and told her that he completely understood. He worked his way down her shoulder to her left breast, and sucked on an already erect nipple. David said, 'do you think your mom will know that we are doing it now?'

There was no doubt that finally this was the time. Eleanor felt an enormous sense of anticipation, and it wasn't just those heavy petting nights as teenagers. It was also their time as Sophie and Hans, she didn't know for sure, and didn't know why she felt this, but she believed they never managed to express themselves then either. She closed her eyes, and gave into David's embrace. He was gentle, and patient as a lover, and he teased the inside of her thighs, further building the tension.

Eleanor said, 'I didn't want you to go to America, I wanted you to stay with me, but I said I didn't care to make it easier for you to leave me, as I knew you had no choice.'

David replied, 'I loved you, and you loved me, I was never in any doubt.'

With this out of the way, she was ready for him. This time when he trailed a very light touch from her knee up her thigh, he didn't stop. She let out a moan of delight, and she reached for him to find him completely ready. They didn't claw at each other, and get frantic, they both savoured the occasion. He almost exploded right from the first time he entered her body, but he managed to hold back, and he got back in control. To her it was incredible, she always managed to orgasm, but it was always once. But after this orgasm, and with him still fully erect, she suddenly felt another coming on, the sensation was beyond sex, it was love physically expressed. She now understood why sex between the right pairing was called making love.

Chapter 41

Eleanor found records of the village where they had lived, only to find that it had been totally destroyed in the War. As the girls were sisters now, and mother and daughter in the past, it was the one aspect of the past lives that at first felt strange, but now they had read David's book on the subject, they understood that it was possible to be reincarnated in any combination of family member.

Eleanor was praising Google for its ability to find answers to her endless questions. She desperately wanted to see a picture of Sophie, and Alicia. She had found copies of their birth certificates, but no photographs. From what she knew so far, Rittershoffen was used for a propaganda movie, which raised the question, did the film still exist? If it did, and they were actually featured, would she recognise them? David walked over to Eleanor.

'You have been on there all day, and you need a rest.' He squeezed her shoulder, and she put her face on his hand.

Eleanor replied, 'I would love to see Sophie, and Alicia ... and Han's, obviously. I wonder if we resemble them?'

'I see real similarities between you, and Sophie. I think it's the eyes.'

'Really!' Eleanor said, 'you can remember me as Sophie!'

'Yes.' He really wished he had kept that to himself, but it was true, and it was the eyes.

Eleanor said, 'oh I wish I could remember more. I want you to regress me again. I want to see you, and Emily back then.' David said that he would, but right now they should get some sleep. He took her in his arms, and gave her a kiss. She said she felt wide awake, but agreed to go to bed as they wanted an early start. 'Why do you think that we are connected to a famous person? What are the odds of that?' she asked.

David said, 'well someone had to be. Maybe the longer a soul has been coming back to earth the more overall experience that person has too. Someone like Hitler may have been building his sense of evil for all we know. But I think it's no more than random luck, or lack of it, in our case.'

David hadn't even finished his sentence before Eleanor was fast asleep, he knew that they must watch Weiss like a hawk. He instinctively felt that he might be trouble, but he couldn't see how, so he would just have to be vigilant. He didn't think it was of any significance in this current life, but he was here a long long time ago, and he wouldn't dwell on it now. He knew the day would eventually come when he would like to know if Eleanor was with him five hundred years ago, a life he glimpsed briefly during regression; a face he saw reflected that he knew was from the very distant past.

Book 4

Chapter 42

Only three people had left D.I.S through various flare ups of Weiss' anger, so there were still thirty eight people in Las Vegas for his annual trip to the gambling Mecca. It was a very hot June evening when they landed, and his gambling was just as hot. Within two days, Weiss was three million dollars down. He was gambling frantically, telling himself that he had just made three billion, and what he had lost in the last two days was irrelevant.

Gambling in Vegas, for high rollers, comes with a lot of comps. The Bellagio had attracted Weiss by offering their best suite, completely free of charge. Amongst the additional sweeteners, the manager had actually said to Weiss, 'your wish is our command.' Weiss, being flippant, asked for lions in his suite. It was an unusual demand, but they did surprise him when they agreed to his request, and his allegiance transferred from Treasure Island. The lions were fed by their trainer, against the instructions of Weiss.

The trainer wasn't going to let them go without sedatives with their food. 'These crazy request from guests should be banned,' he advised his boss. 'They are extremely dangerous animals.' His protest didn't matter though, in the end Weiss' lions joined him in the suite.

Kugel arrived at six pm sharp. It was another of the, BBRW meetings, but Victoria now knew who he was, the Senator wasn't a mystery anymore. For the select few that did know, they were also aware that this was a VVIP, who needed to come, and go incognito, always a complete cloak, and dagger affair.

When Kugel arrived the first thing he said was, 'how the hell did you get these in your room.' Kugel was talking about the lion cubs.

They had an area of around twelve square feet just off the main living room, with chains securing them to the wall. They had keepers around the clock to look after them, and to clean up immediately, to minimise any odours. There was no doubt that they were cute, but Kugel didn't want to go anywhere near them. He had a complete phobia of cats, and that was the small variety, coming face to face with these made him realise it also applied to big cats too.

'I love them,' Weiss said while stroking both of them on the top of their heads. He had an affinity to the beast at the top of the food chain, he felt that he was, after all, a lion in business.

He washed his hands, and invited Harvey into the office, a large fully fitted Business Centre just off the hallway. Richard threw the towel to one of his staff as he crossed the threshold, and said, 'Right, let's get down to business?'

Kugel had come straight from the monthly Federal Reserve meeting, where they set the "Base Rate". Straight after the interest rate is set, Kugel always met with Weiss, and they would arrange the placement of funds, in line with the anticipated movement following the public announcement of the adjusted interest rate. This insider trading was highly illegal, and Kugel wouldn't take the chance of emailing, phoning or any other method for sharing this information with Weiss, so they always met up on the day that the Interest Rate decision was made, this was the secret to how Weiss had built his wealth, and reputation.

Kugel said, 'we are holding the base rate at a half a percent again.' The Federal Reserve controls the interest rate for the USA in the same way that other countries would do with the state owned bank, but the Federal Reserve was different, because it was a private company.

Richard asked, 'right, what is happening in Europe?' Kugel focused on Germany, France, the UK, and Spain when he responded to the question. 'The indicators all point to a hold on interest rates there too.'

Weiss had educated himself on investing, and he saw the USA as still one of the safest economies in the World, but at the same time it wasn't immune to external economic influences. He could see that the ability to instantly buy, and sell shares, currencies, and commodities and in fact, every financial instrument available, influences share price fluctuations. Day traders, both professional, and amateur were all looking for a quick profit, and the law of cause and effect was making the majority of stock market fluctuations than would ever have happened before on line trading. He therefore concluded that he had to do something to remove the risk, and this is why he used Kugel.

Weiss always stacked the deck in his favour, and the Chairman of the Federal Reserve was his ace card. For his part, Kugel got ten percent of the profits, without putting any money in. It was a trade they have pulled off time, and time again.

'How much are you placing?' Kugel asked.

'Put me down for forty billion dollars.'

Weiss was using the bank's money as security to purchase this trade. The bank customers received a competitive interest rate, but they were not aware that the money on deposit was being used for a geared investment, increasing the risk to the capital. It was also one of Weiss' private companies that provided the facility, and made a very healthy profit in the process.

Richard asked, 'can I get you a JD and coke Harvey?' They had a bite to eat in Richard's suite as they couldn't afford to be seen together, outside of official functions, Kugel couldn't hit the tables with Weiss as he would have liked. Kugel took the opportunity to put more pressure on Weiss for a swift conclusion of his water deal. He had three credible buyers, as well as the French Government agreement that was still on the table. Again Weiss refused to sell. Although his stance had softened he said, if he couldn't get an agreement with the USA within a month, he would start to sell off smaller lots.

Kugel said, 'look I want this now, please just do the French deal.'

'Come on Harvey, you have plenty of money, you don't need this to happen straight away. What's the real issue?'

'I don't need it, but I want it. This is it for me. One last big deal, and I am calling it a day.' Kugel was of the opinion that they had got away with it long enough, and he had a gut feeling that it was time to cash in, and call it a day.

Weiss thought Kugel was losing his nerve. Weiss was the Alpha male in this relationship, but it was a partnership that had served them both well, but today Weiss felt like crushing him, just to show him who is boss.

∞

Later that night Weiss played Blackjack with Dr Blake Gibson. Weiss said to him, 'I have a simple strategy that has always served me well.' Richard added, 'every player will win at some point, it is just a matter of how many hands before that win comes along.'

Knowing this, Weiss would double his stake every time he lost a hand. He played a hundred thousand for his first hand, and if that went the way of the dealer, he doubled his stake. When he played this way, within four or five hands he would usually get his money back. Tonight was different, he started big, one million dollars. Eight hands later, and without a win, he was down two hundred, and fifty five million. He believed in his strategy, like most gamblers do, and was therefore convinced it would work. He tried to play his next hand at two hundred, and fifty five million. The casino limit was two hundred million dollars a hand.

The Casino Manager approved the higher stake knowing how much Weiss had already played. Weiss drew a pair of kings, and indicated with a hand gesture, that he would stick. The dealer had a good hand, an eight and a two. A crowd gathered as the pace of his betting had increased. The dealer turned his next card, "Fifteen". An eight ended the hand, "Dealer bust". There was a round of applause as Weiss won his money back. It would be his last win on this trip.

Chapter 43

Dr Gibson was going to do a special project, and Weiss had asked Philippe to assist. Philippe said, 'Richard has changed my life with his investment, and I want to repay him with my loyalty.' The only issue he had was Dr Gibson. He couldn't understand what Richard saw in him. Philippe thought Gibson was a bigot, and that he had an exaggerated opinion of his own ability.

Philippe looked into Gibson's past, and was naturally concerned, so he called Richard, 'Dr Gibson has been struck off.' Weiss told him all about their history, and assured Philippe that Gibson was used as a scapegoat by the implant manufacturer.

Weiss said, 'Gibson works full time for me, and has done for the last two years, and his work has been impeccable.' So undeterred, the operation went ahead as scheduled. Philippe's opinion hadn't changed, but he would later concede that Gibson was a good surgeon, and he knew what he was doing. Richard was a human guinea pig, and was the first person to have NSC's placed inside his circulatory system. They were ready to be used in veins, but as yet hadn't been, as there was still some final testing to do before the ultimate approval would be granted. Richard didn't want to wait, he was completely convinced that this would extend his life. The NSC's couldn't be used in the brain yet, and the smallest veins caused very few death related health issues. Therefore the first patient to receive NSC's for arteries, veins, and the heart was Richard Weiss.

Once in place they would strengthen the artery walls, and reduce the risk of cholesterol issues, and they should work well in the aorta. Weiss had the operation, and one thing that Philippe and Blake would agree on was that it had been a complete success. Gibson had given Weiss a General Anaesthetic, they wanted to get the NSC's into the heart, and they went up through his groin. It was far easier than anticipated, and they knew going forward this procedure could be done with just an epidural. For the majority of the NSC's they were administered through a drip. The unique positioning of the NSC's made the whole process far easier than at first could have been hoped for. Any doubt Philippe once had, he no longer did, it was a complete success.

There was a total of 85% of the NSC's that found their way to their allocated positions, the rest would find their way out of the body through the lymphatic system. Within two days of the original operation, the 15% additional application through further drips saw Richard with 99% coverage. There were no after effects. Richards's blood pressure was perfect, and everyone had good reason to be optimistic about the future use of NSC's to extend life. There may have been a placebo effect, but Richard Weiss felt good, he felt very good indeed.

∞

In the highs, and lows of Richard's life, the following week was another stressful one. The Internal Revenue Service, IRS, was looking into his Trust Assets. Tax avoidance schemes were not illegal, and the American government were particularly relaxed about sensible fiscal control that enables a company or an individual to minimise their overall tax burden. However tax evasion was frowned upon. Weiss spent the week, in and out of meetings with the IRS, his accountants, and lawyers.

Each day he was making the national news. He was accused of acting with impunity following the Regulatory victory, but he didn't respond to this accusation. He was filmed, and photographed every time he arrived at the IRS Headquarters, but he gave no interviews. After a week of "No comment", the Teflon man was giving an Oscar winning performance again in front of the world press. Yet again he had nothing but praise for a system that he said he believed in. And as he did with the regulator, he announced that he would not be suing. He had reached an agreement with the IRS and heads had rolled, His stock price had gone up again.

Victoria remained on his payroll, and he hadn't put a hand on her since that fateful day. The brief personal relationship was well, and truly over. They both knew it was over without having to say a word. However, the resolution with the IRS, his position with Victoria, and the application of the NSC's has done nothing to alleviate his anger, if anything it had got progressively worse. He could still turn on the charm, but if he didn't need to, he was angry, very angry. He still had his daily sessions with Rainbird, and the dreams kept coming. Rainbird was increasingly concerned, she didn't think that she could work with him for much longer, and she was only staying now, to try to influence him for the better.

Weiss was watching whatever footage he could on Hitler, and he loved it. He realised that being here before made him immortal, and he started to feel mentally linked to his old self, at least that's how it felt when he dreamed. In Hitler he couldn't see the evil despot that history had assigned to the man, he saw a brilliant military strategist. He particularly enjoyed reading Hitler's book "Mein Kampf" Weiss had purchased a signed version, and all the time he was really proud, after all it was his old self that he was admiring. He felt that he was shedding his old self completely, and that the new man emerging felt powerful and mentally strong. He said to Hitler on the screen, 'This time we will show them all.'

Chapter 44

The emotions stirred up through regression were extraordinary. Emily was absolutely determined to right the wrong of Richard Weiss, and Harvey Kugel. She had more fight in her than anyone would ever have given her credit for. Victoria had become their eyes, and ears as she too wanted to stop Weiss in his tracks. She knew from the various trips to Tambura, exactly what Weiss had control of, so she stayed with him with one goal in mind, to assist Emily, David, and Eleanor in order to stop him from killing innocent people.

Emily had done some specific work on the prediction of the likely deaths that his actions would cause, and she was planning an expose on National TV. What she didn't have yet, was evidence. Richard covered his tracks well, and it would be difficult to prove any wrongdoing. It certainly wasn't illegal to own land with water on it.

Victoria felt Richard's power had corrupted him, and he was demonstrating that he would do anything to win. She no longer had respect for him, he wasn't the businessman she had always thought he was.

The day that made her see him for the man he had become was her meeting with Rainbird. They met face to face as Rainbird was certain that all calls within any of Weiss' businesses were recorded. She had told Victoria about her revelation that Richard was Hitler, and Kugel was Himmler. "Richard also knows about Eleanor's past life", she asked Victoria to warn Eleanor, not knowing that she already knew. Rainbird didn't want to help Richard ever again, but she did promise Victoria that she would use her ability to see if she could help. Maybe they could stay one step ahead of him.

Chapter 45

Weiss believed it was his ability that made him successful, but everyone needed a little luck. 'I make the most of any opportunity presented.' Weiss said. The right opportunity falling into place may be the fortunate part, but Richard's luck had finally ran out. He was still in Vegas after meeting with Kugel, and the news was a complete disaster. A news station followed the story, "In a shock move today, the Federal Reserve have reversed their decision, and the base rate will move to three percent".

W.I.B.C account holders who believed their money was on deposit, had in effect a straightforward bet on the base rate, and the movement change had moved against him. The way the gearing worked meant that W.I.B.C depositors would lose ten percent of their deposit balances. The money never left the bank, but it was used as security for the gearing. Depositors would be required to pay ten percent of all cleared funds, which was a staggering four billion dollars. The result of this was very simple, it would now be known that Weiss had acted completely illegally, and he would be arrested, this time he knew he would be in trouble.

Across Europe, several countries had announced "Quantitative Easing" as a solution to the economic turmoil, as there was a danger of hyperinflation, not seen since the Second World War. According to various news feeds, the Federal Reserve had a meeting without the Chairman. The F.R. rules allowed for an Extraordinary General Meeting to be held if three or more Board Members called into question the Chairman's ethics. At this meeting, all present agreed that the Chairman did have questions to answer. Kugel went against everyone in the room on a vote to increase the Base Rate, against the economic advisers. It did not make sense. It was after this meeting that the Board met again without the chairman's knowledge, and the meeting led to a vote of no confidence. The Chairman was officially removed by majority.

This unprecedented move led to a concurrent meeting Chaired by the Vice Chairman temporarily Acting Chairman, until the outgoing chairman could be replaced by election. There was talk about how ethical Kugel was. A rumour started by a very senior banker, stated that Kugel made money off the back of interest rate decisions. The acting chair called for the group to not discuss speculation, but as a precautionary measure put to the vote, "Should a full investigation be undertaken"? They voted ten in favour, and one against. One Board Member, Peter Cross, stood out in support of Kugel, and insisted the vote needed to be unanimous for an investigation to be undertaken. The rules were checked, and all that was required was a majority. The decision was therefore made. A letter was prepared to the outgoing Chairman to be hand delivered prior to an official press release.

∞

Within hours of the historic vote, Kugel was on board Weiss' 747 heading for North Africa with Michael at the helm. On board, Kugel kept his eye on Weiss, who had taken to holding a cane, walking around with it held by both hands behind his back. For once Weiss hadn't gone ballistic, but Kugel concluded that he was acting very strange. Kugel didn't know what to do, he was in too deep, and this was not the time to lose the plot. He poured himself another JD, he knew he was drinking too much, but this was a stressful situation, and it was his only way to keep calm.

Kugel said, 'I can't believe they have done this to me.' Cross had called, to tell him about the three votes. Weiss whipped his cane down from right up high onto the arm of Kugel's chair. Kugel went to jump out of his seat, his face furrowed in a scowl. But despite his anger, the look that Weiss gave him suggested today was not the time to have this argument.

Richard said, 'Stop this negativity, feeling sorry for yourself. Do they have any evidence?' Kugel had not considered the large sums of money he made evidence, and there was nothing else.

Weiss was right so Kugel answered 'No' and began to calm down. 'I've had enough of the Chairman role anyway', he also suggested they had given him the push he needed. Feeling slightly better about his own position, Kugel turned his thoughts to the impact on Weiss. 'What will you do about the Hedge?' Kugel was referring to the money that would have to be paid for the currency bet.

'There is nothing I can do, so I am not prepared to worry about it.' Kugel was amazed that Weiss was taking it so well.

Kugel said to Weiss, 'you do know that W.I.CB.C will have to pay four billion dollars in the next four days?'

Richard replied, 'of course I do.'

This time the slamming down of his cane was followed by an instant calm, Weiss was becoming very difficult to predict. The stark reality of the situation was desperate. The payment would have to be made, and the drop in the deposit accounts would trigger an investigation that would cost Weiss his banking licence.

∞

Kugel thought *I need to distance myself from him or he will take us both down.* This thought helped, he vowed to distance himself from Weiss, and this issue. He considered all of the illegal trades, and couldn't see how they would link back to him personally. He was proud of himself for not letting his guard down and always being diligent. There wasn't one piece of paper that would lead back to him. There was however, a document that would put the responsibility squarely on Weiss' shoulders. *It is all in offshore accounts and it is in Trusts, and they would be difficult to trace.* He had a loan account with the Trust that allowed access to his money, but he knew that was not breaking any rules, bending them possibly, but not breaking them.

Kugel didn't like the change in Weiss, he kept losing his temper, and acting strange. So Kugel made up his mind here, and now, *Weiss was going down by himself, I am getting off this sinking ship.* He started to ask himself why on Earth he was flying to Africa. Fuck the water deal. He would get back as soon as possible, for now he decided to placate Weiss. 'You could always pay the margin on the Hedge?'

Richard turned nasty, and shouted, 'I could always pay four billion! Are you paying your ten percent?'

Kugel said, 'Look I have helped you to get incredibly rich. You had ninety percent to my ten on every deal. We never agreed I would pay anything back.' Kugel didn't want to wind him up, but there was no way he would part with four hundred million. That was about the extent of his total wealth. 'You stood to make one hundred million dollars, my share was only ten million. I can't pay four hundred million even if I had it, which I don't. How many times have we done this? Come on.'

Weiss went right up close to Kugel's face, eyes out on stalks. Angry again. 'Do the fucking maths. I made a hundred million, thirty times, three billion dollars, and now you want me to pay back four?' He looked ready to get physical, but Kugel was strong enough to not be intimidated.

Kugel said, 'the three billion has made much more. Come on man, talk sense. How much are you worth? Forbes estimated five billion, but I think you must have more?'

This strange instant mood change, calmness was back in Weiss, and it was disconcerting for Kugel. Weiss now walked back, and forth, cane behind his back. Kugel thought Weiss was like an actor, turning on the anger at will.

Weiss said, 'I have six billion tops, and that's with my profit from Nanostem.'

Kugel suggested, 'pay the four, and we both walk away with our liberty. You still have the water deal. You could even make the money back if you keep your head.'

Richard said, 'I want no further discussion. My mind is set. I can, and will live like a king in Tambura, and I will not go back to the USA. You can stay here with me, and get involved in government issues. We will control our own country.'

Kugel could see Weiss meant it, and concluded that he was mad. Kugel thought, *the pressure must have got to Weiss and he had tipped over the edge.* He would be a wanted man within hours. Kugel made up his mind on the spot, and decided to extricate himself, and fast. He had no choice, and he knew what he had to do. There was one way out for Harvey he would become a whistle-blower to save his own skin.

Chapter 46

Emily said, 'I can't believe it, I have just spoken to the President,' she was with David, and Eleanor at his place. They had all become very close over the last couple of weeks, and Emily's confidence had blossomed. She also had renewed enthusiasm for her research, and had spent the last week revising the AQWA paper, and this time she focused on issues within the USA in isolation. After discussing it at length with her sister, she decided to focus on a home grown solution first, because without making a start on home soil, how could she hope to lead a seed change on rationing between continents.

'Come on then, don't keep it to yourself, what did he say?' Eleanor asked.

Emily said, 'I was on my final draft when I took the call. The operator said I've got the President for you.'

David asked, 'what did he say?'

'He said that Senator Kugel would not be heading up the project any longer, and that he wanted a synopsis from me to be sent direct to his P.A, and he would come back to me.' She was standing as she said this, and more or less bouncing on the spot. 'Thank you both for all of your hard work.'

Eleanor said, 'Em . . . that's great news. You said you would speak to him at some point.'

Emily said, 'I never thought I would actually take a call off the President of the USA! A simple girl from England. Surreal.' She sat back a little in shock.

'I already had what the president wanted, so I emailed his PA straight away. He said the issue was not only a National issue, but an International one, and he would temporarily be taking this under his own control until further notice.' It felt like a momentous occasion, this was a complete change of direction. Emily added, 'He finished by saying "it is a significant piece of research" and he apologised that I had been overlooked until now. He assured me that it would be given the attention it demanded, and deserved.'

David said, 'I wonder why Kugel has been taken off the committee?' It was the day after the vote of no confidence, and the announcement hadn't been released yet. It was almost as if Victoria had heard his question, as Eleanor received a text off her, she read it aloud.

Heading to Tambura. Kugel on board. Keep you posted. X

David said, 'We have to watch Weiss and Kugel for that matter.'

The girls agreed, they all felt that it wasn't over. They spent the night going over Emily's amended report, and presentation. What she decided to also highlight was the water deal that Weiss wanted to do. There was a real chance, now that they were in communication with the President, that they might be able to stop him. Emily did a whole section on Weiss, and she revealed all they knew so far. She also highlighted the potential impact if he did manage to sell to any country. She made it abundantly clear that Weiss must be stopped. So this was the first step, convince the president that it would be wrong to take water en-masse from another country to bolster US supplies, and if Emily's report was accepted at face value, this would be the only logical outcome.

Emily stayed the night as she had drunk a little too much to drive. She was pleased for her sister as she seemed blissfully happy to be reunited with her soul mate. David's character was very accommodating of people generally, but to Emily he was like the big brother she never had. She'd hoped David didn't beat himself up too much about his lack of ability to stop Sophie, and Alicia from being executed. But she suspected it was something he might never forgive himself for. She wanted him to know that "forgiveness" was the only way to not carry any burden in this or any other life.

David had still said nothing about the role of Guardian Angel, mainly because he didn't really fully understand what it would entail, but the overriding sensation was clear. He was here to safeguard Eleanor, and Emily. He knew that he had to protect them from Weiss, and potentially Kugel, and Gibson, but for now at least, that was the extent of his knowledge. He hadn't changed in any other way, it was just this knowing. But his knowledge seemed to be growing. How, he didn't know, but he was becoming more aware of them all as souls. He went to bed happy that they were both under his roof.

They all slept well, it wasn't just David that felt better together. Eleanor was fixing breakfast when she called Emily, and David to the TV. It was Weiss, and Kugel featured together. Emily had still been in bed, it was only 7:30 am, and David was in the shower, but within minutes they were all around the TV. The press release had been issued by the Federal Reserve, and all main news channels ran with this as their lead story. David turned up the volume.

'In a shock statement issued today by the Federal Reserve, there is a warrant for the arrest of Senator Harvey Kugel, wanted for questioning in relation to a rate fixing scandal, after allegedly breaking Insider Trading legislation. The Senator is alleged to have taken payment for releasing sensitive information. The Federal Reserve was keen to point out that it was an "Internal investigation" and the Federal Reserve's integrity was untarnished by this high profile arrest. Well I think that's for someone else to decide,' the newsreader said.

The news item went on to say that Weiss was suspected of providing the funding for the illegal transactions. The issue for W.I.B.C was also under the spotlight. The newsreader continued, 'W.I.B.C needs to pay four billion dollars within forty eight hours, otherwise they will be in default, and depositor's funds will be frozen.' The story continued to unfold throughout the day. The Regulator was very nervous about another wrongful arrest, and was being cautious in their response to the allegations but, nevertheless confirmed that there would be a full investigation. The IRS refused to comment. There was also speculation about the whereabouts of Kugel, and Weiss, who were believed to be travelling together, but their destination was unknown.

Things continued to unfold at a pace, and Emily had received an email from the President's office. It thanked her for her synopsis, and it finished by saying, *Rest assured, America will not be purchasing water from Mr Weiss, or for that matter any other country.* By ten thirty, Emily was asked to appear on the midday news for CNN live, and she also scheduled four other interviews for that day, to be conducted by telephone. She was a changed person, the darkness had lifted and she was a girl on a mission.

By early afternoon the W.I.B.C customers were actually queuing around the block to withdraw their money. The run on the bank was relentless, and the News channels reporting on the bank's demise were the catalysts of further mass fever as more, and more people pulled out, the bank would almost certainly follow in the footsteps of Lehman Brothers.

The story would only be surpassed in the afternoon by one item, and that was the Richard Weiss planned water deal. Because Weiss was linked to the story, this had now been seized on by all the main news feeds. Emily's on screen performance this time was flawless, and her previous appearance was forgotten, this one was perfect. Gone was the talk of rationing and the emphasis was now on home soil. Desalination plants, covered in her report, were seen by the interviewers as an excellent way forward.

In David's apartment the news had been on all day, and the two stories had been repeated until early evening. The White House Press Office issued this statement. 'We are aware that Richard Weiss, and Harvey Kugel are under suspicion for potential fraud.' Nothing specifically was said about their links to any water deal, however, the White House also stated, 'under no circumstances will the US be negotiating with these men.'

Despite not directly linking Weiss, and Kugel to a deal that could cost thousands of lives, in the same statement, the subject of "AQWA" and the valuable work undertaken on behalf of the US Government was also mentioned. The main point made was, "This report would form the basis of the debate at the G10 summit". Apparently the government was going to propose a moratorium on all countries moving water en masse, and to form a coalition to work on an International agreement restricting future movement.

In David's apartment the mood was one of relief, it looked like they really had stopped him. As the day was coming to an end Eleanor had another text off Victoria.

Have you seen the news? Weiss furious, lost temper in front of Michael. I am safe, don't worry. Call you tomorrow. Vic xx

Eleanor replied, *Txs Hon, stay safe. X* within seconds of sending it she followed up with, *where are you?* It was over an hour before she had the one word reply.

Tambura

Chapter 47

The day after the news broke, Weiss was much calmer. He had a luxury hotel on the outskirts of Tambura, and was living his extravagant lifestyle as if nothing had happened. He was still surrounded by many of his team. They had stayed despite the turbulence, after all, he had been an excellent employer for many years. He was disappointed to have lost Eleanor, but she had already served her primary purpose. Though in all honesty he thought, *I liked her being around.*

'I am really glad you stayed,' he said to Victoria. It was one of his cardinal sins that he broke, having a personal relationship with her in the first place. He really did miss Rainbird. She had made her excuses, blaming her mother's illness as to why she couldn't be with Weiss. He loved his yoga, and she was an extraordinary masseuse. But it was her council that he would miss the most. After all these years resisting her spiritual guidance, now he needed it, and she wasn't there to dispense it.

Since becoming aware of his past life, he had a strange longing to have Rainbird closer, not further away. It came to him in a dream that they were all with him when he was Hitler. It was like a portent. Once he was connected to his life as Hitler, more instinctive knowing filled his mind. David had not highlighted this to the sisters, but just because Hitler was evil, he was still part of their soul group, no matter how uncomfortable that felt, and Weiss seemed to be coming to the same conclusion.

Without the advantage of the book that David had, Weiss questioned himself more about the principal, and wasn't drawn to act upon it at this stage. He would have to replace Rainbird straight away, if he couldn't find one person for all three elements of Rainbirds skills, he would hire three people. This decision lifted his mood. He thought, *I am such a positive person, why let a setback like this rock my world.* Some part of his brain said, *you have just lost your bank, and your reputation, you are entitled to feel down.* No, he decided that his first thought was right, onwards and upwards.

He had emails from the Federal Reserve, the board of W.I.B.C, and seemingly endless others, along with voicemails he hadn't responded to. Some were sympathetic, some indifferent, most angry. He took no calls. He let them leave a message, and no sooner had they done so, he would listen to them. The recurring theme of these calls was that the bank was finished. It was in its death throes in less than forty eight hours since the run had started, and it was sinking too fast to save. Secondly, his assets were frozen. The serious fraud squad had issued an International stop on all known assets.

In truth it wasn't enforceable what they had tried but it was no less effective, as no bank wanted to have any come back on any transaction to do with Weiss. The third message, there was a warrant for his arrest if he ever again landed on US soil. The French had officially pulled out of the water deal, after initially denying that the agreement had ever been discussed. He rationalised, *I have full access to my Trust funds, and they totalled something in excess of three billion dollars.* He could live like a king here with that amount.

His Trusts owned all the land, and he controlled the trust, so ultimately the water was under his control. If the western world turned their back on him, he would make new allies in the East. He could look at Asia or even the Middle East, he was well connected, and he would win, of that there was no doubt.

Richard said to Victoria, 'tell Harvey I want a meeting in one hour.' He thought, *Kugel will know whose door to knock.* These positive thoughts were putting him in a good mood.

She replied, 'apparently he has left.'

'What do you mean left? Get me Michael.' Within ten minutes, Victoria came back with the news that Kugel had definitely gone, and Michael had left a message with one of his team that he was taking Kugel to the airport, and would be back within the hour. It was quite normal for Michael to drive Kugel. He was the only person who worked for Weiss that had always been aware of who he was. 'Victoria, get Michael on the phone, NOW! I do not want Kugel on my plane, make sure he doesn't leave.' There was little Victoria could do as no one was picking up. By lunchtime it was confirmed that Kugel had taken off with Michael piloting the aircraft.

∞

If the BBC World News was accurate, Kugel would be arrested as soon as he landed in the USA. Weiss knew that this was not good. Kugel hadn't discussed that he was leaving. Weiss had wrongly assumed they would stay in Tambura together, and he wasn't happy with Kugel or Michael. In fact he was very angry, once again. He broke his cane lashing out. He decided that he needed to lay low for a couple of days, and decide his next move. He had plenty of direct staff with him, but he didn't have his core business team, they sat on the board of the bank.

Also, his team of share traders used bank intelligence so they were now redundant. He looked at himself in the mirror again, very close up, *think . . . think, I am a great thinker*. He hadn't suddenly lost it. 'This all began with the water deal, and Emily Myers', he said out loud to himself. She would get her comeuppance. Kugel, now that was far more serious. He would pay the ultimate price if he betrayed him.

Weiss' suspicions were confirmed when Kugel landed in Washington, the police arrested him as soon as he disembarked. Before the police took him away, Kugel made a statement to the waiting press, claiming his innocence, and the fact that he would very quickly prove this. When pushed on Weiss, he made this quote, and it was seized as the headline in newspapers around the world.

'Richard Weiss is an evil man. I travelled with him to try, and talk him out of a deal he is trying to do.' When he was asked about his arrest for controlling the base Rate of Interest, he said that they were missing the point. Hundreds will die and that was what he had focused on. When it was pointed out that he was avoiding the question, he said, 'I am completely innocent, and I have nothing to answer for.'

Within 2 hours Kugel's representatives had put up a ten million dollar bail bond. A judge ruled that Kugel could be released on bail, and cited his voluntary flying back to the USA as being sufficient evidence that he wouldn't try to skip bail. The lawyers for Kugel went straight to work, and they were equally bullish about their client's innocence.

∞

Weiss was getting very drunk. He rarely did this. Victoria made sure that everyone kept out of his way. He sat in front of the TV, watching the news while he ran through how he would get his revenge. Eventually he slumped where he sat. He looked like a completely different man within just a few weeks. How had all this happened? He connected more, and more with his darker side. People were going to pay, he would show everyone.

Tomorrow he would immediately stop any water leaving his land. He wanted these Jewish Bastards to die. In reality, the Jewish population in Tambura was minimal, and this fixation must have been filtering in from his past life. He ran through what he would do to get his revenge. He thought of funding weapons, and warring havoc. He reflected on his darker side, the side he now thought of as his better half.

'In my past life I would know what to do,' he said out loud and so he tried to link mentally to Hitler. When he lay half asleep, his thoughts were all of revenge and he was dragging up evil from deep down inside.

No one went in his room. If they had they would have heard him mumbling all night. He wanted the world to know that he was in command, not Kugel, not the Police or the Courts, not the Regulators, he was. He would call on Hitler's strength, and he would not lose again. When he finally drifted into a deep sleep, he had a final thought about Kugel, and how he would pay. Kugel would die.

Chapter 48

The last few weeks had flown by, and things had progressed at a pace. The President required some amendments, and lots of additional information to be considered prior to the G10 Summit, so Eleanor worked with Emily proof reading the amendments to her report. David insisted that Emily also move in with him, at least in the short term, as he believed she would be safer. He decided it was time to take advantage of his constitutional rights, and he purchased a handgun, and was taking lessons in how to use it. He had always hated guns, but under the circumstances he thought it was a sensible precaution.

After asking Eleanor if "The shares are in a safe in a hotel", meant anything to her, she recalled what Weiss had said to her in Gibraltar, about Bearer Shares. She also linked it to the Hotel Du Paris, where she knew Weiss had a permanent safe. They went to their connection at the White House, and he promised to follow it up.

Emily presented at the G10 summit, and it went perfectly. There was a unanimous agreement from all countries represented that the distribution of water would not be done to the detriment of the country of origin. The world leaders also agreed that no person should ever again be entitled to own water for their personal use, even if they did own the land the water was on. This extended to aquifers, and any water that could be extracted from underground.

The overall effect would stop Weiss from selling the water under his control. He could still potentially sell to countries outside the G10 group, but he was certainly in a weaker position now. All of Emily's areas of concern were being addressed. The issues that she had at the top of her list were the population growth being catered for, and it was treated as a high priority.

∞

David had a large office space, and all three were now set up to work there. Eleanor was on her cell phone, David and Emily could see from her face that it was important. As she finished the call she said, 'that was Victoria.' The first thought the other two had was that Weiss had again been aggressive with her again, but that wasn't the case. It was a long call, and Eleanor wished now that she had taken notes. But she first of all told them the essential message, 'she said we have to find his yacht, but he has a new one, and she doesn't know the name.'

'Why do we have to find it?' David asked.

Eleanor said, 'you won't believe this! His crew are waiting for a shipment of anthrax, and he is going to use it to poison the water. Apparently, the crew don't know what it is, but they are waiting for delivery from North Africa, and his further instructions when it arrives.' It was a worrying twist, and it justified David's insistence on continued vigilance.

'Weiss is planning to contaminate the water system . . . I thought he owned the water, why would he do that?' David asked.

Eleanor said, 'not his water, our water.' According to Victoria, when he was swearing revenge on Kugel, he had also fixated on Emily, as she had stopped him doing the water deal. Eleanor hadn't said anything yet, and didn't know if she should, what could they do about it. He'd had such bad press that the buyers that were still in the running wouldn't pay that much, he would be lucky to get his money back, so he wanted revenge on Emily.

Eleanor added, 'she also said that, Weiss has surrounded himself with a whole new raft of people, including links to terrorist groups. Victoria promised to call as soon as she could with any more information, but she was really scared.' David, and Emily said nothing, waiting for Eleanor to recall the rest of the conversation. 'She said we have to stop him. She thinks he has actually gone mad, and may even just dump it into the Mediterranean.' Eleanor stood before them biting her lower lip, she flopped into a chair feeling the weight of the world on their shoulders.

'If she doesn't know the name of the yacht, how are we going to find it?' Emily asked.

Eleanor replied, 'what she did say was that they are definitely in the South of France. He only ever goes to three places in France, Monaco, Cap Ferrat, or St Tropez.'

'But there must be hundreds of yacht's there, and without a name..?' Emily said.

Eleanor sat upright as she recalled another important part of Victoria's message, and told the others. 'His old yacht was held in his Trust, and couldn't be seized by the authorities, he is taking no chances, and has sold it in favour of a new one, and he had changed the entire crew.'

'But he will have a very large yacht, and there will only be so many of those.' Emily replied.

'Just call the police.' David said.

Eleanor told them the final part of the conversation, scolding herself for not saying this straight away. 'She also said that he knows we have all been around before, Rainbird told him so.' Emily explained to David who Rainbird was.

'Did he mention me?' Emily asked.

'Yes.'

'Why did Rainbird tell him anything?' David asked.

Eleanor told him all she knew. 'basically after fifteen years with him, she felt that she couldn't lie, but moreover, she didn't think for one minute that knowing would initiate such a dramatic change in his basic personality. She hadn't been able to predict what would happen as she was too close to it. She also said it was fate, and she had warned of a final showdown.' She thought that David would be their ace card.

They discussed what they should do. David said again, 'I will call the police,' and the sisters agreed with him. Eleanor called Rainbird to see if she could use her psychic talents to find the yacht, but she couldn't get hold of her, she tried several times, and just got her answer machine. After making several calls to try, and find someone to take him serious, David concluded that it was far harder than they expected. Everyone he spoke to didn't take the threat seriously.

David said, 'what about emailing the President, you have his PA's contact details?'

Emily replied, 'do you think I should, what if Victoria is wrong?'

'I agree with David,' Eleanor said, 'you should say something to him, after all it is about water and he knows all about Weiss.'

Within an hour the President had responded, and he was prepared to help. He did say it was a big stretch of the imagination that a once very successful banker with a completely untainted past should suddenly turn into a megalomaniac. However, he promised that the Foreign Secretary would make contact with his French counterpart, and make them aware, and see if they could at least make some enquiries. What he could confirm was the Bearer Shares were found in Weiss' safe at the Hotel Du Paris, and they hoped this would be the evidence they had been searching for to directly link Weiss to the "Insider Trading", but ideally they needed the Trustees to confirm that they did actually belong to Weiss. There was an arrest warrant out for the Trustee, Andrew Harris.

Despite this good news, they were no closer to finding the yacht, and they felt helpless. They didn't just want to wait around doing nothing. So they decide to search yachts owned in a Trust, but they soon concluded that there were too many. So they narrowed the search to Trusts in Gibraltar, and the Isle of Man. Eleanor knew from the Tambura meeting that he used these two domains for his Trusts.

'Tambura, let's try that name,' but still nothing.

Emily said, 'it's like looking for a banjo in a butchers shop.'

David went to retrieve some papers in his consultation room, on the way he stopped at the water cooler dispenser, the sort with the large upside down recyclable bottled water. He filed a plastic cup three quarters full, and he downed it in one. Within seconds he was feeling ill. The girls heard him tumble, and went rushing to assist.

'What happened?' Emily asked. David had passed out, but was coming round.

'I'm not sure, I just went dizzy, it's nothing, I feel okay now.' He was quite pale, and Emily suggested he lay down. Eleanor thought of Rainbird, it was something akin to deja vu. Then it popped into her head, Rainbird warned her about this on the first day they met, *when your boyfriend is ill you are to call an ambulance immediately*, so she took her advice.

'Lie still, there is an ambulance on the way,' Eleanor said. His head cleared slightly, but his stomach was cramping, and he felt sick in waves. It then occurred to him that it was the water, and he made them aware. They said they understood, and wouldn't touch it. When the ambulance came Eleanor went to the hospital with him, Emily choose to stay at the office, and keep looking for the yacht while waiting for the President to make contact.

It was touch, and go throughout the night, and at one point his throat was constricting so much that he was struggling to breath. He couldn't talk, and had to make gestures. The medical team that looked after him said he would have died if he hadn't been in hospital, as the poison they identified affected all organs in the body, and if it wasn't for the antidote, he would be dead. They also confirmed that it had been deliberate.

By early the next day, David was out of intensive care, and off the critical list. He needed to be kept under observation, they had used a stomach pump, and given him a blood transfusion. They said he may need further treatment, so he was being kept in for at least the next three to four days. David said to Eleanor, 'go help Emily, and see if the President has made any progress.' She agreed and as she left, she promised to keep him informed.

Emily had got nowhere searching for the yacht. Finding a list of recently registered crafts was the latest dead end. Eleanor asked her, 'has the President made contact?'

'Yes, but the French government said there are something like 1900 yachts in the South of France alone, and they would like to help but they would need a name, or at least the name of the captain.' They were stumped, and weren't sure what to do next. The police came to take away the water cooler, and the bottle feeding the dispenser. As they took it off the girls saw the label around the neck. RW Pharmaceuticals.

Chapter 49

The same day that David was rushed to hospital, Harvey Kugel was officially released without being charged. He was no longer a Senator, and he would never be allowed to sit on any Board again. But he got what he wanted, his liberty. His wife stood by him, and completely believed him to be innocent, and he wasn't about to alter her perception. They appeared everywhere together, and they always posed for the paparazzi arm in arm.

The investigation couldn't prove conclusively that he had been paid for intelligence leaked to Weiss, but it was clear that he had received a lot of money. No one involved in the investigation doubted that Kugel had taken advantage of his position, and taken money off Weiss, but his release was negotiated because Kugel had something to trade. He had used Weiss as his bargaining chip. He had supplied conclusive proof of the water deal that Weiss had tried to do, and the amount of lives that would be lost if he had pulled off the deal.

This information would allow the Government bodies involved to apply for a "Proceeds of Crime Award", against Weiss. The reason for this was simple, even though the assets of Richard Weiss had all been frozen, without a good reason, the order would have to be lifted, at some point. This way, the Government, through its Regulator, would be able to keep the funds. The amount was an undisclosed sum, the speculators were quoting two predictions, the first was that the fine would be the largest ever levied, and the other stated that it would decimate the assets in the name of Mr Richard Weiss. His Trusts were not mentioned, but in his own name, it was estimated, they would be talking anything between two, and three billion dollars.

Kugel had also made an ex-gratia payment of fifty million to the Federal Reserve's Widows & Orphans fund. He was allowed to announce it as a charitable donation, but it was part of an agreed settlement, allowing him to avoid further investigation and potential consequences. In reality, the Federal Reserve wanted the case closed quickly, so that the public confidence could be restored as soon as possible.

The focus switching to the water deal, and the thousands of predicted deaths being ignored, it took the spotlight off the "Insider trading". In all interviews, Kugel did actually look quite humble. He knew that he had had a close call, and for his self-preservation humble was the only way to be. His wife had been encouraging him to slow down, and take a long holiday. She had never been to the Cote d'Azur, and he had never been to Monaco other than for business, and she knew he would love to go to the casino.

Samantha Kugel was always seen at public functions at her husband's side, they were both still committed to each other. As a couple they had fallen into a habit of not sleeping in the same bed, this was followed by not being intimate at all. But When Samantha's relationship with their gardener became physical, she thought she had all that she needed. She assumed Harvey had an alternative outlet for his personal needs and thought, "what I don't know won't hurt me". The gardener wanted to get serious, but Samantha would never leave Harvey because of her public profile, and the gardener didn't fit into her social circle anyway. So instead of changing husbands she changed gardeners.

As a Senator's wife she had full use of a private jet, and the public and private life of a woman in her position was intoxicating, and served her sense of self-importance and it was a status in life that she wanted to hold on to. So Samantha stood by her husband's side.

'I always believed in you sweetheart.' His wife said as she searched flights to "Nice" France. They were both in no doubt that it was a very close call. Kugel knew he was lucky to get away from Weiss, and to avoid prison. He answered the phone, Samantha stopped what she was doing, sensing the call was important.

When the call ended he said to Samantha, 'the President wants to see me.'

She asked, 'what now?'

Harvey said, 'he probably wants to apologise for not stopping my arrest.' She trusted him, but believed that he had probably not protected himself enough, and left himself open to the arrest, but she wasn't that gullible to believe Harvey would get an apology.

Samantha asked, 'Shall I still try, and book the flights?'

'Yes you can book them. The President wants to ask me about Richard Weiss, nothing to do with the Interest Rate, just about his water deal, and I had absolutely nothing to do with that', he lied. By late afternoon he was with the President. The topic of conversation was about an Anthrax threat, and Kugel genuinely knew nothing about it, absolutely nothing about it at all. 'To be honest Mr President, I think that Weiss has lost the plot. This is why I wanted nothing to do with him. He couldn't care less how many Africans die.'

The President said, 'we both know Harvey that you couldn't care either, and I have that on good authority.' Kugel was going to jump in, and defend himself but he knew there was a time to just listen and take your medicine. This was one of them. So he let the President speak as he listened.

'I believe that you could make a decision without proper consideration for the impact when money is involved, but I don't believe you would ever be involved in a scheme to poison our drinking water.'

The President paused, and Kugel managed, 'thank you Sir.'

The President said, 'my question is, would Weiss?'

Kugel replied, 'I have known him for a long time and the man I knew would not do anything like this, however he is a broken man and he could be looking for revenge.'

'Revenge for what?' The President asked.

Kugel said, 'He wanted to sell "Water" to the USA sir. It hasn't happened so he may well blame the Government or the Myers girl who did the report I commissioned.' Kugel couldn't help himself, he had to get that one in.

'Let's not go there, you are lucky to not be behind bars. Do you think it's a credible threat?'

Kugel decided to cut the smart talk. It may have worked with some people but certainly not with this man. 'I would take it serious sir.' They continued to chat but it was clear that Kugel couldn't actually throw any light onto the potential whereabouts of a yacht or its name, other than suggesting it would most likely include Weiss' name.

The President said he didn't want to ever hear Kugel linked with even a misdemeanour otherwise, 'You will have to answer to me'. He did also add that if Weiss was to make contact, Harvey was to immediately call the Foreign Secretary with the details.

∞

After the meeting, Kugel called his wife to say he was on his way home, but he never made it. It was normal for him to call every night wherever he was, so this was not like him. Kugel did not go home to his wife. In the morning he still wasn't home, and his wife was now getting very concerned. Two days later the police called to take a full statement, and the former Senator Harvey Kugel was officially listed a missing person.

Chapter 50

It didn't take many phone calls to establish that RW Pharmaceuticals do not supply bottled water. It said a lot about the mind-set of Weiss. Not only was he prepared to kill anyone who happened to drink out of the poisoned bottle, he wanted Emily to know, if she happened to survive, that it was him behind it. The police had no credible leads. No one could track the company that dropped off the bottle. The normal delivery was once a month and the suppliers had on record that the order had been cancelled just before the last delivery was due. Whoever delivered it just had to turn up acting as the usual provider.

When Eleanor said, 'the perpetrators would need to know that David had bottled water delivered,' the detective leading the investigation pointed out that it wouldn't be difficult to sit in a car on such a busy street, and just observe.

They could decide the best way to implement a crime like this. She pointed out that there was also a specific link back to water, but the detective said this was most likely just coincidence, and it would be easy to find some other way of bringing poison into the home, and the label was no more than leaving a calling card. A calling card may indicate to the victim, the ultimate person behind the crime, but this was not enough to lead to a successful conviction.

Eleanor said, 'how would you find someone to actually do the crime?' He didn't need to answer, his look suggested that he knew of a different world, where a job like this could be arranged quite easily. There wasn't any better news with the search for the yacht, and with very little to go on, nothing was going to happen. But the bottle in David's consultation room was all the evidence the girls needed. Weiss was behind this, no one denied that, but was he really going to try to poison the drinking water of innocent American citizens? Yes. The girls believed he would.

Eleanor said she would go to France herself to try finding it. From her time in Marbella, she knew that there were only a dozen or so really big crafts at each port, so it wasn't as mad as it seemed. Her mind was made up when she took a call off Victoria.

'Richard is not far away,' she whispered.

She still had no idea of the name, or the captain, or the exact location, but she had overheard Richard say *It will be there in six days*, and the yacht was definitely still in the South of France. They decided that Eleanor would go, and Emily would stay behind to keep the pressure on from this end. Eleanor left on the next flight. She arrived in Nice with only five days to find a yacht.

∞

Within minutes of landing Eleanor was heading east in a hired car. She decided it would be easier to get around this way. She decided to head straight to Monaco, one of Weiss' favourite haunts. From up by the Palace, the task looked impossible. She hadn't realised that there was more than one port in Monaco, they were all along the coast. Eleanor decided that she could only do her best, and she couldn't afford to waste any time. She called home for an update, and spoke to Emily.

Emily said, 'I had a good chat to Rainbird, as you suggested, and she was really lovely. She said we should be looking for a name that links Weiss to the past as he is now completely fixated on Hitler.'

Eleanor said, 'okay that's good to know, let's hope it helps. Are you going to put a list together of the most likely names for me to look for?'

Emily replied, 'already done. I have just emailed you. Hitler believed that everyone betrayed him in the end, apart from Eva Braun, his wife, whom he married on the day of their joint suicide, and Blondi, his German shepherd. But I have also sent you thirty of the more likely names.' As she said this Eleanor's phone pinged, indicating a new email. She clicked on it to confirm it was the one Emily had sent. Emily said, 'take a picture of every boat you think is a possibility, and email them to me, and I will see if I can trace the owner. To see if we can rule them out. If I can't, I will cross reference the name to see if I can identify a link to Hitler.'

Eleanor said, 'ok thanks. I better get going, talk to you later.'

'Hold on, before you go.' Emily said. 'I'm also convinced that you should look at numbers too! Apparently Hitler was very superstitious, and liked certain numbers. He was born in eighteen eighty nine, and died in nineteen forty five, so there are two straight off. I have done a list of what I think are the top ten, that you should look out for.' They both agreed the number could be a feature on the boat or the berth.

'I would also look out for eighteen. People still to this day talk of eighteen for Hitler. The 1 representing his first initial, "A" and the eight being for the "H".' Emily said she was cross referencing berth numbers with names too. Between them they felt that they had reason to be optimistic. Emily said, 'it is more like a nail in a haystack rather than the proverbial needle.' The other news was also good. Delta Force, the USA's Counter Terrorism Unit, had been put on high alert through the President's intervention, and they were ready to act if the girls could get the information required.

Emily had argued that it would be better if the Delta Force could do the job they were trying to do, but she was reminded that it wasn't actually seen as a credible threat, and the Delta Force would step in when, or if, substance was added to the accusation. So the girls would have to stay on plan, and do their best to find it themselves. Emily kept searching for any useful information to pass to Eleanor, who continued the physical pursuit.

∞

After searching all day in vain, Eleanor was in a hotel room with sore feet, and sunburn. She had been exposed to the sun, without thinking of sun cream, and despite her relatively comfy shoes, her feet were still suffering. Even though Monaco had more than one main port, the really large yachts were still grouped together. So they were able to narrow it down to about 60 yachts that fit the profile. They were able to rule out some because of their names, as they were so obviously linked to a famous brand or person. Nineteen were identified by Emily as being registered to a named individual. The other twenty-nine the sisters both worked on concurrently.

Emily cross checking names against either Hitler or Weiss himself, while Eleanor went to each yacht, and spoke to owners, Captains or crew. Most were helpful, and confirmed who the owners were. Others didn't wish to reveal who the owner was. Eleanor asked them to compromise, and confirm if it belong to a Mr Richard Weiss, and they were more relaxed about answering. Enabling her to rule more of the yachts out.

Two owners that personally spoke to Eleanor were very open, and friendly. She was soon left with just four possible crafts in Monaco, and even though it was the height of summer, all four were unoccupied. Eleanor found the harbour master, who was quite off at first, until he realised she was fluent in French. He was able to confirm the owners of the four crafts, and they didn't belong to Weiss either. She had to stay, and drink strong black with him, while he leered at her and was overly flirtatious, in order to obtain names of the last four owners.

Eleanor had wanted to go on and keep looking, but Emily had advised her to call it a day, get some sleep, and start again first thing in the morning. It was good advice, and Eleanor felt better for a good night's sleep. On the third day she repeated the exercise a little further west on Cap Ferrat, with similar results to the previous day. Many were ruled out for various reasons in the same way. There was a berth numbered 1889, but the friendly owners were on board. They were welcoming, invited Eleanor to stay for lunch, but as tempting as it was, she politely declined so she could push on.

It was good news from home, David would make a full recovery, and would be released within the next 2 to 3 days. His doctor was pleased with his progress. Eleanor said she would call him when the day was over. She had drawn a blank again, and ended the day with nothing more than a puncture to show for it. Emily pointed out that at least she could move on to the next port, and as she had less to get through, there was a statistically higher chance of success tomorrow.

They knew that they were running out of time. Victoria had said five days before the Anthrax would arrive. If the captain, and crew were on standby, they would probably set sail the same day. And so it was with a sense of impending doom that Eleanor set off to St Tropez. When she arrived she had the presence of mind to think, *I will come here with David for a holiday when all this is over.* As soon as she reached the port, she went straight to the Harbour Master, she realised this was the fastest way to find the right boat. Armed with this advice, she went to the line of large yachts that she was assured were the right candidates. After looking at several she called Emily and said, 'I am at berth eighteen in St Tropez and guess what . . . the yacht is called Blondi.'

Eleanor couldn't attract anyone's attention, and assumed that there was no one on board, so she went back to the harbour master to ask about this particular craft. She was told that Blondi was not booked to be in the Port tonight, and if it was still there, it would be going out today. On her way back she saw Blondi actually leaving the port. She ran towards it as fast as she could, it had pulled away a good eight feet, she shouted 'STOP' as she ran, but no one heard her, so as she got to it she jumped, landing heavily on her knees, but she was ok. There was no one on the back of the boat, and Eleanor was extremely nervous, it crossed her mind that it could easily be the same people that planted the contaminated bottle. She proceeded with caution feeling exposed, thinking to herself, *how on earth did I get into this position.* She was on board and they were pulling away from the shore, and still no one had come to the back of the boat.

She called out, 'hello . . . hello, is anyone there. Bonjour?' She didn't go inside, but instead used the walkway around the cabin.

'OH SHIT . . . you made me jump,' it was the captain at the helm. An Englishman, and thankfully he was friendly. He really had jumped out of his skin. It turned out that he was alone, because he was taking the yacht just off shore where it would be anchored, he didn't need his crew for this ten minute trip. The people he was expecting tonight had rented the yacht for two weeks and no, it wasn't a Mr Weiss, it was a Swedish timber merchant. The owner's name was strictly confidential, but he said that it was a woman, she was a famous actress, so Eleanor was definitely mistaken.

The captain said, 'look . . . I can't go back into the berth as I need crew to reverse a craft of this size. But I will take you back to shore in the tender when I have dropped anchor.'

Eleanor gratefully accepted, and she was profusely sorry. She felt defeated and consoled herself with the fact that it was always a long shot, and she had done her best. Weiss may be mad enough to do this, but she was a translator not a superhero, she felt defeated, and was ready to throw in the towel. As she thought this she saw a craft at anchor in front of the famous restaurant, "Club 54". As soon as she saw it she knew it was the one. Its name was "Rittershoffen".

Chapter 51

The Tambura Trust, or more accurately a subsidiary, had inadvertently paid for a shipment of Anthrax, and the Senior Trustee of Harris & Tarling Trust Corporation was arrested, and held under "Anti-Terrorism Laws". He was accused of having complete control over the funds, and if found guilty he was facing multiple life sentences. As a Trustee for Weiss, Andrew Harris had become independently wealthy, and didn't want to betray his clients' confidentiality. Agent Winterton of Delta Force explained the situation quite succinctly.

'We have arrested the crew of the yacht "Rittershoffen", and we have seized a shipment of Anthrax bound for New York'.

Apparently the crew had a history of delivering precious cargo around the world, and Winterton said their story checked out. They had no idea what they were about to carry, and they didn't know who they were taking it for. They had one link, and that was to the Tambura Trust. Winterton said, 'I put it to you Mr Harris that you are acting as a terrorist.' The Delta Force officer, Winterton, was trying to put the fear of God into Andrew Harris. This strategy was to flush out Weiss, they didn't actually believe Harris was behind it. The Tambura Trustees were just pawns acting under instructions from Richard Weiss.

Winterton said, 'look Andrew, do you mind if I call you Andrew?' Harris responded positively with a nod, 'from what I am led to believe, it is quite common place for Trustees to receive instructions off a beneficiary.'

Harris said, 'I have been a Trustee for an excess of $3 billion dollars. The money is not mine, I work on behalf of the Beneficiaries, and I have a duty of Nondisclosure. I cannot give you any information on this Trust, or any other for that matter.' Winterton was secretly impressed. This was a pen pusher, a bean counter who didn't scare easily. He was facing life for conspiracy, and yet he still protected his client.

Winterton said, 'you personally made $20 million dollars last year alone! according to your accounts and you work out of Gibraltar which I believe is for tax purposes. How do you think a jury will look at you Mr Harris, we will get a "Proceeds of Crime Order" against you, and won't leave you with a dime.'

Harris replied, 'well if I am in prison as you keep suggesting, I won't need any money.' Winterton thought, *Touché*, but kept the smile inside. Harris said, 'find the Bearer Share Certificates, and you will have the owner.' That was just what Winterton was hoping he would say. The interview came to an end, and Mr Andrew Harris was still not charged with a crime, but was asked to go, and sit in a cell. An hour later Winterton was back for the interrogation to start again.

'It's your lucky day,' the mood had changed. Winterton was playing good cop, bad cop, all by himself. He brought cakes, and coffee. 'We have the gang in custody that was to take the anthrax to its final destination, Staten Island, in New York. It would have killed at least a million US citizens Andrew. We also have the Bearer Shares Certificate as you confirmed, and it links straight back to Mr Weiss.'

Harris was starting to query the facts that he was being bombarded with. There was no way on earth he would protect Weiss if he really had planned to do this, but he didn't believe Winterton. He felt that he was being tricked into divulging his client's identity, and it was sacrosanct in his world to protect the anonymity of his clients. He had known, and worked for Richard Weiss for nine years, and he was his main client. Harris didn't believe Weiss capable of such a crime. He decided to play it safe, and keep his mouth shut. As it turned out, he didn't have much longer to endure, and the interview was drawing to a close. Winterton finished with, 'you haven't heard the last of this.'

Harris replied, 'Does that mean I am free to go?' When Andrew Harris was released without charge, he tried, unsuccessfully, to contact Weiss. The following day Harris' lawyers had the full picture, Weiss really had purchased enough Anthrax to kill hundreds of thousands of people. It was seized while being delivered from the manufacturer in North Africa to the South of France, to a yacht owned by a subsidiary of the Tambura Trust. A subsidiary that Harris was aware of, but not under his control, so if it was an inadvertent purchase or not it was no longer something Harris had to lose sleep over, particularly now that Agent Winterton had confirmed that they had a confession by the criminal gang that were to receive the Anthrax in New York. They had provided absolute proof that they were working for Richard Weiss.

Chapter 52

Eleanor's current concern was Victoria. It had now been a week since the public announcement concerning the anthrax, and still no word. She called Rainbird who said, 'I know she is physically fine I can sense that much, and I don't think she is in any imminent danger.' She went on to say that Richard had lost the plot. Switching between his dual personalities of Weiss, and Hitler, it was like he had become schizophrenic. 'I have visions in my sleep, but they aren't dreams, they are my psychic link to him, and I know he hasn't hurt Victoria.'

Eleanor was comforted by this, and went into the bedroom to tell David. He was lying in bed still convalescing, even though he had been released from hospital after extensive tests confirmed he no longer had any trace of the poison in his body. He just needed bed rest to get over the ordeal his body had been put through. He proposed to Eleanor when he was semi-conscious in hospital, and she thought he would forget all about it. But as soon as he was home, he asked again and this time she accepted, so they were now engaged, and even this news made the TV.

The detective who investigated David's water contamination called to say they had found spittle on the tear off strip off the bottle. Apparently the perpetrator had used his teeth, and part of this strip had DNA, and they had a match, it was Dr Blake Gibson. Eleanor couldn't believe it.

Eleanor said to David, 'he is one of Richard Weiss' staff, the really weird one I told you about. Richard refers to him as his personal surgeon. No doubt his medical background allowed him to obtain the poison.'

David told her what the detective said, apparently Gibson had served 6 months in prison for having child porn images on his computer, and that is how they had his DNA on file. But more concerning, 'now they know who it is, they have been looking at CCTV and interviewing residents in the apartment block, and they know Gibson has been back again, and he said we should be very vigilant.'

Eleanor said, 'I can't believe this, what should we do? He is dangerous, I don't think we can go out until he is caught.' They sat, and talked about their options, and concluded that they would take extra care, but they must go on as normal.

∞

They were all quite the reluctant celebrities of the day, but they knew that it would all die down soon. David was reading the Washington Post in bed and as it had a picture of Weiss on the front, he felt the need to remind Eleanor again, not that she needed reminding. 'You must remain vigilant all day, every day, as Weiss may try again . . . also Kugel, and Gibson are still at large.' He turned to the inside story, this time the heading said, We Admire the Myers, and it summarised what had happened:

> A plot to poison New York's tap water was foiled by the incredibly brave Myers sisters. Today New York's Mayor Julian Reynolds hailed the sisters, Eleanor and Emily as heroines and called for them to receive the "Freedom of the City", after they single-handily thwarted a criminal gang headed up by the disgraced pariah ex-city Golden Boy Richard Weiss.
>
> Questions are being asked why Delta Force didn't act sooner, but instead left the sisters to search for a yacht owned in a Trust, ultimately controlled by Weiss, that was suspected of being involved in terrorist activity. A White House press statement indicated that the President himself had communicated with the Myers sisters, and they confirmed that the deadly poison Anthrax was destined for the USA.
>
> The sisters identified the craft in question, called the "Rittershoffen" the day before a shipment was due to arrive. Delta Force then occupied a vessel anchored close by, to

catch the perpetrators in the act. A Delta Force spokesman said, they had readied a rapid response team, and acted immediately after the Myers tip-off. The Captain and Crew of the Rittershoffen were not suspects, and neither were the Trustees. But the criminal gang making the delivery would spend many years in prison.

The article used the opportunity to rehash a previous story on Weiss, which mainly said, "It is widely accepted that thousands of Africans have already perished and their blood is on Richard Weiss' hands, after he stopped whole villages benefiting from fresh water". But the last sentence was the one that Eleanor read three times, it directly quoted the President and said:

> The World wants to know where is Richard Weiss? A reward of $1 million is offered for information leading to his successful capture. We found Osama Bin Laden and we will find Richard Weiss.

∞

Victoria's phone rang again, but she didn't answer it. Richard said, 'is that the sister of the bitch?' Referring to Eleanor calling. 'I know it is, answer it, and I will speak to her.' Victoria refused. She had no more work to do for Richard, he had gone underground with only 4 of his D.I.S team, and Victoria was one of them. He had a secret fallout shelter that he had built to survive a nuclear war, and it was fully stocked with everything they would need to survive for months if not years. Sanitation, power, water, and oxygen were all catered for in a self-sustaining system. Until they arrived, Victoria had no idea that this facility even existed. She was amazed that he had all this without her knowledge.

She had got to the point where she only stayed with Weiss to leak information to Eleanor as she knew she could be instrumental in stopping Weiss in his tracks, but it was a dangerous game. Weiss spent hours talking to Gibson. They were always strategizing, but over what, Victoria didn't know as there were no deals being done that she was aware of. Weiss was drinking every day. He drank, and got angry with everyone and everything, and then drank some more. He had all communication devices on lock down unless strictly authorised by him, and through him. Any calls that were allowed were recorded, Weiss would be able to listen in, or read a text or email.

The last contact Victoria made was when Weiss passed out, and once done she cleared all trace of the call. She was always aware that Dr Blake Gibson was now Richard's only ally, and he seemed to be Richard's eyes, and ears. He hadn't done anything specifically to her, but he didn't have to, his look was enough. It was cold and calculating, and she knew he was watching her. As well as Weiss, the Dr tended to only one other patient full time, in a separate annex of the sprawling underground complex, and all employees were not allowed in there. Weiss said his Mother really wasn't well.

They had a brief conversation, which had been quite rare lately, Richard said to Victoria, 'where did it all go wrong?' He actually had tears in his eyes, and for a brief lucid moment, Victoria was looking at the man she once knew. 'I am truly sorry you know.' Victoria didn't reply, she didn't know what to say, but she did hold his gaze, and gave him a smile full of pain. Richard added, 'about what I did to you. I'm really sorry.'

She didn't want to comment on what he had done, but as a conciliatory comment she said, 'I don't mind caring for your mother, I have nothing else to do, and I can't imagine Gibson's bedside manner is anything to write home about.'

Richard replied, 'Blake said she is to receive no visitors, and I just do as he says, so leave it, but thank you for offering.' The way he said it, left no doubt that the subject was closed. He would continue with the silent treatment.

Richard was awake around 20 hours a day, and he still had more energy than most, but Victoria knew that he was having daily medication to stay awake. She had no idea what he was being injected with. He knew he was a wanted man, and didn't want to get caught under any circumstances. His money was all around the world, the Tambura Trust was one of many, so he would be fine financially. Many of the accounts were not in his real name anyway, he would keep going.

Victoria had to remind herself that this was a man who the world was after as a terrorist. But she thought that Weiss would find another way to wreak havoc, and if he did, she vowed to stop him. She was almost beyond caring about her own safety, moreover, and contrary to what he said she didn't think he would ever let her go. He said if she wanted to go, she would be blindfolded and driven off, so she couldn't reveal the location of his hide out. But she didn't believe him. Everyone could go with just two exceptions, Dr Gibson and his patient, Richard's mother. Dr Blake Gibson, was now clearly Weiss' only true confidante.

Whatever strategy Weiss had, he no longer shared with Victoria. A week went by in the bunker without incident. Weiss had even reduced his drinking, and seemed more relaxed than he had been for a while, but Victoria couldn't take any more pressure. She was, after all, living in an underground fallout shelter with the world's most wanted man. She wasn't to know she would soon be free. The last conversation she had with Richard, he likened the bunker to Hitler in Berlin under the Reich Chancellery, and his monologue was about what he referred to as Hitler's heroic suicide.

He said to Victoria, 'I needed to be a martyr then, but I won't be this time, you wait and see.' She didn't know much about World War 2, but she was confident that no one else would use terms like "Heroic" and "Martyr" when discussing Hitler.

After another fitful sleep, Victoria rose early. The stress was getting too much. As she walked to the kitchen in the shelter it became obvious that something had changed. It didn't take her long to find out that Weiss, unannounced, had left. She was all alone, every room was empty. She soon concluded that he must have left with his number two driver, his surgeon, his butler, and his Mother. Victoria went straight to the exit, and found the whole site unlocked, where it had always been securely locked since their arrival, some 10 days ago.

It only now sunk in that she hadn't seen the light of day since.

She stepped outside, it was hot, very hot. She took a deep breath in, it felt far better than the filtered air of the shelter. It dawned on her that she was free. She hadn't really contemplated the fact that she had really been a prisoner, but now she did. She immediately called Eleanor.

'He's gone . . . Richard he has gone.'

'Thank God, I wasn't sure you would ever get away, and I was going mad with worry.'

'He left me here without saying a word. They left while I was asleep. I wonder why he left me. I didn't want to be trapped with him any longer, but I wonder why?' Victoria started to sob before Eleanor's reply.

'Clearly it was a goodwill gesture towards you, he left you behind so you can make your way home.'

Victoria wasn't panicked, he wasn't coming back, she didn't know how she knew this but she did. He had given her back her liberty. Her only problem now was that she had absolutely no idea where she was. Standing outside still talking to Eleanor, she could see nothing but desert as far as the eye could see.

'Your mobile obviously works, turn on your find my phone,' Eleanor said.

It did work as the fallout shelter had its own Base Station, and Transmitter Tower. So it was that simple, Eleanor now knew the location coordinates of Victoria's whereabouts. She was in the Djurabin Desert in Northern Chad, North Africa. The day unfolded fast, and with the help from the President's Personal Secretary, and the United States Air force Victoria was headed for home. Within eight hours of waking up in a fallout shelter in an African Desert she had never heard the name of before, she was with her friends in Washington DC.

Eleanor had insisted that they unite in celebration, and so Victoria went straight to David's. She was exhausted, but ecstatic, as they all were. She felt very comfortable in the group. She had never met Silvio, and whispered to Eleanor, 'you never told me Silvio was so attractive... and funny.' The close bond the group had was undeniable. Eleanor felt happier when Victoria was around, and she told her so, for her part Victoria replied 'I came here to you, David and Emily, even before going to my apartment, and there is nowhere else I would rather be.'

Chapter 53

Victoria had only been back from Africa for a week when Eleanor talked her into a blind date with Silvio. She told Eleanor that she was worried she wouldn't have anything to talk about. So Eleanor suggested that they could double date. Victoria had worried unnecessarily as the conversation between her, and Silvio flowed quite naturally.

David and Victoria shared the same sense of humour, and the same taste in music. They had got on like a house on fire right from the first day they had met. Eleanor was equally relaxed around Silvio, and the four grew closer. Victoria and Silvio were very soon inseparable, and like Eleanor and David, they felt a connection beyond the amount of time they had known each other.

David knew that their soul group was not yet complete. His knowledge of their past lives had continued to grow. It was as if his memory from past lives, was a file downloading straight to his brain's hard drive. He told the others that he thought it was possible that they may be all part of the same soul group, and they had all been together before, but he didn't expand on this and nobody asked him why he thought this. Victoria was completely up for regression to prove it, but Silvio asked her to wait. He had become far less sceptical, but he argued that he wanted to know her in this life first. Since that first blind date, they had met as a foursome every weekend ever since.

Their social life was spent eating in nice restaurants. They all had eclectic tastes, and were happy to indulge in foods from around the world. But tonight they were going back to Pinocchio's, their favourite place. It was also in walking distance from David's, so no one had to drive, and they could all enjoy a drink. Before departing Silvio went to turn off the TV and shouted, 'quick look at this!' They all rushed into the room.

He turned up the volume, the news item featured Dr Blake Gibson, as the newsreader said, 'The Government has offered a reward for information leading to the capture, and arrest of Dr Blake Gibson, the fugitive is currently on the run, but still believed to be in the USA. Police have advised that Dr Blake Gibson is armed, and dangerous. Members of the public should not approach this man. He was known to be involved in a plot to kill thousands of innocent Americans.'

Behind the newsreader the picture of Gibson was replaced by one of Richard Weiss, the newsreader did a segue from the one to the other, explaining the relationship before going on to say. 'The former banking mogul, turned terrorist, Richard Weiss, was killed today by an angry mob. Some viewers may find the following footage disturbing.' It was a scene reminiscent of the murder of Colonel Gadhafi, the gang surrounding him could be heard shouting insults. Someone shouted you killed our children, and then they all started chanting, "Diablo, diablo, diablo". The scene was captured on several mobile phone cameras, and despite being frenetic in parts, it was clear to all that it was Weiss. The footage became pixelated as it apparently featured Weiss being shot, and killed. The newsreaders final comment was, 'we confirm that the world's most wanted man, Richard Weiss is dead.'

There was a stunned silence in the room. David switched off the TV as he let out a big sigh. 'That's how I feel,' Victoria continued, 'It's a horrible thing to say but I feel relieved . . . I actually feel happy he is dead . . . I'm sorry that's a horrible thing to say.'

'No it's not, well at least it's not for a man like Weiss,' Silvio said. 'I never even met the man, but it feels like a weight off my shoulders too.'

'I will up the ante,' Eleanor said. 'I am over the moon, let's go and celebrate.'

∞

They all started to settle in their lives, and move on from the danger they had all been facing. But moving on didn't mean moving away, they were all closer than ever before and they spent much of their time together. Tonight the whole group would be meeting up again, Pinocchio's was busy as always, and Marco was on top form. Tonight's special was line caught Sea Bass baked in sea salt, but Eleanor loved the Sea Bass cooked on the bone with garlic and lemon, with crispy skin. She was so fond of it that she found it hard to order anything else. She recommended it to Victoria who had become a pescetarian since she started dating, soon to be best man, Silvio.

Victoria said, 'I only used to eat chicken and fish, but since I moved in with Sil I only eat fish. Whenever I was cooking for both of us I cooked fish, and I decide to drop meat altogether.' Victoria had been dating Silvio for three months now, and they got on so well that she had already moved in with him.

'How is your book coming on?' Silvio asked Eleanor.

'Slowly . . . no, it's not going too badly. It is hard work believe it or not, it's like being a child again, and being given lots of homework to do when everyone else seem to be outside enjoying themselves. I'm just trying to avoid it reading like Die Hard 8, or whatever number they are on.' When Eleanor told David of her desire to write he had encouraged her saying, *there is no time like the present.*

'So is it a thriller?' Silvio asked.

'It's Fifty Shades of Grey, meets The Green Mile, written in the style of Woody Allen.' They all laughed. 'It's supposed to be a thriller, but I don't seem to be in charge.' As Eleanor was writing her first novel she had read several instructional books on writing, and they all made it sound about as much fun as studying Quantum Mechanics. But then she read Stephen King's book, "On Writing" and his approached gave Eleanor permission to completely relax into the story, and let the plot take care of itself. Eleanor said, 'well I've had such a full life, I was sure there was a story in me.'

'What about your past life experience, are you leaning on that?' Silvio was asking the questions, but they were all listening.

'No. I didn't want it to be in any way autobiographical. I read a quote, I wish I could remember who said it. It was that "absolute power corrupts absolutely" and I thought that was a good starting point for a story.'

Emily said, 'It was George Orwell in Animal farm.'

David said, 'she writes every day for at least three or four hours.

I've no idea where all the ideas come from. I don't think I'm very creative, I couldn't do it.'

'Here's Emily and Rainbird.' Victoria said.

The table tonight was for six. When Eleanor found out that Rainbird was going on a yoga retreat for six weeks, she suggested that Emily should go too. She said "After what you have been through, it will be the perfect tonic." Emily expressed concern as she hadn't even met Rainbird, "What if we don't get on?" she had said, but she did go, and by all accounts they had a wonderful time. They had only been back a couple of days, and were joining the others for dinner.

After introducing Rainbird to David and Silvio Eleanor said, 'you two look fantastic. I've never seen my sister looking so healthy.' The deep brown tan that they both sported made a big difference, but Emily was a changed woman, the tension was gone out of her face. They all embraced.

David said to Rainbird, 'I tried to Google you, but I couldn't find anything. No LinkedIn, no Facebook.'

She replied, 'Owww!! that's like trying to go through my knickers drawer.' Everyone laughed. 'I don't do computers Darrrling.' Emily noticed that Rainbird spoke a little more theatrically when she met people for the first time. The wine flowed as they caught up on the stories of the last couple of months in Thailand. They made the others laugh, such as when Rainbird had insisted that Emily join her for colonic irrigation, but it wasn't great dinner conversation.

'But I'll never be able to use a garden house again.' Emily joked. Not once did they talk about Richard Weiss, Harvey Kugel or Dr Gibson, and they didn't even talk about his death. That whole part of their history was already starting to be firmly in the past. David still had his gun, probably because Kugel had never been found, dead or alive. But they had all moved on and tonight wasn't the night for dragging up the past, and the more nights like this, the better. Time is definitely a healer.

'Can you really tell someone's fortune Rainbird?' Silvio asked. Everyone else felt slightly embarrassed by the question as they all completely believed in Rainbird's ability. But she liked being the centre of attention, and was always asked this question.

'Well Darrling,' she replied in that exaggerated Eartha Kitt style, 'are you asking me to look into your future?' She looked right at Silvio, square in the eyes, and never blinked. He looked down, like a naughty schoolboy. 'I'm joking,' she said, 'of course I can. Let me have your hand.'

While she had been in Thailand, she had consciously avoided any mental interference. Being psychic, she was often aware of potential messages, like an overfull inbox on your iPhone, commanding attention. But she could tune in and out at will. She could turn off the voices, and completely tune out, and she had actively switched off for the last six weeks. She briefly explained this, and then got herself into the right frame of mind to read for Silvio.

She said, 'you have to be very careful of your knee . . . your right knee. You will have trouble if you keep jogging on it.'

From this first statement Silvio was knocked sideways. But when he had got over his initial surprise, he thought, she must have seen me walk to the men's room, but then he countered to himself, it isn't playing up right now, so he wouldn't be walking with any sign of a limp. Rainbird continued, 'you are discussing renting out the spare rooms at the practice, and you have a dentist in mind. You are questioning if it is a good fit. Go for it, I can see this working well.'

David said, 'I didn't say anything.' He had favoured the dentist, but Silvio was a little sceptical.

Rainbird had more to say, 'your Mother is no longer here with us, but she wants me to tell you that she approves of your choice of future wife, and you should ask Victoria for her hand in marriage before someone else does.' Silvio's mother died three years ago. The fact that Rainbird knew this was extraordinary enough, but she put all of Silvio's scepticism to bed when she told him, 'your Mother said look after my ring, it was you Great Grandmothers,' his hand went to his pinkie finger of his left hand, where he wore the ring. There were oohhhs, and ahhh's around the table, and tears in Silvio's eyes. No one needed any further confirmation that Rainbird had been right. Victoria put her head on his shoulder for a comforting hug.

'Right enough of that. Let's have a drink, and relax. I'm off duty for a while. The voices can keep a girl permanently looking over her shoulder darrrling.' The mood was temporarily less jovial, but it was warm, and cosy rather than down. Another table in the restaurant had a birthday, the lights were dimmed. A large hand bell was rung as Marco and the table in question were singing happy birthday.

When the lights came back on Emily said, 'I have some news.' She paused to make sure she had everyone's attention. 'I have been nominated for an award for my work with AQWA.'

Eleanor was the first to speak, 'brilliant!!' Everyone else offered their congratulations.

'There's more. I have been invited to an awards ceremony in Vegas, as a special guest, and the best news of all is, I have 6 all expenses paid places, and I want all of us to go together.'

From what Emily could gather, the event was hosted by an Argentinean company who had adopted her rationale in South America. It was an Argentinean Government initiative with the same ideals as AQWA. It would be a lavish affair with over a hundred guests all being looked after in style at the Bellagio hotel in Las Vegas. Confirmed guests included representatives of most of the main suppliers in the Water industry. It would celebrate a turning point in history, in the way the world views the international control of such a precious commodity. From what Emily had been told, she had been nominated for the main award of the evening.

'I wouldn't miss it for the world. Can you have the time off?' Eleanor asked David, but Silvio replied for both of them.

'We can, and will close for the week, we will definitely be there.' Everyone felt the same, and so it was decided, and they would put the date in the diary, it was only three weeks away. David always said that there was something special about living a life with close friends, and as your history unfolds together you become even closer. Going through any trauma is never good, but going through it together had drawn this group closer.

'Victoria, can you sort out the flights please? I have to book them, and claim the cost back on expenses.' Emily asked.

'Leave it with me.' She was instantly comfortable being in charge of logistics, and happy to help.

Silvio asked Rainbird, 'If I gamble in Vegas, am I going to win?'

'Have you seen the girl on your arm? I think you have already won darrrling. No more predictions from me, we have been on this path all of our lives.' That summed it up for David too, it was their destiny. He didn't have any of Rainbird's psychic ability, but he had what he now thought of as "knowing" their past lives. 'It is written in the stars Darling. This is our soul group. Some things are fate, but this is our destiny.'

Book 5

Chapter 54

Gradually they had all stopped worrying about Gibson returning, and life had been good. The first draft of Eleanor's novel was completed just in time for their Las Vegas trip. She would relax on holiday, and come back to it with fresh eyes to do her editing. David wanted to get married in Vegas and had said, "let's just go for it, we have the six of us here." Eleanor was tempted, but she wanted her Mother there too. They were trying for a child, and David wanted to be married before she got pregnant. She promised they would agree to a date straight after their break. Victoria had a full itinerary, tonight was the awards, tomorrow, Cirque du Soleil Beatles, "Love" show, all finishing with a helicopter ride over the Grand Canyon.

The awards ceremony itself was a formal affair with dinner, and a guest speaker with a live band to finish. The gang had gone from four to six as Emily and Rainbird had become a couple, and joined the others at the weekend. Emily had finally come to terms with the simple fact that she was happier with a woman. Rainbird was comfortable with her sexuality, and had always been bi-sexual, and made no judgment. Her attitude was, live and let live, and they had both decided to commit to a long term monogamous relationship to see where it would lead. Emily thought breaking the news to her mother would be difficult, but Elizabeth was really pleased for them, and said, "as long as you are happy, I am happy".

None of them had ever been to Las Vegas before, and they were all completely blown away. The strip was spotless, and it felt safe. Every hotel was a famous landmark, which made it all familiar. They all thought that it deserved the reputation as an adult Disneyland.

Emily had a three bedroom suite on the top floor of the Bellagio, so they could all stay together. The men had gone out sightseeing. Eleanor knew they wouldn't get beyond the first poker table. David's attitude was, "you just have to, when in Rome and all that." The four girls all had their evening dresses hanging up. The long black Stella McCartney for Eleanor, with Victoria also in black, and the other two in white, it looked planned, but they had all chosen independently.

'Eh look at those beautiful legs.' Eleanor said to Rainbird. 'You should have them on show more often.' Rainbird considered herself a hippy chic and always wore jeans. Nice jeans granted, but nevertheless still jeans.

'I can do swanky darrrling. Check out the heels.' She had three inch heels on her shoes, white with a gold trim to set off the dress.

Victoria made them all laugh when she said, 'I heard they are called Jimmy Choo for symbolic reasons, the JC, because everyone says, "oh my God" when they see the price.' The men were back, Silvio was up, and David down, Silvio had a very brief winning streak, and felt he should give David gambling tips while they changed into evening wear. Within mere minutes the lads were in the sitting room in their Tuxedos. David was all in black with matching cummerbund, and a bow tie. Silvio, on the other hand, always tended to go against the flow, and was in a white tux with a red bow tie, but they both looked the part.

'Right, let's have an aperitif while the girls finish getting ready.' Silvio said.

The girls had been getting dressed for about three hours and were running late as they were still not quite ready. 'What do they take so long over?' David shouted to the girls, 'Come on!! Or we will be late, the invite says 7:30pm for an 8pm start.'

'David, stop panicking! No one will be there yet,' Eleanor said.

'I am not panicking, it's ten to eight, and I think it's rude to be late.'

'You are wasting your breath mate.' Silvio said. David knew he was right, and mixed another Margarita for them both. He was going to offer one to the girls, but decided that would only delay them even more. By eight fifteen the girls all came into the living room.

'DA DAAAA!!' They said in unison.

'Jeeez, look at you. Give us a twirl.' Silvio said. The girls obliged and Silvio whistled appreciatively.

David was a little more reserved in these matters but he offered up, 'You all look beautiful. How lucky are we?'

'Speak for yourself mate. You might be punching above your

weight, but I think I am a perfect match for my finance,' Silvio said.

'Are you marrying me then? Thanks for letting me know.' Victoria said.

Rainbird said, 'haven't you proposed to her yet? What did I tell you?' Silvio the permanent comedian of the group got down on one knee in front of Victoria.

'Will you marry me?' Everyone thought he was joking but he pulled out a box from his left inside pocket, and opened it to reveal a diamond engagement ring. 'I wanted to wait until the right time, and I thought Vegas would be perfect.'

'You sly old dog.' David said, 'you didn't even tell your business partner.'

Victoria cried happy tears, and said yes.

Silvio asked David to be his best man. 'It will be my pleasure.' They embraced in the way men do these days. David said, 'Now come on or we will be late.'

The Ballroom capacity was for one hundred, and it looked like it would be a full house. There was a seating plan outside the entrance to the dining hall, and the group were on table one. It was the top table, and apparently they would be sitting with the host. Even though it was now around eight thirty, all the guests were still mingling in the bar area. Emily saw some colleagues who had worked on the AQWA project with her, and went to say hello, and to introduce Rainbird. For the first time tonight, Rainbird noticed that Emily had started referring to her as "My partner". Victoria was too much in love to have eyes for anyone but Silvio. He had always said he would be 40 at least before he settled down, but here he was captivated by his new fiancé.

David looked across at them, and reflected on the path they had travelled together. All six of them had been together in past lives, how many, he didn't know. He hadn't told the others yet that Rainbird was also in Rittershoffen with them, as he wanted to recall her name before he told them. Silvio was no longer in any doubt that the soul group concept was real, he had to suspend his medical training to just have faith, but since he had been amenable to the principal, he no longer felt the need for a scientific explanation.

There was a loud thwack of wood on wood as the "Master of Ceremonies" banged his gavel down. The room went quiet. 'Ladies and Gentlemen, please make your way to your tables, dinner is served.' The general hubbub of noise came back, and everyone started to filter through to the hall. David led his group through to the hall towards the stage, and the large round table where they would be seated. The place names had Emily to the left of the host, a Mr Carlos Perkins, with the others in her group to her left. The host hadn't arrived yet, and so they found their places, and stood behind the chairs. There were 12 guests per table, and they all introduced themselves. Within 5 minutes or so most people were seated.

The lights were dimmed, and over the PA system they heard, 'Ladies and Gentlemen, please be upstanding for your host, Señor Carlos Perkins.'

The stage Vari Lights came on, and out walked a sprightly elderly gentleman, to music. It was Ringo Star singing "Honey Don't". He was flanked by two dancing girls in full Brazilian dance outfits with large feather headdresses, with stocking legs that accentuated their length. They each had one hand on opposite hips, elbows held out for Perkins. He was flanked on both sides by these striking women, and held their offered arms as they walked together like a South American Hugh Hefner. If it wasn't for the Buddy Holly type, thick rimmed glasses, you would have said he looked a little like Liberace. Other dancers joined the two girls as Carlos walked down from the stage to greet his guests. He waved just like Bollywood Bhangra dancers unscrewing the light bulb dance, as he negotiated the steps.

'Who is this guy, Elvis?' Silvio said directly into David's ear. The walk down the steps was that of an elderly gent. Left leg first, and the right leg joining the left on the same step before tackling the next, not daring to step onto the alternative step as most people would.

Perkins said, 'Good evening. Good Evening.' He shook hands with a couple of people as he went past, just saying good evening to others. 'Ah. My special guest Miss Myers. May I call you Emily? I am Carlos Perkins. It is my pleasure.' Emily wondered how old he was, he could be anything from fifty five to seventy five, a lot of his movement was that of an arthritic man. Carlos was a real charmer. He very quickly dropped Emily, and used the more familiar Em when addressing her. Emily was left in no doubt that he knew plenty about the water industry. They didn't talk about the bad press, and Emily hoped he hadn't seen it. He certainly didn't mention it, and he talked a lot. In fact he never stopped, she was quite engaged with him, and oblivious of everyone else.

Most guests talked to the person to their immediate left or right, as the general noise level from a 100 people talking at the same time, made it difficult to hear beyond those closest. Carlos had a young Russian blond to his right, and Emily felt a little uncomfortable because this woman was left out, and was sitting there looking bored stiff, Carlos seemed oblivious.

'Hello my dear.' Carlos acknowledged Rainbird to Emily's left. He leaned over Emily, 'Excuse me Em please,' and put his hand out to shake with Rainbird. It was one of those light grips where mainly the fingers of both parties meet rather than the palms.

'That is one beautiful diamond Mr Perkins.' Rainbird said. 'Well thank you, but please, with friends it is Carlos. It is a 7 carat yellow diamond you know.' He had turned his manicured right hand to let the girls have a closer look.

Carlos said, 'between you and me, it was from my own mine in Caracas.' He winked as he said this. 'Well, are diamonds a girl's best friend?' he asked, not looking for an answer. He sat back indicating to Rainbird that the greeting was over. He looked over at the others, and waved at the men and blew a kiss to Eleanor. As the plates were cleared, everyone returned to speaking to their nearest fellow guest again.

'Tell me about your friend?' Carlos asked.

Emily struggled at first, 'I mean . . . what is there to tell? She is a yoga expert . . . a psychic and my best friend.'

Carlos said, 'psychic you say. And what does she say about your award, will you win?' He laughed.

Emily said, 'she is taking a break. It was all getting too much for her.' They talked about lots of things, Carlos was pleasant company, and dinner came and went without a gap in conversation. Emily and Eleanor excused themselves to go to freshen up.

'Well what have you found out?' Eleanor asked, 'you were deep in conversation?'

Emily replied, 'Oh . . . he is easy to talk to. He is widowed, his Mother was from Argentina and his Father was from America, hence his name. He is the key sponsor of the awards, and he just seems like a really nice man.'

'Who is the blond with him, I haven't seen her say a word all night?' Eleanor asked. They were headed back to their seats. Emily was just about coping with her heels that were new to her.

She said, 'apparently she is from an escort agency, he didn't want to come alone.'

When the coffees arrived, Rainbird declined, she wasn't feeling well. Her gift could be a burden on nights like this. She was receiving too much psychic interference, and for some reason she was finding it hard to block it out. Without tuning in properly, the messages were just like static from a radio, not quite locked into the right frequency. When this happened it was often of significance, typically something imminent that someone or something somewhere thought she needed to know. If she didn't tune in she paid the price, as she was now. She stood up and said, 'would you mind awfully if I excuse myself? I have a terrible migraine, and I need to take some medication and lie down.'

'But of course my dear'. Carlos went to get out of his chair to say goodnight.

'Please stay seated.' She said as she bent over to kiss him on both cheeks. 'Are you sure you don't mind.' She asked Emily.

Emily replied, 'of course not. Do you mind if I don't come with you? I will be up soon.'

'You are to stay until the end, do you hear me. It's your night. I'm just sorry that I can't stay any longer.' With that Rainbird excused herself, and went to say goodnight to the other guests.

Emily said to Carlos, 'she has been open to all manner of extrasensory information coming through, and she is exhausted, so she is actively avoiding being a receiver. But as a result of suppressing these signals she suffers these migraines.' They talked some more about Rainbird, and then got back to water, and how Carlos was a real "Green ambassador". Emily put her left hand on his left arm. He was a father figure type, and she felt really comfortable.

The lights were dimmed and the master of ceremonies introduced the guest speaker, an Olympic swimming gold medallist that no one knew, but within an hour everyone loved. He was an excellent choice of after dinner speaker.

'He should be a full time comic.' Silvio said to Victoria. Half way through the guest speaker's slot, Carlos excused himself, and went backstage to get ready for his hosting role. He had a sense of theatre about him, and didn't want to be seen leaving the dining room floor to go up the steps to the stage. He had his grand entrance planned. As the speaker left the stage, the lights dimmed and an unseen announcer over the PA system announced, 'Ladies and Gentlemen, please stand for your host, Carlos Perkins'.

Carlos came on to the stage to a standing ovation. He revelled in the applause for a good minute or so. It was deserved, it had been an excellent night. With his palms facing down, held out at waist height, moving up and down 3 or 4 inches, indicating for everyone to sit. David thought, "This will go on for hours" but he was wrong, Carlos seemed aware that he shouldn't lecture, and kept the presentations at a sensible length. He introduced a guest from the industry, who announced the contenders. The first was a nervous person who said, 'this award is for technical achievement in water filtration.' There were three contenders, as the names were read out, the guest table that had representatives of said company cheered.

'And the winner is... Creative Filters PLC!' They had been reinvesting their profits into a fair-trade scheme designed to provide filters to Africa at a net cost, and they got a lot of applause from the crowd. A representative of the winning company went on stage to collect their trophy. With the host on the left and the guest announcer on the right of the winners, photos were taken. With the hand shaking, air kisses, brief thank yous, it was taking about five minutes per award. The first four were done in quick succession, and it came to the main award for "Water Personality of the Year", the category that Emily had been put up for. The same pattern followed before the announcement.

'And the winner is... Emily Myers!!' There was a standing ovation. Silvio was whistling through his thumb and index finger. Eleanor was really proud, it was a great end to the last few months of highs and lows. When she came back to the table everyone in turn gave their congratulations. It really was turning into a fantastic few days, and what a night. If anything tonight had gone too fast, and with the awards over it was time for the last act of the night. It was a live band, a Beatles tribute act, "Sgt Peppers Only Heart Club Band" were introduced, and they opened with "I Feel Fine". It was explosive feel good music, and the dance floor filled straight away. David was looking a little worse for the drink and was happy to sit back and watch. His bow tie already untied, and hanging around his neck. Silvio loved dancing, and the Beatles so he got the girls up to dance with him.

'Are you coming to dance?' Eleanor asked her sister.

'I'm going to go up now, if you don't mind. I'll go and see how Rainbird is.'

Eleanor said, 'ok I'll come with you.'

But Emily said, 'no you won't, don't be silly, you stay and enjoy the band.' Eleanor really wanted to party, but was happy to walk Emily to her room, and come back down.

'Let me escort you to your room. I am not as young as I used to be, but I know how to take care of a lady. You are on the top floor aren't you!?' Carlos said. It was arranged, Carlos would see Emily back to her room.

'I can walk myself you know,' she said, but offered no resistance, she too had over indulged. Emily took Carlos' arm, and they set off. As Silvio walked towards the dance floor, he pointed towards Emily and Perkins and said, 'who is holding who up.' They were soon distracted when the band ripped into "All My Loving".

In the lift, Emily adjusted her hair in the mirrored reflection of the brass coloured metal back wall. Carlos was looking tired but was still immaculate, he hadn't even undone the top button of his shirt. Carlos said, 'can I invite you back for a night cap?'

'I think I should get back, and see how Rainbird is.'

Carlos replied, 'she will be fine. I am a good judge of character, and that is one very strong, independent woman.' She knew he was right and thought it would be rude not to. He told her he had something in his suite that she just had to see . . . so she thought, "One drink won't hurt". Their suites were on the same landing, but his was bigger, and it had the best view in the hotel. It had three separate balconies, and from them they could see the gondolas. From the largest of the three balconies you could see the strip in all its glory, from the New York Skyline to the most famous tower in Paris. But the big surprise was chained to the wall.

Emily said, 'lions? I can't believe it, who has lions in their room.'

Carlos said, 'only in Vegas my dear. Anything is possible in Vegas.' The lions were lying down on their sides, up against each other. The one closest, lifted its head for a cursory glance, looked at them, and lay back down again.

Emily asked, 'can I stroke them?'

'That depends. How much do you like your fingers?' Emily wasn't sure if he was teasing or not, she asked, 'aren't they tame?'

Carlos said, 'they see you as prey. When they are hungry they would have no problem attacking us.'

Emily was sure he was exaggerating. They were obviously allowed in a hotel room or they wouldn't be here. 'I have saved a treat for them and you, you can watch them eat before you go. Now, let me get those drinks. What can I get you?' Emily flopped down on the comfy sofa, and slipped out of her shoes, in the background she could still hear the band, she said she would join him with a port.

Chapter 55

"I saw her standing there" was one of David's favourite Beatles tracks, and he decided to join them on the dance floor. The other three had their arms around each other's shoulders dancing and singing. '*Well she looked at me, and I, I could see,*' he sang as he joined them. He had by far the best voice, but he couldn't dance, not that that stopped him. They really were all very happy together. They all did the "OOOH" bit into Silvio's rolled up place setting, to double as a microphone.

∞

Rainbird was sleeping, but her sleep wasn't a deep sleep, she was fitful, dreaming about Weiss again, and the demonic personality he adopted towards the end of their relationship. He was the reason she tried to block the psychic information, because she kept having thoughts of him. He came to her in her dreams as the devil incarnate, not literally the horn, tail and trident version, but a force of such malevolence that was able to be reincarnated, was a scary concept. Her dreams were projecting into the next life when he would re-emerge again in a new guise. These visions always left her sad, because one day he would be back. Anyone in the room with her now would have heard her mumbling "Emily", followed by "Richard".

∞

Carlos sat on the end of the sofa with his hands on his knees. Emily was getting comfortable and it was making her more tired, so she decided to get ready to excuse herself. She had an inch or so of the port left, and she had already declined a top up. 'I have something to show you,' he said.

He had a remote control in his hand, and he used it to activate a large screen that was unfolding on the wall in front of them. Emily hoped, whatever it was, that it wouldn't take too long. Carlos pressed play and the projector lit up. On screen came the now familiar footage of the demise of Richard Weiss. He probably had some exclusive footage that he wanted her to see, but Emily thought, this was hardly the time or place. 'I really need to be going. It's been such a lovely night, and I don't want to spoil it by being reminded about him of all people.' She reached for her shoes, and slipped her feet into them.

Carlos said, 'oh don't go just yet. You haven't seen the best part, just another two minutes.'

∞

Rainbird sat up with a jolt. She knew in that instant that Emily was in danger. She rushed out of bed, and got dressed. She had Emily on speed dial, she heard "Hello this is Emily please leave a message". She hung up and called Eleanor, another answer machine, she left a message. 'Eleanor it's urgent!! I think Emily is in danger, call me back.' She left to find Emily, she hoped she wouldn't be too late.

∞

The guests were all joining in with the band for the "La . . . La, La, La la la la" section of "Hey Jude". Silvio and David both had an arm raised swaying, and one arm around each other's shoulders, singing along. The girls went arm in arm to the rest rooms, as only women can. When they were away from the noise of the dining room, Eleanor's saw her phone flashing. 'I've got three missed calls off of Rainbird.' She listened to the message. 'Something's wrong. It's Emily.'

They rushed over to the lads, 'what's happened?' David asked.

'It's Emily,' Victoria replied. They all went to the lift, it was on the way down.

Eleanor said, 'we don't know what happened.' The lift opened, and it was Rainbird who had made her way down.

'Is she not with you!' Rainbird asked of all four.

'No. What's wrong?' Sil asked as they got in. Eleanor pressed the top floor.

'I don't know. All I know is Emily is in danger.'

∞

In the suite with Carlos, Emily felt uncomfortable, why bring Weiss up now. On screen the view changed to a distant perspective, this camera was set up to film the scene below. It was the sort of footage shot for a documentary on the "Making" of a film. There were clearly two or three angles that had been used to create this clip. The action below stopped on cue. The whole event was staged, on screen, Weiss had a towel wiping away the blood as the camera went in for a close up of him smiling.

In the hotel suite, Emily sat open mouthed and mesmerised. Weiss was alive, he had faked his death. The enormity of the news was still sinking in as Carlos removed his grey curly wig and the thick rimmed glasses. Next came the false teeth. Emily didn't react quickly enough as Weiss removed his disguise. Out came the coloured contact lenses and finally the prosthetic skin below the eyes. Finally he stood at full height rather than stoop as Carlos, no longer frail or old.

In his own voice he said, 'good evening Emily, we haven't formally met. I am Richard Weiss.' He offered his hand to shake. He looked calm and in control. The hoax was so elaborate that he got away with it. To Emily it felt like minutes since she had sensed danger, but in reality it was mere seconds. She came to her senses and ran for the door. Weiss didn't give chase as he didn't need to, he had locked it, and the only key was in his pocket. 'Going so soon, we have only just met?'

His pulse was a steady 70 beats a minute, and he remained in complete control. Emily pulled at the locked door, and felt more frightened than she ever had in her life. Weiss was going to kill her. She came close to breaking down, just cowering on the floor there and then, he had her completely trapped. She took a deep breath and fought the fear . . . she wanted to survive.

∞

In the lift the tension was palpable. Silvio broke the silence. 'It's this Perkins fella I bet. I don't think it is his real name, but I didn't want to say anything. Wasn't there an old rock and roller called Carl Perkins?'

'Richard Weiss.' Rainbird said as the lift slowed to a stop. 'He is still alive, that's why I can't get him out of my mind.' As the door opened they heard an ear piercing scream. They ran in the direction of the noise, Eleanor said, 'The Presidential Suite.'

∞

Her scream was almost a war cry. A call to action, and she ran. It was a large suite, she would hide and gather her thoughts. She ran to the right, avoiding the lions. There was an office, but it was through an alcove without a door, so she ran past this into the next room. While running she decided to barricade herself in, so she was ready to find something . . . there, a large heavy dressing table, she leant against it and it moved, just. Thankfully the room had a key in the lock. Her hands were shaking so much that she took longer than she should have, but she did eventually get it locked. Weiss still hadn't given chase, he was taking his time. He was filling a syringe with an aesthetic concoction with a succinylcholine base. It was a muscle relaxant that he was going to use to temporarily paralyse her while still conscious. With the syringe full he walked to the room Emily was in. He had a master key.

There was banging at the front door and voices. Weiss ensured that no one in the hotel had a key to his suite, so he wouldn't be disturbed. He had one very clear objective and he said to himself, 'payback time.'

∞

After locking the door, Emily had pushed the sideboard into place to start the barricade. There was a hospital bed with someone in it. She had seen it when she entered the room, and all that registered, was that person was no immediate threat. This room's balcony was at a forty five degree angle to the main balcony, separated by a ten foot divide, but Emily still locked the balcony doors. She looked over at the patient, and it was a stomach churning image as the full extent of the person's condition was sinking in. The shaved head was missing the bulk of the skin, and cartilage that make up the ears. The eyes were dried out and odd, they looked like they had been pushed out of their sockets; it was a full thirty seconds before Emily realised that he had no eyelids, top and bottom on both had been removed. The nose was still there but it looked like it had been broken several times. The body was propped upright on several pillows, and was strapped to the bed, with his head locked into position by a metal frame. The restraints didn't have padlocks, but the poor fellow had no arms or legs. The torso had horrendous scars and it was clear that this person had been through several operations, some very recently. From his side of the door, still taking his time, Weiss said.

'I believe you already know my other guest, Senator Harvey Kugel.' She heard the words and looked at those eyes, and saw the different colours. "Oh the poor man", she thought, not only did she feel sympathy, she felt an overwhelming sense that he needed her forgiveness and despite their history, she would give it gladly. It dawned on her there, and then that this wasn't an ill person being treated to make well, this was a well person being taken apart, body part, by body part. It was a torso, and head and that was it, a man barely alive, how, she didn't know.

Emily had left the key in the door, but Weiss managed to push it out of the lock from the other side. The furniture she had managed to push against the door was gradually moving. Emily looked to bolster the obstacles and noticed the bed was on wheels. She took the brake off and pushed Kugel to the other side of the room. 'Errh errh erh.' He tried to talk, but she couldn't understand him. There were drips, and machines here there and everywhere, keeping him alive, they remained attached. She wondered what sick surgeon would pander to Weiss desires. Eleanor had never had cause to mention Dr Blake Gibson to her sister.

Weiss said, 'I have saved his final night for you to savour. Tonight we are feeding him, alive, to the lions.' He smiled, reminiscent of Jack Nicolson playing the Joker. 'They have so loved his body parts, haven't they Harvey?' With the eye lids removed, and his head locked in position, Harvey had been forced to watch feeding time.

∞

David couldn't believe he wasn't carrying his gun, especially as it was this very possibility that it was purchased for. He grabbed a fire extinguisher and with a hand each end, he had raised it high and brought it down hard against the lock, removing his left hand from the bottom at the last second. The door being steel reinforced was holding up against the blows. Silvio saw this working if they hit it enough times, so he ran down the corridor and grabbed another extinguisher and they rained blows down on the lock one after another like lumberjacks working in pairs on a large tree.

∞

Victoria didn't have her cell phone, so she went to their suite to call the police. Rainbird and Eleanor tried neighbouring doors, in the back of their mind, if they gained entry, they would hope to access Weiss' suite through a connecting door or the balconies. They saw to their right, a door saying "Fire exit". Without speaking they went through and rushed up the stairs. They were on the top floor so the stairs must go to the roof, where they could possibly drop down to the balcony. They had to at least try. It suddenly occurred to Eleanor that Weiss had booked the whole hotel. Other than the party downstairs, none of the rooms were occupied, there would be no staff, and security cameras wouldn't be on, a typical condition of his bookings.

∞

As Weiss pushed his way into the room, Emily stood by the balcony doors. It was the furthest point from where Weiss would emerge. She was trapped and had only one option, to fight. 'I hope you have said good evening to or guest?' Weiss said now he was in the room, he was smiling at Kugel.

Weiss added, 'oh silly me, I forgot you don't have a tongue. That was the first thing to go wasn't it . . . I find that is the easiest way to stop someone talking about me behind my back.' Weiss was sideways on to Emily, and she decided it was now or never, she had stepped out of her shoes and ran at Weiss.

∞

They could see as well as hear the helicopter from the roof. 'It's coming for Weiss.' Rainbird said. But one thing she didn't want to know, would Emily survive, as she didn't want the answer.

∞

David said, 'The hinge. Let's try that side.' The lock was resisting the savage blows, and David had decided that it was unlikely to be penetrated. They were tiring but determined and they moved their efforts four feet to the right.

∞

Emily ran at Weiss and hit him as hard as she could on his left side. She hoped to knock him off his feet, and run past him, but he didn't budge. He grabbed her and she fought like a wildcat, managing to connect with his face. A nail had drawn blood on his cheek, but he wasn't hurt at all, and he soon had her in a vice like grip. She tried to bite him as the syringe went into her leg and within seconds, she was limp in his arms.

'Now was there any need for that.' Weiss said as he laid her across the bed, where Kugel's legs should have been. He wiped at his cheek with the back of his hand as he effortlessly moved the furniture, and once the doors were de-cluttered, he wheeled the bed through to the lions for feeding time. Weiss didn't know they had already been fed, so they were not hungry, certainly not enough to kill. They were still being dosed with sedatives in their food by their trainer, and this had rendered them docile.

∞

There were no obvious steps down from the roof, to the balconies below. The drop was about twenty five feet, so far too high to jump. The facade did have obvious hand holds, and they were tempted to climb down, however they both had heels on and it would have been impossible barefoot. Eventually they found a way down, it was a fire escape that led to the neighbouring suite and from there a short gap to the left hand balcony of Weiss' suite, they hoped to get there before it was too late.

∞

Weiss was still calm despite the banging on the front door. He was singing to the Beatles "Yesterday", that could be heard from downstairs. 'I'm not half the man I used to be.' He laughed at his own sick joke and said, 'sorry Harvey that was a little insensitive.' The helicopter went past the balcony, and landed on the private landing pad that can only be accessed through this suite. 'Ah, there's our transport.' Weiss said, to no one in particular.

Emily could only move her eyes, and they followed Weiss around the room. As he made ready for their departure, he said, 'not him, just you and I. My wonderful surgeon gave me such pleasure, but Harvey is alive but only just. When you can't elicit a response, it takes away the fun.' He said this with a detached interest. 'But I think the big finish may well squeeze out some reaction. At least out of you, if not out of him.'

∞

Rainbird and Eleanor had jumped across the gap, it was only three feet, but the drop was sure death, and it made it look much wider. His balcony doors were locked as they expected. They looked for something to break the glass. Just after the helicopter landed they ran at the window with a large metal plant pot, it was toughened glass and it didn't break. They could see Weiss standing, and Emily's legs hanging off the bed, not moving, they feared the worst.

∞

Just as David and Silvio were going to admit defeat, there was a loud splitting noise as the bottom hinge gave way. They continued their attack on the top of the door with renewed vigour. They would be inside in no more than two or three minutes.

∞

Eleanor was banging on the glass with both fists, she didn't know what else to do. Rainbird put her hands up to her face, as if she was holding binoculars, to shield the light, which was reflecting off the glass, to get a better view. Weiss waved and smiled. It was the smile of a man who would kill your favourite pet to see the look on your face. Weiss knew he was running out of time, as the door sounded like it was less secure that he had been advised, when he booked the hotel. Still, there was only one door through to the helipad, and he had the only key. He also had his gun so he got it out and placed it on the bed to use if someone did break in before he made good his escape.

Outside the girls felt helpless. They could hear the helicopter, its blades still rotating indicating that it was waiting to take off again. They saw Weiss pick Emily up, and throw her over his left shoulder. Now they could tell she was still live and Rainbird said, 'thank God.' Eleanor went to see if they could get across to the helipad from here, but the divide was far too great.

Weiss pushed the bed over to the lions, they didn't move at first. The larger of the two got up and sniffed the bed, scent marked it, and went back to lie down. 'Well would you believe it? Weiss was incredulous, he planned this as his big finale for Kugel, but soon recovered his composure. 'Never mind, it was fun Harvey.'

Chapter 56

He left his suite, and the door shut behind him with seconds to spare, the front door finally gave way. Rainbird and Eleanor saw the men break through, and banged on the window. Silvio let them in as David went towards the bed. He stepped into the perimeter of the lions for a brief second, and pulled the bed away. The lions had been prepared as always by their trainer, and were not going to be bothering anyone, but still their presence made everyone cautious.

Eleanor said, 'there is a gun on the bed,' she continued, 'through that door, quick he has got Emily.' The door was locked, David picked up the gun and shot at the lock and they all burst through the door. When the pilot saw Weiss with a woman over his shoulders he turned off the engine. 'Don't stop the engines,' Weiss shouted as he placed Emily on the floor.

'What's going on!? I don't want anything to do with this,' the pilot said to Weiss.

David shouted, 'STOP or I will shoot!' Weiss heard him but had no intention of being captured, he went to grab Emily again, he was sure that Prost wouldn't shoot him, he was no killer. Weiss still feeling really calm reached for his gun. 'Damn,' he said as he realised he had left it on the bed. He decided to take Emily to the edge to use her as leverage to get his gun back.

Weiss said, 'I will throw her over the edge unless you put the gun down and kick it over to me.'

David could take no chances, he wouldn't let Weiss kill Emily, and there was no way he would pass him the gun. He was absolutely certain that he could take the shot without harming Emily, and so he took aim and fired. As he did so he said out loud to himself, 'I'm sorry Sophie, I never did forget you.' He shot Weiss right in the middle of his chest, and he dropped to the floor.

Eleanor and Rainbird rushed to Emily who was still not in control of her body. They carried her inside. Victoria said, 'the police are on the way.' Silvio looking for Victoria, also came in from the helipad, followed by David, who said, 'I had to shoot him. He's dead.'

Kugel had been kept alive with various machines and once Weiss moved the bed, his body had finally shut down, and he too lay dead. 'Looking at the state of him, I think it's for the best,' Victoria said.

'I don't know what this man did, but no one deserves to suffer like that.' Silvio said. They placed Emily on the sofa, and they saw her foot twitch, followed by her hand. The succinylcholine concoction was wearing off.

David came in to join the others. 'Who is that poor man?' He was pointing at the thing on the bed.

'Innrach carrcul.' Emily tried to speak. They all looked at her, relieved that she appeared to be coming round, 'Issh corlgul.' She tried.

'Kugel?' Rainbird asked. They all understood Emily's reply.

'Yesh.' The others all sat down exhausted. 'I'm going to jail for this.' David said.

'You can't, we all know what happened.' Eleanor said.

'It's not like in the movies. I can't say, he was going to kill Emily so I had to kill him.'

'It will be okay,' Rainbird said. 'I had always known this day would come, not the detail, always ephemeral and just out of reach, leaving me with the thought that we would be okay.' She didn't like to say that she had always resisted the truth as she couldn't face the consequences of losing to Weiss.

'Look we will deal with it together, come what may.' Eleanor said.

∞

Weiss was lying where he fell. The wound would have killed anyone, but it hadn't killed him. As he lay there, his body was repairing itself. He had the NSC's all through his arteries, and veins, and they were working. The bullet had penetrated them but the NSC's had instantly closed the leak by re-joining, just as they were designed to do. His left lung had suffered irreparable damage, but he would live. As he lay there he knew that he had to move. He could hear the police sirens so he had to move now. He knew his body was damaged but the NSC's had stopped him bleeding to death. He got to his knees, he was recovering, and he knew his brain function hadn't suffered.

A part of his mind said, *I wouldn't have survived a shot to the heart, we need to improve the technology.*

Another thought occurred that went, *why are you thinking this now?* The third concurrent thought that formed part of these multi-layers of thought all occurring at the same time, *fascinating.* The blood flow had improved, and he felt well enough to get to his feet.

∞

'Richard is still alive,' Rainbird said.

'It's not possible. He had a big hole in his back where the bullet exited.' David said. Eleanor and Victoria went to the door to see for themselves as they knew Rainbird was rarely wrong.

Weiss got to his feet, and was trying to think how to get away. He was like a drunk as he walked towards the edge, he wanted to see if there was a way down. He had more of the multi-layered thinking and thought, *this must be the life passing before your eyes that people talk of.*

Emily managed to sit up just as the police came in. She had more or less fully recovered all of her motor skills. 'Out there,' she said to the police.

Weiss knew he was caught, he also knew that given the opportunity his body would recover. But for now it was over, he would meet them all again, he promised himself, next time, no more Mr Nice guy. Why did he need to feel liked, he was evil personified, it energised him. Weiss had a minute or so of these multi-layered thoughts, and then had a moment of complete clarity. A police officer shouted, 'Put your hands on your head and lay down on the floor.' They had their weapons out pointing at Weiss to make their arrest.

'He is unarmed.' David said. Weiss was trapped like an animal in a snare. He backed up to the edge of the helipad, and stepped over the perimeter cable. As the police moved in to make their arrest Weiss shouted, 'you will never rid the world of pain. You deserve all that you get.' He put his arms out in a cross position, and fell backwards to his death. His final thought before he hit the floor was, *next time, I will make them pay for this.*

Chapter 57

David went to get a glass of water, old habits died hard. They had dispensed of the water cooler, and would live without one. David had been questioned, but the police hadn't pressed charges. For a while it had been uncomfortable, because he had shot an unarmed man. The post mortem of Weiss helped, as the NSC's had worked so well the pathologist confirmed that the bullet would not have killed Weiss, and he had died from a massive head trauma, and the cause of death was officially recorded as suicide. What the post mortem also showed was that the NSC's were repairing a lot of the damage, they worked remarkably well, and from injuries that were not so severe, they would undoubtedly save lives.

Emily used her contact at the White House, and The President personally intervened, the whole story was almost beyond belief, but the President said, 'we owe a debt of gratitude to Dr David Prost, and it would be a complete miscarriage of justice if he was charged with any crime.'

∞

David was at his desk reading about Dr Blake Gibson. He had been arrested, and charged with the murder of Harvey Kugel, and suspected of being involved in other atrocities. He had been held in a High Security Hospital wing, after entering an insanity plea. While detained, he kept quoting A.E.L, but no one knew what that meant. But he had escaped, and was currently on the run, thought to still be in America. David was interrupted when Eleanor shouted from the kitchen. 'Can you get that love?'

The gang were all coming to dinner. David logged off, and went to let them in. The night was pleasant as it always was when they were together. Silvio was funny, as he constantly was. David was more reserved until he had a couple of drinks. Tonight he wanted to share something of which he was certain.

'Rainbird, you were also with us in Rittershoffen. You were known by the single name Paris.' The similarity to her being known by a single name then, and now didn't escape anyone's attention. 'When Hitler came to the village many people perished, but you survived. You went so far down inside yourself that you were ignored, they thought you were dead.' No one spoke, they hung on his every word.

'Your mother had unofficially adopted you from a prostitute in Paris, so you never had her surname. She loved you, and lost her life attempting to defend you. You were always psychic, even then. You would find Alicia's lost toy, you would close your eyes, and the answer was there. You also told me that you knew what was going to happen to you, and that you knew you would be okay. After that fateful night, I went AWOL, and took you with me.'

Silvio asked him, 'did she say darrrling then' and they all laughed.

'We did our best to trace your birth parents, but we never did find them. We stayed in close contact for the rest of my life.' David hoped that Silvio, and Victoria were part of the same soul group, but so far he had not established a link. The last thing he said about it was, 'if it wasn't for you, I wouldn't have been able to carry on after losing Sophie, and Alicia.

They all talked about this, Victoria and Eleanor always had so much to say to each other that David said, 'how on earth can either of you be listening, as you are always both talking.' Rainbird was always fun, and tonight she was talking about crystals, and the healing power of Amethyst, and how using these, Emily now had a clear aura, whereas in the past it was almost pitch black, as a manifestation of her stress then. But it was Emily who summed up the feeling of the group when the subject of the recent past came up.

'You know . . . he was right, the World will have pain, but we don't deserve it at all, that is complete nonsense. But pain does seem linked to pleasure, the best analogy I can come up with, it is as if without the dark we wouldn't appreciate the light. But I do know that I will never be a victim again. That was my choice.'

Rainbird understood the principle, but had a different slant on it, and she always said, 'it's not what happens to you, it's more about how you feel about what happens to you, and how you feel is entirely up to you.' David felt it was time to let go of the pain he felt for Sophie, and Alicia, he would make amends in this life. The Sardine Packing was so wrong, and so painful, but he didn't want that experience to taint this life.

Emily said, 'as a soul I needed to experience this, but I don't need to be a victim. Love will always overcome evil, and you know what, I forgive him, and as long as I do . . . as long as we do, he can never win.'

'Hear hear.' Eleanor said, and she raised a glass. 'To us. Forever'.